For my good friend, Louise Marte,

with thanks and gratitude,

Frank

8/29/89

NORTH POINT PRESS

9 STORIES BY

within the
RIBBONS

FRANK MANLEY

SAN FRANCISCO 1989

The author and publisher gratefully acknowledge prior publication of "The Rain of
Terror," in *The Southern Review*, "An Errand of Mercy," in *The Kenyon Review*, and "The
Baptism of Water," in *The New England Review and Bread Loaf Quarterly*.

ISBN: 0-86547-379-X

LIBRARY OF CONGRESS
CATALOGING-IN-PUBLICATION DATA
Manley, Frank.
  Within the ribbons: 9 stories / by Frank Manley.
    p.   cm.
  Contents: Within the ribbons—The rain of terror—The concisest
  tenant—An errand of mercy—The baptism of water—Chickamauga
  —58 Babylon dread bean—The call of nature—A joy forever.
  I. Title.
PS3563.A517W58   1989
813'.54—dc19   88-34433

FOR CAROLYN

Contents

within the
RIBBONS

Within the Ribbons

Daisy Feed was having a Coca-Cola next door on Amelia Thorlew's side porch.

"I've never been to a wedding," Daisy Feed said.

Amelia Thorlew went into a sort of spasm, laughing and coughing.

"You've never been to a wedding? I can't believe it."

There were a lot of things Amelia Thorlew could not believe. That was one of the main things about her.

"I never married," Daisy Feed said. Even now after all these years, she still could not believe it herself—not even after she came home from her mother's funeral and caught a glimpse of herself in the mirror and realized how old she was. It was as though, having just been buried, her mother had reappeared, and Daisy had to take care of her all over again. It was like a dream. Her whole life had passed, and she roamed through the house like the last survivor searching the wreckage for some sign of life.

Amelia Thorlew laughed again. "I know all about never getting married." The smoke from her cigarette caught in the sunlight and ignited. "You got yourself to blame for that. But I'm not talking about being in one. I mean going. You've gone to one, haven't you?"

"No, I haven't."

"Why ever not?" Amelia Thorlew fell back on the sofa and tapped her front tooth to show she was thinking.

"I don't have any relatives."

"You got them," Amelia Thorlew said. "Just like dreams. You may not know who they are, but you still got them anyway."

"They don't ask me to weddings," Daisy Feed said.

"They would if they knew how."

It was a conversation they had had before—not about weddings, but about relatives. "Reason I got so many relatives," Amelia said, "is I can afford them. That's what my daddy always said. He'd pick me up and swing me and say, 'The reason you got so many brothers and sisters is I can afford them, that's why, honey. Children're a blessing and so is money.'"

"I go to a wedding once a year," Amelia said. "Sometimes twice. And sometimes it just comes in bunches. I don't even get back home and take my bicarbonate of soda sometimes when here comes another and I got to get sick all over again." She laughed at her own joke and sat up. "Next time," she said, peering at Daisy Feed like a threat, "I'm going to take you."

And that's how they went. The last Friday in October they got in the car and drove over to Montgomery. It was a lot like driving to the grocery store. Once they left Atlanta, they were on I-85 all the way, with no towns and nothing to see except trees and old fields with nothing in them but weeds and broom sedge. And then suddenly they came on two fields of cotton no more than a mile apart. It was like a miracle. Daisy Feed was still trying to figure it out when all of a sudden they were in Montgomery, and it looked just like Atlanta. They might as well have stayed where they were for all the good it did to the landscape. Daisy Feed did not know who was getting married, and neither, she suspected, did Amelia. The skein of relationship was too complex. "If they had their eyes set too close together from counting their money," Amelia said, "and were named Thorlew, they were related. The rest were the ones marrying in."

At Exit 3, Ann Street, they drove up the ramp to the Windermere Hilton and inquired about the wedding party. "You got a block of rooms reserved, don't you?" Amelia asked.

"Yes ma'am," the desk clerk said. "Right by the pool."

"Well, put us in there," Amelia said. "We're here from Atlanta come down for the wedding."

"I wish I could," the young man said. "But I can't do that. You're not on the list."

"Not on the list?" Amelia said. "Let me see that." And the desk clerk, a fat young man who could rise from his chair only with difficulty, struggled up and waddled over. He handed her a smudged typewritten list.

"That's not the one," Amelia said, looking it over. "You sure you got the right list? This might be a convention of salesmen."

"Yes ma'am," the desk clerk said. "That's the only wedding I got."

"Not a name on there I know," Amelia said. "All Roys. Where're all the others?" she asked the desk clerk, rummaging in her pocketbook as though she might have misplaced them in there. "Where're all the Thorlews?"

"This all they give me," the desk clerk said. "They're all from New Orleans."

"The groom's family," Amelia said to Daisy Feed. "Roys from New Orleans. We're in there with them." She turned back to the desk clerk. "Well put us down. Amelia Thorlew. This is Daisy Feed."

And the desk clerk put them down. The room they were given was reserved for A. P. Roy, Sr., father of the groom, and it was a prime one, right by the pool. The name Roy meant nothing to the desk clerk. Thorlews, on the other hand, owned half of Montgomery.

"How you like it?" Amelia asked, blowing smoke into the fetid air of the room.

"Looks like oatmeal," Daisy Feed said.

Amelia laughed. "What you mean?"

"All beige and white."

"That's so it won't be offensive to people," Amelia said and fell over backwards on one of the beds, kicking her shoes off.

"What do we do now?" Daisy Feed asked.

"Whatever you want. That's how we do at weddings down here. I'm going to take a nap and get ready." Amelia wound her arm around her head and dug at the pillow.

Daisy Feed sat and watched her. Amelia looked much older sleeping than she did awake. Daisy Feed thought of her mother and how she went to bed after her father died and how Daisy sat like this and watched her, not knowing what to do, until her mother got up again after three or four weeks and mooned around the house in a stained flannel robe and bedroom slippers, refusing to go out, refusing to see anyone. She never got dressed again in her life. Daisy thought of all the years that had passed and how much she had loved her mother and how she could never do anything to help her.

She got up suddenly and put on her shoes. It was time to get up and go when she got to thinking things like that. This was a wedding. She tiptoed to the dresser, put the extra key in her purse, and eased out the door.

The air was fresh, and the sunlight blinding. After the smoke in the room and the air conditioning, it was like coming back from the dead. She walked purposefully toward the pool, sat down in one of the plastic chairs, and watched a young mother play with her child. The child was laughing and jumping off the side of the pool into the water. The mother would hold out her arms to catch her. Then they would both fall down in the water, laughing and splashing.

Daisy Feed thought of herself and her mother and how she had wasted her life on love. Then she thought about happiness. As soon as she got whatever she wanted, she always wanted something else. That was the terrifying thing. It was like a compulsion. At the innermost core of her being, there was something she could not name—a void she could not fill, a hunger, a wild longing of the heart. She sought happiness the same way a rock falls in the darkness, a seed grows toward the light. And suddenly she remembered a tangle of ribbons snarled like a fishing line and rolled in a ball and stuffed inside a grocery sack. She had found it in the back of the pantry and taken it out and opened it and seen at once that it was not ribbons. It was alive. The white sprouts like dead men's fingers, yellow, embryonic leaves, and at the bottom the shriveled potatoes growing any way they could without soil, without light, inside a paper sack in the pantry. She had carried them out of the house to the garbage and thought how it was not in her power not to want happiness. Alone at night, after her mother had gone to sleep, she would sit and listen to Bach and hear the music swirling around her like her own thoughts and obscure desires. They rose in her heart and filled the room like a tangle of ribbons.

The pool slowly filled with children. Soon they were everywhere, running and squealing. Then the sun clouded over. The afternoon chilled, and the children left, scrunching their shoulders. The last ones to leave were shivering, huddled in the warmth of their mothers' towels.

Daisy Feed watched them leave and thought how she had come to fear love almost as much as happiness. She remembered reading something once that impressed her so much she put the book down and went upstairs and got out her father's typewriter and painfully, letter by letter, wrote: "The horrible thing is that we can never get drunk enough." The whole world would not suffice, and yet, despite the enormity of her desire, she could imagine it fulfilled. "Make haste, my beloved, and be thou like to a roe or to a young hart upon the mountains of spices." It was the innermost prayer of her heart.

The afternoon grew dark, and Daisy Feed got up and made her way back to the room and lay down on the other bed beside Amelia. She was finally at the wedding, and it was not what she had imagined.

That night was the rehearsal. Daisy heard the shouts of the young people as they left for the church threatening to throw one another into the pool. Two hours later she and Amelia were on their way to the rehearsal dinner. They drove down Zelda to Vaughn, across the East Expressway, and then suddenly, as though they had passed through a hole in the wall, they were in the country. A short while later they turned left at a white painted sign that said "Private Road." They rumbled across a cattle guard, feeling the vibrations shatter the car. Then another. Horses loomed up like apparitions in the beams of the headlights. They entered a woods, broke free again, and came to a stop on a concrete pad beside an Olympic-size swimming pool. Around the pool the lights were set like campfires. No one else was there except one man who wandered among the lights touching the tables.

"That's Wesley!" Amelia cried, struggling to open the door. She couldn't find the handle, she was so busy shouting his name. Daisy Feed helped her out.

"Come on," Amelia said. "That's Wesley." She started trotting.

The man had apparently seen them approaching and was walking slowly toward them, still touching tables.

"Wesley," Amelia shouted. "Wesley, it's me. Come on," she said to Daisy Feed. "He wants to meet you."

"This is my sweetie," Amelia said, drawing up to Wesley and stroking his cheek. "Kiss me, honey. I've come home to see you." She kissed him full on the mouth.

"Here's Wesley," she said to Daisy. "He married in."

"Fresh blood," Wesley agreed. "The rest of them intermarried so much, they'd have died out if it wasn't for me. I got me six children."

"And all of them Thorlews!" Amelia said. "They can't even see, they got so much Thorlew. Their eyes overlap." She bent over suddenly, laughing and coughing, then straightened up and lit a cigarette. "Old Wesley," she said, caressing his arm. "I sure am glad to see you again. I might have married him myself," she said to Daisy Feed, "except he didn't want to marry me."

"I was too young," Wesley said.

"He wanted me," Amelia explained. "But not to marry."

The accusation hung in the air just over their heads like the thin haze from Amelia's cigarette caught in the unearthly light from the pool.

"Come on in and see Cathy," Wesley said. He led the way through the maze of tables to the dark form of the house. It was low and rambling. That was all Daisy Feed was able to make out. Much of it was hidden by shrubs.

Inside, it looked like a Hollywood set full of overstuffed chairs and lush rugs on marble floors, with bars set up in the corners and colored waiters in red jackets behind them. Daisy counted three already, and they were still on the way to Cathy.

A few minutes later, the first guest arrived. Daisy saw him through the window, a man walking alone in the garden. He passed in and out of the shadows. Daisy was not certain at first whether he existed or not. One minute he would materialize, the next minute he would be gone. He looked like a thief. The doorbell rang, and Daisy assumed he had come in the house. But she never saw him again all evening. It had been the bridal party instead. They rushed in like a storm and swept through the house.

"Here's the party," Amelia said. "Give me a refill."

Daisy headed toward the food. She found herself beside two young men. Each had a drink in one hand and a stack of white sandwiches in the other. The sandwiches were so white they looked like they were made of lard.

"Are you in the wedding?" Daisy Feed asked.

The young man closest to her nodded his head. His mouth was too full to talk. The other young man suddenly shot his neck forward and swallowed. It was the same motion she had seen dogs make eating large chunks of meat.

"Yes ma'am," the young man said.

Daisy Feed nodded and reached for a plate.

"You know how to eat that shrimp?" the first young man asked, pointing to a large silver ewer. Daisy Feed looked at it and suddenly realized that all the food on the table was white—a chafing dish of white sauce with white lumps of something in it, white sandwiches, white dressing for the white shrimp. Even the icing on the cake. Even the tablecloth. Even the flowers. They were all white.

"You realize all this food is white?" Daisy Feed asked.

"Goddamn," one said, checking it out.

"Son of a bitch," said the other.

They were galvanized. She might have just hit them with a board.

"That's because it's a wedding," the first young man said. They started laughing.

Other people were beginning to drift into the room. The laughter made them uneasy. They had smiles pasted on their faces and expectant looks. Daisy Feed decided to move on.

"Wait a minute." The young men rushed up. "Look here," one of them said. He held out a plate of shrimp.

"How do you eat it?"

"With a fork."

"There aren't any."

Daisy Feed looked at the plate, then at the table. There was nothing to eat the shrimp with.

"I don't know," Daisy Feed said.

"That's what I mean," the young man said. "They got it fixed where you can't eat it."

"Hey, try a toothpick," one said.

"Look how I do," the other one said, and he opened one of the sandwiches and with a piece of bread dug at the pile of shrimp on his plate as though he was mopping it up with a towel. Then he thrust it in his mouth. Most of it got in. The rest rolled down the front of his suit onto the floor.

"Goddamn," one said.

"Son of a bitch," said the other.

They both stooped to clean it up, and Daisy Feed left.

All evening she kept coming across plates of uneaten shrimp deposited on end tables and bookshelves, stacked on the rug in the corners of rooms and on shelves in the bathroom. It was like following their spoor.

Later, after the party, lying in bed between the air conditioner on one side and Amelia breathing on the other, Daisy Feed thought of the shrimp as an emblem. Abandoned in odd places about the house, the plates of uneaten food seemed to signify her whole life. She shuddered under the covers. The air conditioner was too cold. She got up and turned it down, then went to the bathroom. She lay down again in the dark with her eyes open, staring at the light on the ceiling. It reflected the surface of the swimming pool and shimmered there like something alive hovering a few feet above the bed. It was like being in the dark underwater and seeing the surface shining with light. All we have to do is break through it, Daisy Feed thought. She imagined the water shattering like glass, the air piercing her lungs like knives, and then nothing but light: endless plains of light stretching out on all sides, in all directions at once as far as the eye could see. She had longed for it all her life.

Suddenly there was the sound of voices.

"Throw him in."

She saw the splash. The light from the pool leaped over her head.

"Son of a bitch getting married."

Then the entire ceiling shattered.

"Get out of there, Jimmy. You'll drown him that way. Leave him alone."

There were more splashes. More people jumped in. The ceiling was on fire.

Then another voice—older, gruffer. "What's going on here? You guests here or what? It's four o'clock in the morning."

"Rehearsal party. Just horsing around."

"Rehearsal for what? Killing him?"

"Hell no, Officer. He's getting married."

"Get him to bed."

"Yessir."

"You're bothering the guests."

"Yessir."

The ceiling shattered again as one jumped in, then another. They struggled, shouting.

"Get him to bed or drown him one," the officer said. "I don't give a shit which one."

"Yessir. I'm going to drown him."

A few minutes later the ceiling subsided, and the air conditioner kicked back on. Daisy fell into its rhythm, breathing when it breathed. Then she was dreaming. In her dream she was lifted up by a great wind. Beside her was the man she had seen walking in the garden. He was still not fully materialized, but Daisy Feed thought he looked familiar. She had waited for him all her life. No wonder I saw him in a garden, Daisy Feed thought. No wonder he was all shadow and light. "Open to me, my sister, my love: for my head is filled with dew, and my locks with the drops of the night."

She woke to the sound of Amelia coughing. By that time she had forgotten her dream. She did not remember it again until they were leaving to go to breakfast. As they passed the pool, Daisy Feed checked it out, looking for dead bodies, but all she saw were some beer cans on top, bobbing like buoys. On the tile around the pool were cigarette butts and more beer cans. Attached to the side of the diving board was a forked stick with a brassiere hanging down like a trophy head. Stretched across the lip of the diving board was a torn pair of women's panties. Looks like they had the wedding already, Daisy Feed thought.

Then she saw him again. It was the same man she had seen in her dream. He seemed to be opening the door to their room. She stopped to watch.

"What's the matter?" Amelia asked, pulling up short.

"I thought I saw something."

"Me too," Amelia said. "I can't believe it. You see those panties? That's a big woman, wear panties like that."

The man was coming out of the room. He turned left and walked down the far side of the courtyard. Then he disappeared into the shadows. Daisy Feed could not be certain she saw him. She could not be certain it was their room. She could not be certain he even existed. She had never dreamed something and wakened the next morning to find it true.

After breakfast they returned to their room.

"What's that?" Daisy Feed asked.

"What?"

"That smell."

"I don't know. The air conditioning."

"Smells mannish," Daisy Feed said. She remembered a colored maid they had had: the dog would run its nose up her dress, and she would scream and say, "Don't be so mannish!" That's what it smelled like— thrusting, aggressive.

"Mannish!" Amelia said. "Don't you just wish. There's no man in here since time before us." She flopped on the bed and kicked her shoes off.

"What's this?" She was holding what looked like a white envelope. It was about the size of a large postage stamp. "Look what I found on your pillow."

"What is it?" Daisy Feed asked. She felt the blood rush to her head.

"Open it up," Amelia said. She crawled across the bed, holding the message up in one hand.

"Whose name's on it?" Daisy Feed asked. She was afraid to touch it.

"Nobody's name. Just a blank envelope."

"You read it then."

"It was on your side."

"Give it to me," Daisy Feed said.

She took the envelope and opened it. Inside was a card. On the card was written in perfect Italic script: *Within the ribbons.*

Daisy Feed suddenly felt half asleep. She could hardly keep her eyes open.

"What's it say?" Amelia asked.

Daisy did not trust herself to speak. She handed the envelope to Amelia.

"That's nice," Amelia said.

Daisy was stunned. Amelia was not only not surprised, she acted as though she knew what it meant.

"Better get going," Amelia said, rolling over and lighting a cigarette and coughing.

"What does it mean?" Daisy asked. It was like seeking an oracle. The sibyl would speak, and the rest of her life would unroll like a movie.

"We get to sit with the family, that's all."

"Within the ribbons."

"That's what it means. They rope off the first few pews with white ribbons. Kinfolks sit in them. Let's get going."

At the church she saw him again. They were seated on the bride's side within the ribbons. Daisy Feed heard a commotion. An old woman with a walker was pushing her way into a pew that was already fully occupied. One of the ushers was trying to help her. Daisy Feed turned around. The man the old woman was trying to run down was the same man she had seen in the hotel. She turned to Amelia.

"Who's that?"

"Who's what?" Amelia was a devout Catholic and barely whispered.

"That man back there," Daisy Feed said. She turned to point him out, but the man was gone. The old woman was seated in his place. Beside her was a bug-eyed girl in a black hat.

"I don't see him now," Daisy said, but Amelia was already looking at the altar and mumbling.

The wedding took place in the oldest Catholic church in Montgomery. "The oldest and the only," Amelia said. "They don't have but one." All during the ceremony she stared at the altar and mumbled under her breath. She looked blank about the face as though she had just taken medicine that had an extremely adverse effect. Daisy Feed had never seen her look so old except when she was asleep. The animation she usually assumed to conceal her weariness was gone. She was as open and vulnerable as a child.

When the wedding was over, the bride and groom kissed. Someone began to clap, then someone else, and the entire church soon filled with applause. Daisy Feed was completely surprised. What were they applauding for? All they did was get married. And then she thought, "All?" and her heart filled with wonder. There was no way to express the wonder she felt. Tears ran down her cheeks, and she could not have said why she was weeping.

The reception was at the home of the bride's family. The houses were large and imposing, set on five- or ten-acre lots. Some were wooded, some were in grass. Either way they looked alike, as though they were created not by God, who laid out natural woods and meadows, but by a committee of yard men. As Amelia and Daisy Feed drew near, a policeman suddenly stepped out and stopped the car.

Amelia instantly became excited. "What is it, Officer?" She rolled down the window.

"Turn here," the officer said.

"What for?" She turned to Daisy for assistance. "We're going to a wedding up the street."

"Wedding party turns here," the policeman said. "Just circle the block."

At the next intersection another policeman waved them on. By that time they were nearing the house, and Amelia pulled in beside the curb and parked. Daisy knew which house it was because of the balloons: two huge rafts of them were moored to pine trees in the front yard. They bobbed above the highest branches, pink and white like exotic fruit. If it were Martians come to the wedding, Daisy Feed thought, they'd know where to find it.

Inside the house, on a landing above the entrance, was an orchestra. Below the orchestra was the bride book. Food was piled up everywhere on every flat surface in the house except those holding presents. The presents were wrapped in white paper and tied in white ribbons with huge white bows.

At the reception she found herself talking to an old woman on a camelback sofa.

"I'm the patriarch of this family," the woman was saying. Her hands shook with palsy. The backs were spotted all over like frogs.

"You mean matriarch," Daisy said.

"Same damn thing," the woman said and looked at her. "What's the sense in being old as I am?"

Daisy Feed did not have a ready answer. She was preparing to leave when the old woman reached out and grabbed her arm.

"Sit down and talk to me for a minute."

Daisy Feed sat down beside her.

"I pray every day," the woman said. "That's all I'm good for." She leaned forward and wheezed in her face. Her breath was hot and smelled like cat food. "You Catholic?"

Daisy Feed shook her head no. "I lost my religion." Even to her it sounded bereft, as though she'd been widowed.

But the woman was no longer listening. Daisy Feed might have said she poisoned her husband with French toast and arsenic, and the woman would have kept on talking.

"Every Catholic does one thing a day they don't want to," the woman was saying. "That's the main difference between them and Baptists."

"Lots of folks do that," Daisy Feed said.

"Don't interrupt me," the woman said. "Just be quiet and offer it up. That's how I do." She smiled. "I get to talking to some old fool, I say God must have sent me to relieve her burdens. Who's going to listen to her but me? That's part of my religion, relieving others and offering it up."

"What do you offer it up for?" Daisy asked.

"Sins," the woman said.

Daisy was still not satisfied.

"What exactly do you offer up?"

The woman looked at her with suspicion.

"Pain and sorrow," the woman said.

"I see."

"You take this wedding. There's lots of things wrong with the married state, most of it due to human beings. The other part . . ."

"What other part?"

Daisy Feed had not considered that marriage might have another part besides human beings.

The woman reared back and looked at her.

"The sacrament."

"What sacrament?"

The woman continued to look at her.

"You really did lose your faith."

"I never had it," Daisy confessed.

The woman nodded. "All right," she said. "There're three partners in a marriage. There's the bride." She held up one finger. "There's the groom." She held up another. "And then there's God."

"What's he add to it?"

The woman looked away as though seeking help, then turned back to Daisy Feed.

"Himself," the woman said. "That's what makes it a sacrament."

"The part God adds to it," Daisy Feed said. The idea was bizarre. God interpenetrated them. They united in ecstasy.

"That's right," the woman said, patting her knee. "Grace on grace. It pours down on you in invisible showers. Blessing on blessing. Now help me up. I don't have to hurt myself. God don't ask us to burst our bladders."

Daisy laughed and stood up.

"He just asks us to be faithful to him," the woman said.

Then she was gone, pushing her way through the crowd.

Daisy Feed thought of her own lack of faith. She was an empty pot, a broken vessel. She had taken the love she was given and hidden it deep within her heart. If he should come to claim it again, what could she offer? She stood in the middle of the room and listened. The noise of laughter and music crashed around her like a dark sea. The waves heaved and lifted, swollen with passion, but there was no light, neither sun nor moon nor distant shore.

"There you are," Amelia said. "I've been looking for you. You ready to go?"

Daisy Feed nodded.

"I figured you would be," Amelia said, "talking to *her*. You talk about God?"

Daisy nodded.

"That's because she's old," Amelia said. "She's fixing to die. They all get like that. The curse of this family when they get old. Religious fantastics. That's what a maid we used to have called them. Said, 'You all must be religious fantastics, the way you go on. I never heard about most of that stuff, and I been a Baptist all my life.'"

Daisy laughed.

Suddenly the orchestra ceased. The sound of voices swelled in the room and crashed against the walls like surf. Then the orchestra blew a fanfare.

"Come on," Amelia said and dragged her by the arm into the central hall. There was a clear space and in it six bridesmaids in blue silk dresses. It looked like some sort of ritual. Their faces were raised in supplication. The orchestra blew another fanfare. The bride appeared on the balcony, shouldering a guitar aside. She leaned over the railing. The groom laughed and pretended he was flinging her off. Daisy Feed looked at the uplifted faces around her. And then it fell at her feet like a bird that had suddenly fallen from the sky. The ribbons were wrapped around it so tight it looked like a gull she had seen in Florida. It was high overhead, tumbling and falling. She saw it splash in the surf and ran forward to see what it was. The waves dragged it back and forth. When she got there it was hardly recognizable. The feathers were wet and wrapped in fishing line so tight it looked like a golf ball that had become unraveled. She never found the beak or legs, only one eye that looked out from the feathers as she turned to leave. The sea dragged it out and returned it again. The bridesmaids swarmed on it, and the guests swarmed on the bridesmaids. Daisy Feed stepped back out of the way.

"Why didn't you get it?" Amelia asked, trying to kick it with her foot. The bridesmaids were still screaming and scrabbling. "You could have got it. She aimed it at you."

"I didn't want it," Daisy Feed said. "I wouldn't know what to do with it."

"You could have thrown it," Amelia said. "That's what I'd do."

But Daisy Feed was already out the front door. Amelia followed her, coughing and laughing.

"There's Cousin Bobby," Amelia said. "Just in time to say goodbye."

"Goodbye, hell," Cousin Bobby said. "I'm stationed here to keep you from going." He held up a bottle of champagne. "You want some?"

"We're just leaving," Daisy said.

Cousin Bobby lifted the champagne and drank from the bottle.

"Where's your glass?" Amelia said. "You're wasting good champagne that way."

"You sip it," Daisy said.

"Sip it, hell. I paid for it."

Cousin Bobby was obviously drunk. His mouth was becoming indistinct. His lips were fading into his face.

"Say goodbye to Cousin Bobby," Amelia said. "Tell him what a good time we had."

"We had a good time," Daisy said, suddenly recognizing him as the father of the bride.

"Bullshit," Cousin Bobby said. "Nobody leaves. Listen, I mean it. There's a walkaway coming." He grabbed Amelia by the sleeve and pulled her over to Daisy Feed. He wrapped his arms around both their necks and bent their heads down. He spoke like a conspirator in a play. "Nobody leaves. There's a walkaway coming."

"What's a walkaway?" Amelia asked, adopting the same tone.

Cousin Bobby winked and led them toward a clump of azaleas. Behind the bushes, screened from the house, was a no. 5 washtub full of bottles, their snouts sticking out.

"Private stock," Cousin Bobby said, winking. He reached in and pulled out a bottle. "This is a holding pattern," he said, leading them toward a group of lawn chairs. Most of the chairs were already occupied. The people looked like an audience sitting there waiting.

They were barely settled in their seats when Cousin Bobby thrust the champagne at Amelia and said, "I'll be right back." He ran toward the driveway. An elderly couple was trying to escape. Daisy heard the word *walkaway*. She wondered what it meant. The only thing she could imagine was a car like the Shriners have for parades. The bride and groom get in it all dressed up to go on their honeymoon. They start to drive off, and the car comes apart. The front seat drives away, and they're left sitting in the back, which settles on the ground like a seesaw where somebody got off the other end.

"What is it, some kind of joke?" She told Amelia of the car she imagined, the walkaway.

"Something like that," Amelia said. "When Bobby was married, Cousin Henry and I let the air out of all the tires at the wedding, including the police cars. And Bobby came out and Sally—that was his first wife—going on their honeymoon." She lit a cigarette and stared at the tip.

"You let out all the tires?"

"That's right. One tire from each car. Two hundred and fourteen tires."

"What you let them out with?"

"A stick."

"Why'd you do it?"

"I don't know. Cousin Henry said do it, I did it." She laughed. "Policemen were pissed."

"What about Cousin Bobby?"

"I don't know. He went back in the house. Got their suitcases out of the trunk and went back in the house. People talked about it for months."

"He must have been ashamed of himself."

"How come?"

Daisy Feed thought of herself walking back to the house. She imagined Bobby walking beside her. They were inept and inadequate.

"He liked it," Amelia said. "That's how Thorlews do at a wedding."

"Well then, that's it!" Daisy Feed said. It was like a sudden illumination. "Walkaway means they *walk away*. They're going to walk away this time. He wants you to see it."

Amelia looked at her, then at the champagne bottle. She reached for the bottle and upended it. "You got a plan?"

"A plan?"

"How to stop them."

"No, of course not. I don't want to stop them."

"Then what's the sense in talking about it? You going to watch him?"

"Yes."

"Not me. That ain't how you do at a wedding." She took another swig of champagne. "Let's go. You ready?"

That's when they heard it. Low at first, like an incoming missile. There was no mistaking where it was headed. The sound grew louder and louder, like fate. People began running from the house. They came out the front door and jumped off the terrace as though they were escaping a fire. Daisy Feed saw Cousin Bobby. He had a picnic hamper in one hand and two bottles of champagne in the other—one in his fist, the other tucked beneath his elbow. Behind him were the bride and groom, still dressed for the wedding. The bride had the train of her dress hooked over her arm. They were holding hands and running. They were all running. The whole wedding party was running. Cousin Bobby stayed just in front of the bride and groom like John the Baptist, bumping people out of the way and shouting something. Daisy Feed could not make it out. The noise was too great. The trees were all roaring. Then the leaves started lifting. Pine needles rose as if by magic. They leaped out from underneath the azaleas and swept across the lawn like bugs.

"There it is," Amelia shouted.

And there it was, ten feet above the tops of the tallest pines, hovering and shaking the air. It seemed like a vision. The rafts of balloons were caught in the whirlwind. They clashed together, ducking and bobbing in the eddies of air, and then floated free. Daisy Feed watched them disappear into the endless blue of the sky. They seemed like thoughts or earthly pleasures lifted up and exalted. Seeing them rise she was filled with longing.

They had come to the end of the driveway and were still running.

"Hold on," Amelia said. "I can't get my breath."

She came to a sudden stop and was almost run over by a large woman in a pink dress who was still clutching a sandwich.

Fifty feet away, at the intersection of Adams and Hancock, the helicopter made its last pass and hovered. It hung in the sky like a giant bug. Daisy Feed looked up and saw the red-and-white design on the side, the black markings underneath, numbers and letters mixed up together, and for one brief moment it seemed like a language she once knew and had almost forgotten. The words were there on the tip of her tongue. Then it started its descent, coming toward her. Daisy Feed felt her throat constrict. She could hardly swallow, it was so tight. There was no room for the helicopter to land. On all sides were rows of telephone poles with swags of wires hanging off them, looping down from one to the other, and behind the wires bank after bank of pine trees and oaks, their tops interlocking. The only free space was the intersection, and that was full of people standing still and gaping, watching the helicopter descend on their heads.

A policeman began shooing them back like a child herding geese. He rushed at them, flapping his arms. His clothes fluttered in the blast of the rotor like fins on a fish or some sort of unearthly aura of light. The other policeman was pulling up the street sign. Everything had been thought out in advance, measured precisely down to the last foot. As soon as he finished lifting the pole, he put it aside and began running at the crowd with the other policeman until they finally cleared a space. People circled it on all sides cheering and clapping.

"There's Bobby," Amelia said. "Look at Bobby." He was beside the door on the passenger's side, loading up. First he put in the hamper, turning it sideways, stowing it somewhere behind the front seat. Then he packed the champagne bottles, half climbing inside the cockpit. Then he backed out and waved for the bride and groom, who ran forward clutching their clothes to keep them from being torn from their bodies. Halfway to the helicopter a policeman grabbed them and bent their heads down until they almost touched their knees. Then he sent the couple forward again bent almost double. Only their feet moved. Once they got to the helicopter the other policeman helped them in.

"Look at Bobby," Amelia said. "Look over there."

On the other side of the helicopter Bobby had opened the pilot's door and was pulling him out.

"What's he doing?" Amelia asked.

"Getting in," Daisy Feed said. She couldn't believe it. The pilot was bad enough. He seemed older than the oldest guest at the wedding and stood beside the helicopter bent in a perpetual crouch, cringing and looking confused. But at least he was sober. Bobby could hardly climb up in the cockpit.

"He know how to drive?" Daisy Feed asked.

"You mean a car?" a man standing beside her asked. "I don't think so." He laughed.

"They revoked his license," Amelia explained. "Who are you?"

"Wilbur Thornton," the man said. "Don't get me wrong. I love Bobby like a brother. I just wouldn't want to ride in a car with him."

"Who would?" Amelia said. "But this isn't a car."

"It's not exactly an airplane either," Wilbur Thornton said.

"Too late now," Amelia shouted.

The helicopter was already lifting. The crowd roared, cheering and clapping, expecting to see it rise straight up and disappear over their heads, but all it did was hover a few inches above the ground and rock back and forth. Bobby opened the door and stuck his head out. The crowd yelled again and surged forward. The policeman beat them back. Then Bobby leaned over and checked the pavement. He was still only a few inches off the ground.

"Hey Bobby," Amelia shouted. "You got a flat tire." She beat Daisy Feed on the arm. "I told him he got a flat tire," she shouted.

O God, don't abandon him now, Daisy Feed prayed. Let him get away this time. Don't just leave him there like that, rocking back and forth like a yo-yo, wearing himself out with the motion. And suddenly she saw an image of what she thought was a rag in the water. It was caught in the surf and washed back and forth, rotting with motion. She thought of her own life. O God, she prayed, set us free. Exalt us, O Lord.

Bobby popped his head out the door again. He leaned over and checked the pavement.

"He lost his keys," Wilbur Thornton said.

"That's not funny," Daisy Feed said. "What's the matter?"

"He can't drive it," Wilbur said.

Just then the helicopter roared and leaped straight up. It jerked to a stop and hovered there, its engine gunning ominously. The dust rose on a column of air and drove the skirts of the women against their legs. Their thighs looked fuller than in real life, richer and more voluptuous.

"Can't drive it?" Amelia said. "What you call that?"

"I don't know," Wilbur Thornton said.

"What if he kills them?" Daisy Feed asked.

"He knows what he's doing," Amelia said. "He's just playing around, what he's doing."

The helicopter kept jerking and rising as though someone had it tied on the end of a string and was pulling it up hand over hand. Every so often Bobby stuck his head out to check, until finally it was ten or twelve feet above the ground—just far enough above a man's head to have lost all connection with the earth. Seeing them there, Daisy was lifted as by a dark tide, her heart swelling with the motion like a boat tied at a mooring. And suddenly she knew what the old woman meant about marriage. It took ordinary men and women and struck them again and again with grace until they were not only blinded like Paul, they were utterly changed. They were lifted up and exalted, for whatever time they were given—the rest of their lives for some, growing together like vines in a thicket, or one brief moment of glory for others, in ecstasy.

She shaded her eyes against the sun. The helicopter seemed to burn in the air. Then it suddenly surged with power and swooped up and out in the curious sideways motion helicopters often have straight into the wires hanging from the row of telephone poles on the left-hand side of the intersection. It was like flying into a net. The wires wrapped around the rotors and began unraveling, pulling off the poles and twisting like ribbons. She thought of the message the man had placed on her bed. It was not what Amelia thought. She had been sent for. That's what it meant. She had come at last to the place appointed.

In the sky above her head the ribbons unfurled like tentacles, leaping and swirling until suddenly the rotors wobbled and stopped. Something exploded. The sparks fell like stars around her, as though they had been swept from the sky. Just before the helicopter fell and exploded, she caught a glimpse of the man she had seen the night before in the garden. He was standing alone in the sunlight, burning as if he was on fire. She realized she was burning too. They were both burning, lifted up together and soaring. She was dressed in a white gown and carried a bouquet of flowers. He was more handsome than she could have imagined. It was more than just beauty. He leaned forward and kissed her, and she felt something in her quicken. All the longing she had felt in her life, all the years she had ever lived and all the accumulated desire fell away, and not only was she a girl again, it was as though she had never been born, she was so innocent, her heart was so pure. She looked down and saw only the tops of trees. She had never known they were so soft and green. The people were standing in the street still waving. The policemen were cheering. Then they began to look smaller and smaller. The houses were like a Christmas village, the cars like toy cars. And then there was just the sky and in the distance a puff or two of cloud. Daisy Feed felt something beating in her like bird wings beating, throbbing like the throb of the rotors. Blessing on blessing, she thought as they soared. Grace after grace.

The Rain of Terror

"My name is Oletta Crews."

It sounded like a public announcement.

"This is James Terry Crews, my husband." She indicated the old man on the sofa beside her. He was dressed in khaki trousers and six-inch work boots. The woman had on a print dress, a bold floral pattern like slashes. She wore no shoes.

James Terry Crews gestured silently, acknowledging himself.

"Don't act like an idiot," Oletta Crews said, and the man dropped his hand.

"Just sit there." She turned away from him.

"This is James Terry Crews, my husband." She spoke in a powerful voice, lifted like a singer's from her diaphragm. "He's retired. We're both retired," she added significantly. "Him from work and me from housework. I got a bad heart, and I'm stout besides. You can see that. Doctor says I'm hundreds of pounds overweight, shortening my life with every bite of food I take. But what if I didn't? You think that'd help?"

She leaned forward and spoke confidentially. "There's more dies of hunger than does of the other."

She leaned back and gestured toward her husband again. "He helps me," she said. "He does what he needs to."

James Terry Crews sat beside her and stared straight ahead. He looked afraid.

"Listen to me," Oletta Crews said.

James Terry Crews started to get up, but she held out a hand and restrained him.

"Sit there," she ordered.

"Listen," she said. "I live here alone all by myself, a poor old woman, except for him. He lives here, too. Both together."

There were one or two aluminum windows, an aluminum door, a dinette set; strings of laundry overhead; a scattering of shoes and other debris on the floor; aluminum cans, some in plastic sacks, some loose, piled in the corner. The feeling was that of a cave or a nest—a secret, bestial place.

"This is a trailer, you notice that?"

James Terry Crews corrected her. "Mobile home."

"Same damn thing." She was suddenly angry. "I told you that. Pay attention."

James Terry Crews ignored her. "Trailer's something you trail after you," he explained. "That's what it means, trailer. You hitch it on the back of a car and hit the trail."

"And mobile home's mobile," Oletta Crews shouted. "That means it moves."

It seemed like an argument they had had before, the lines already memorized, the positions taken not only well known but entrenched and fortified.

"Tell them about the rain of terror."

"The rain of terror," Oletta Crews said, repeating the words, savoring them. She turned to James Terry Crews. "They don't want to hear about mobile homes. They want to hear about the rain of terror." She bugged her eyes as she said the last words, but the effect was not comic. Her eyes were filled with something other than fear.

"It was at night."

"Two nights ago." James Terry Crews sounded incredulous.

"It was two nights ago," Oletta Crews said. "And it was dark. James Terry was already home, soaking wet from the weeds where he'd been, and changed his clothes already to dry them. He was picking up aluminum cans. I'm too stout to get out and help or else I'd be there driving the truck, but I can't even drive no more. It's bad on my heart, and the pedals are too close anyway. They're all underfoot. It's hell to be old." She leaned forward. "If I was you, I'd die before I got there." She laughed silently, baring her gums.

"I used to be a house painter," James Terry Crews announced suddenly. "Twenty-eight years and every day sober on the job."

"That don't matter," Oletta Crews shouted. "They don't want to hear about that. You're retired. He sells aluminum cans," she explained. "That's what he does now. They got a yard in town buys them. Beer cans and such as that."

"I didn't always do it," James Terry Crews said. "I used to paint with the best of them."

"That was then. This is now. I'm telling this," picking up where she had left off. "He came in sopping wet from the rain of terror where he been out in the weeds all day looking for beer cans, and I told him what I saw on TV so he don't fall too far behind. And he was changing his socks. I can close my eyes and still see him sitting right there." She pointed across the room at an overstuffed chair that matched the sofa. The arms were shiny and greasy with wear. The seat was piled high with clothes, the upper layers of which had toppled over onto the floor. "Sitting in that chair right there changing his socks, when I heard this knocking at the door."

"What did you think?" James Terry Crews asked.

"I thought, Who's that?"

"Me, too," James Terry Crews said. "I thought, Who's that?"

"I thought, Who's that knocking on the door in the dark? I knew it wasn't nobody I knew. His children are gone, and I don't have none, and all my kinfolks are dead before me."

"Tell them about the news."

"I don't generally watch the news if I can help it," Oletta Crews said, "but this night was special. The good Lord led me to it this night. It's like I almost heard this voice say, 'Don't touch the TV. I got something on the news.' I was too tired to get up, and it said, 'Don't do it, then. I got something better for you to do than get up and change the channel. I got something to show you right here on this one you're watching.' It's like I almost heard this voice beside the still waters, leading me on in the valley of the shadow of death where I fear no evil for thou art with me. Thy rod and staff they comfort me."

"And you were afraid," James Terry Crews said.

"Of course I was afraid after hearing what I heard and knowing it was some kind of message delivered on TV special for me. Of course I was afraid. Who wouldn't be? I knew he'd protect me like he done. That's why I'm alive and the other one's dead because I could walk through the valley of the shadow of death and fear no evil. So the answer is no. No, I wasn't afraid. But I *was* interested. When I heard how he escaped from the work camp and killed two men, and it wasn't more than five miles down the road and was coming this way, I wasn't afraid, but I *was* interested."

"She heard the knock," James Terry Crews explained.

"I heard the knock and wondered, Who is it? But I already knew. I said, 'It's him.' "

"And I said, 'Who?' "

"Let me tell it," Oletta Crews shouted. "You weren't even there when it happened. I'm telling it. Listen," she said. "This is how it happened. I heard the knock, and I said, 'It's him,' and James Terry looked up from his sock and said, 'Who you mean?' and I said, 'The one on TV when you wasn't here escaped from the work camp and killed two men. It's him at the door.' And he put on his sock"—indicating her husband—"and said, 'What you want to do?' And I said, 'Let him in. He might have some money hid.' "

"And I said, 'Money? What you mean, money?' "

"Where he hid it after he stole it," Oletta Crews said. "I thought he might have some, and I said, 'Let him in. He might have some money hid.' And James Terry went to the door, one shoe on and one in his hand, and it was him. I was sitting right here where I always sit on this side of the sofa, and I saw him standing in the door soaking wet where it was raining outside in the dark as far as the eye could see. Looked like silver knives. And he said, 'Can I come in? I'm awful wet.' And I yelled, 'I can see you are, honey. Let him in, James Terry. Let him in to get dry.' And he came in, and I said, 'Get him a towel.' And James Terry got him a towel and sat down and put on his shoe. And I said to him, 'I know who you are.'"

"She knew who he was," James Terry Crews said.

"I told him I saw his picture on TV, and I knew who he was, thanks to God, and what he was there for."

"What was that?" James Terry Crews asked.

"You were there. Don't ask things you already know. He was there to rob us. He came there to rob us."

"Your life was in danger."

"My life was in danger. As soon as I saw him, I knew I might not live."

She paused, staring at something in the distance.

"Go on."

"I told him his name. I said, 'You're Q. B. Farris, escaped from the work camp.' And he said, 'Yes ma'am. I can't fool you, I can see that.' And I said, 'That's right. There's many a one better than you tried all my life, and they didn't do it, so why should you?' And he laughed. He was good-hearted. I can say that for him. He might have been mean, but he was good-hearted. He didn't care."

"I liked him," James Terry Crews said.

"Then he said, 'You know who I am? You know what I done?' And I said, 'Some. I know the most recent.' And I told him he killed two men. And he said that was exaggerated. And I said, 'It's on TV.' And he said he didn't care, it was exaggerated. And I said, 'Don't kill me. I'm just a poor old woman. It won't help to kill me. I don't know where your money's hid.' And I saw him looking at James Terry where he just finished putting on his shoe, and I knew what he was thinking. I said, 'Don't kill him either. He got to help me. I'm retired.' And he laughed like he done and said, 'What you retired from, momma?' And I said, 'Don't call me momma. I ain't your momma. I ain't nobody's momma.' And he said, 'You look like you ought to be. You got a kind face and a big bosom.' And I thought then, he's going to rape me. Been in prison with men too long."

"His name was Duke," James Terry Crews explained.

"Q. B. Farris. He said his name was Duke. He said, 'Call me Duke. I don't know who Q. B. is.'"

"And I said, 'What's the Q. B. stand for?' And you know what he said? He said, 'Queer Bastard.' I didn't know what to make of that."

"Except he wasn't queer," Oletta Crews said. "Else he wouldn't have wanted to rape me."

"Unless he was both."

"I'm telling this," Oletta Crews shouted. "We already agreed on that." She looked straight ahead. "That's the kind of person he was, full of useless jokes like that. He didn't care. You know what he said when I said don't kill me? He said, 'I wouldn't kill you or him either, momma. I got a momma of my own.'"

"What did you think?" James Terry Crews asked.

"I thought, Well, where is she? I said, 'You say you got a momma, where is she?' I figured she might have the money. And he said, 'Oconee, Tennessee—in the graveyard,' and looked at me and laughed. And I said, 'You laughing because she's dead or you laughing because you broke her heart?' That straightened him out. He quit laughing and said, 'Neither one. I loved my momma. She's the only one I trust.' And I said, 'I reckon. I'd trust her too, state she's in now.' That's when he hit me."

"He hit you?" James Terry Crews glanced at her, then turned away.

"He tried to," Oletta Crews said. "Then he looked at me and said, 'She died when I was still in prison. I never got to go to the funeral because it was out of state.' Said if it'd been in the state, they'd have let him, but she was buried in Tennessee, and that's a whole other system. And I thought, So what? She wouldn't know if you were there or not—chained like a wild dog at a funeral. 'They all die. That's a common fact,' I told him. 'She'd have died if you were in jail or not.' And he said it wasn't the dying he minded. It was they wouldn't let him out to be there. That's what he hated. And that's when he told me about the nine years. He said, 'I ain't been my own man in nine years, and nine more to go.' And I thought, Whose fault is that? Don't come crying on my shoulder. You should have thought about that when you decided what you wanted to be."

"What do you mean?" James Terry Crews asked.

"What do I mean? I mean a robber—steals money and hides it somewhere. And I said, 'Your momma's house still standing? That where you going? And he said no, he liked it here. And I said, 'I don't got no money. You might want to go and get yours.' And he said, 'Mine?' like he didn't know what I was talking about. He said, 'I don't got no money. What are you talking about?' And I said, 'That money you got hid you come out of jail to get.' And he said, 'I don't got no money hid—I come out because I couldn't stand to stay in,' and laughed like he done, so I knew he was lying. I said, 'Where's your home at in Oconee? You from town?' I figured that's where he hid the money. And he said, 'Oconee? I ain't from Oconee. I'm from right here.' He was born and raised in this county. Reason his momma died in Oconee, she was living with her sister, and they buried her there. That's when I knew he had it on him. All the money he stole and buried, it was right there beside me. Only difference was he had it, not me, and he was fixing to leave if he could."

"I didn't know what that meant," James Terry Crews explained, "but she said it was stolen already and buried nine years, and besides they're all dead anyway . . ."

"I said I'd tell it," Oletta Crews said, each word heavy with its own weight.

James Terry Crews did not look at her. He did not answer.

"And that's when he said, 'How about some supper?' He was looking at me. And I said, 'You talking to me?' And he said, 'I was. I ain't now,' and laughed like it was some kind of joke. He said, 'You look like you might be hungry. How about you and me eating something?' And I said, 'I ain't hungry.' And he said, 'Well, then why don't you rustle up something for me?' And I said, 'I don't cook. I'm retired.' And he said, 'Retired? What are you retired from?' And I said, 'The human race.' That took him back. And he said, 'Lord God, I thought you had to be dead for that.' And I said, 'Some do. Your momma maybe.' And he said, 'Don't talk about my momma. She's some kind of saint in heaven when you rot in hell.' And I said, 'I don't believe in saints.' And he said he didn't care. He knew her, I didn't, and started doing these things on his head like he was beating up on himself. And I said, 'What's that?'"

She turned to her husband. "Show how he done."

James Terry Crews looked surprised. He took off his glasses and slapped at his forehead, then at his ears. First with one hand, then with the other.

"I saw Duke do that," Oletta Crews said, "I said, 'What you do that for?' And he said it was something he learned in prison. Means you're sorry for what you done. And I said, 'What for?' And he said, 'Whatever. It works for all.'"

"I thought he was crazy," James Terry Crews said.

"Me too. I figured he was going to kill us both or else stay there and keep us for ransom."

"What she means is hostages."

"That's right. Stay with us here till he was safe and then kill us as soon as he walked out that door heading to California."

"She wants to die in California," James Terry Crews explained.

"That's right. I'm a poor old woman. That's my only hope, to see California and die happy there. That's all I want."

"That's all she wants."

"They got the Pacific Ocean out there. I got a picture in the bathroom from *National Geographic*. You ever see that one on California? That picture I got's the best one in it. I see that picture, I get all smooth inside. The jitters fall off like leaves off a tree. Shows the ocean and the sun going down, smooth and calm as far as the eye can see. Another thing—it don't ever rain. There ain't no rain of terror out there. Nature is mild. They got orange trees, bloom all year, and you want an orange, you pick it yourself."

"They got retirement," James Terry Crews said.

Oletta Crews turned and stared at him. James Terry Crews fell silent.

"What he was saying is they take care of you out there even if you don't got no children."

"I got a daughter."

"There ain't no minimum social security," Oletta Crews said. "No matter how much you made, they fix it up so you live like a prince. It ain't like here. They care about you in California. All it takes is getting out there. You got a bus ticket to California, you got a ticket to the Garden of Eden. It's like what they call your Heart's Desire. 'Lay up for yourselves treasure in heaven, where neither moth nor rust doth corrupt, and where thieves do not break through nor steal. For where your treasure is, there will be your heart also.'"

"They know all that," James Terry Crews said. "Tell them what happened."

"That's what I'm trying to do. He was going to California, and we stopped him, that's all." Oletta Crews stopped suddenly as though slamming a door. "We already told the police."

"That was yesterday. This is today," her husband explained.

"What do I care? I'm old." She paused, "I said, 'Fix your own supper. I'm too old.'"

"I fixed it for him."

"He fixed it."

"I told him I'd fix it. I said, 'I generally fix the meals around here.'"

"Duke said, 'You know how to cook?'" Oletta Crews turned to her husband. "I'm telling this."

James Terry Crews stared straight ahead as in an old photograph. He gave no sign of having heard. He looked as though he might have been dead the last twenty or thirty years.

"All right," Oletta Crews said, leaning forward. "Listen to this. Duke said, 'You know how to cook?' like he was surprised at a man cooking. And I said, 'How you think you ate in prison?' And he said, 'With my hands.' And I said, 'What?' And he said, 'I ate with my hands. Haw haw.' And I said, 'I thought you might have used a spoon.' That straightened him up. And then I said, 'He learned in the army'"—meaning James Terry Crews. "He was in the Second World War and cooked for generals, when he wasn't killing folks."

"I cooked for General Eisenhower." The memory seemed to stir the ashes in James Terry Crews. "I cooked steaks and eggs for breakfast, and he drank whiskey. He didn't touch a drop of coffee. He said, 'I'll have whiskey, Cookie. You got some bourbon?' And I said, 'Damn right. I'll make it myself.' I didn't even know what I was talking about. He was the most famous man in the world. This was overseas in France."

"They don't want to hear about that," Oletta Crews shouted. "That's too long ago, and he's dead anyway. They want to hear about Q. B. Farris."

"He's dead, too."

"He died more recent."

James Terry Crews turned away.

"Now, where was I?" Oletta Crews asked.

"Cooking supper," James Terry Crews replied.

"You were out cooking supper. I was entertaining him. I asked what he robbed to get in the work camp for eighteen years. I figured it must have been a bank. And he said, 'Robbed? Who told you that?' And I said, 'I don't need nobody to tell me nothing. I can figure it out by myself.' And he said, 'Then in that case you tell me.' And I said, 'A bank. I figure you for robbing a bank.' And he looked up quick under his hair. Had this hair over his eyes. And that's when it came to me. If he robbed a bank, there must have been a lot of money. Where was the suitcase? I said, 'You got a car?' And he said, 'Not yet. I'm fixing to.' And I said, 'How'd you get here then?' And he said, 'Through the woods. I walked.' And that's when I knew he had it on him, thousands of dollars wrapped up in plastic inside his pocket. And I said, 'You going to California?' And he said, 'Not if I can stay with you, momma. I love you too much to go off and leave you.'"

"Then we ate supper," James Terry Crews said, "and I told him about the army. He said it sounded a lot like prison, and I told him he was wrong about that. 'There's a world of difference between them,' I said."

"They just talked about this and that," Oletta Crews said. "Most of it him and the other one. I didn't listen. I was thinking about what comes next. And then I asked him, 'Are we prisoners?' And he said, 'Not any more than I am.' And I said, 'What's that supposed to mean?'"

"That was what you might call a threat," James Terry Crews explained.

"A threat?" Oletta Crews asked.

"Meaning we were hostages."

"That's right," Oletta Crews said. "We were hostages. It was a threat."

"Then we finished supper."

"We finished supper," Oletta Crews said, "and he said, 'Here, let me help you.' And I said, 'Help what?' And he said, 'Clean up. Don't you clean up the dishes? You let them stay dirty or you got dogs?' And I said, 'Dogs? What dogs got to do with it?' And he said, 'A joke.' He was joking. He was a jokey fellow, he said. That's one thing I got to get used to. And I said, 'What for?' And he said, 'What for? To understand what I'm saying. That's what for. To get the good out of me.' And I said, 'I don't see nothing funny about dogs.' And he said he meant lick the dishes. Clean them that way. And I said, 'James Terry does the dishes. And besides that, I never had a dog in my life. Dogs unclean. It says in the Bible.' Then I told him, 'They don't have dogs in California.' And he looked surprised at that and said, 'California? You ever been out to California?' And I said, 'Not yet. I'm fixing to.'"

"As soon as she can sell this place," James Terry Crews explained. "She's been talking about it ever since she retired. 'Going to California,' I told him. 'That's where she wants to go and die happy.'"

"And he laughed at that," Oletta Crews shouted. "I said, 'What are you laughing at? That some kind of joke like dogs?' And he said, 'No ma'am. I was thinking about dying happy.' That struck him funny. He said, 'I can't figure that one out.' And I didn't even look at him. I told my husband, I said, 'You better clean up the dishes before he calls in some dogs to do it.' And he laughed and made like he was going to hug me, but I flung him off. And he said, 'That's why I like you, momma. You're so fast and full of jokes.'"

"Then we went and washed the dishes," James Terry Crews said. "He called me dad."

"Same way he called me momma," Oletta Crews shouted. "He didn't mean it. I told him, 'I ain't your momma. Your momma's dead. I wouldn't have a son in the work camp.' And he said, 'It'd break your heart. It'd break your heart, wouldn't it, momma?' And I told him it'd kill me for sure if I had a child and he ended up in the work camp for eighteen years. And he said, 'Nine'—like he was setting me straight. He laughed and said, 'I stayed for nine. I ain't fixing to stay for the rest. That way I'm ahead.' He didn't care."

"Tell them about the dictionary."

Oletta Crews reached under the sofa and pulled out a book. The covers were torn off, the pages dirty and dog-eared. She held it up for inspection.

"This is the dictionary," Oletta Crews announced. It was like an exhibit, a piece of evidence. "I was reading it."

"Reads it all day, that and the Bible, when she ain't watching television," James Terry Crews explained. "That's what she does. She does that to pass the time."

"It's all in there, everything you need to know," Oletta Crews said. "One's the head and the other's the heart. I got something to figure out, I read the dictionary till I find what it is."

"The Bible's the heart," James Terry Crews explained. "She reads it to ease her heart."

"When it gets too full," Oletta Crews said. "When I get to suffering too much. It puts my weary heart to rest. But I couldn't find it. It was there, but I couldn't find it."

"Find what?" James Terry Crews asked.

"What comes next," she said. "And then it came to me. I was in the bathroom, and I heard them washing dishes and talking like bees in the wall, and I was looking out at the ocean, that picture I told you about of the water. And that's when it came to me."

"That's when she decided."

"I didn't decide. Something told me."

"Something told her."

"Like a voice in California. I got up and flushed the toilet and went back and sat down and turned it over in my mind."

Oletta Crews held up her hand. "Listen to me," she said. "This is the main part. I knew what he was fixing to do, and he knew I knew. He already killed two men to get here. I heard that where God led me this far on TV, and now he was telling me what to do next."

"God," James Terry Crews explained. It was like nailing a pelt on a wall. "The voice she heard. It was God."

Oletta Crews looked at him with contempt. "They know that. Who else got a voice? Of course it was God. Speaks in your heart just like he led me on TV to know who it was came to the door in the rain of terror. And he opened it"—indicating her husband—"and I looked out and knew who it was like in a mirror, he looked so familiar."

"You were afraid."

"Yes."

"You killed him because you were afraid."

"Yes." And then, "I didn't kill him."

"I killed him."

"Don't listen to him," Oletta Crews shouted. "Listen to me. He don't know nothing."

"I don't know nothing."

"He just did it. I heard the voice."

"She heard the voice. I'm the one murdered him."

"It wasn't a murder. The police said that. They say, 'You shoot whoever you want to, lady, breaks in your house and keeps you hostage.'"

"Damn right, wouldn't you? She was afraid he might kill her."

"Yes, and I was afraid he might kill him, too," Oletta Crews said, indicating her husband. "I need him to help me. Besides, I heard the voice. It spoke in my heart." She stopped as though reflecting. "'You can't serve two masters.' That's what it said. 'No man can serve two masters: for either he will hate the one and love the other; or else he will hold to the one and despise the other.'"

"That's right. Then what?" James Terry Crews asked.

"I thought how to do it."

"How to kill him," James Terry Crews said.

"I thought of ways of how to do it. Like roach tablets, putting them in his grits at breakfast. And then I thought, What if they don't work? What if they just work on roaches? Then I thought of rat poison. But what if he tastes it? Drano. That's too strong. Lysol and Clorox. He might have to drink a gallon. Poison is out."

"I told her about the nail."

"That was later, when he went to bed."

"You were still thinking about it."

"Not that way I wasn't."

"In the ear . . . ," James Terry Crews began.

"Let me tell it," Oletta Crews shouted. "I'm telling this. It was all over by then. I already figured it out. He said, 'What about a nail?' And I said, 'A nail?' And he said, 'I read about it in the paper.'"

"No, I didn't. It was in the *Police Gazette*. In the Charlotte, North Carolina, bus station. I was there waiting, and I went to the newsstand and picked up the magazines like you do, looking for pictures . . ."

"They got pictures of half-naked women where they been raped, in the *Police Gazette*," Oletta Crews said. "That's what he was looking at."

"No, I wasn't. I was just looking, waiting for the time to pass till I got my bus, and I picked up the *Police Gazette*, and the first thing I turned to, that was it. Nail murder. All about how this farmer in Kansas and this girl-friend he got killed her husband by driving a thirty-penny nail in his ear."

James Terry Crews glared about him in triumph. "They killed him by driving a nail in his ear." He leaned forward. "You know why they did that?"

"So it wouldn't be a wound," Oletta Crews shouted. "They know that. The nail went in, and they wiped up the blood and burned the rag and called the doctor and said, 'He rose up in the bed and shouted and fell over dead.' And the doctor didn't even look in the ear. Said, 'Must have been a heart attack.' And they almost got away with it except for the farmer. He went crazy and confessed it all. Otherwise they'd have joined the farms, his and the one she got from the murder, and made a million dollars by now selling it off for shopping centers."

"You ever hear anything like that?" James Terry Crews said proudly. "That's what you call a perfect crime, except he went crazy."

"That's where he went wrong," Oletta Crews said. "That's why it ain't perfect. So I told him the nail was out." She lowered her voice. "I even thought of cutting his throat. Waiting till he was asleep and then creep in the light at the end of the hall shining in so we could see the vein in his neck beating and then pull the razor across it. But what if it's too deep? What if the gristle is too hard to cut through? I ain't that strong, and I knew he couldn't do it," indicating her husband. "He can talk about nails all he wants to, but I knew he couldn't even hold it still. He's too soft. He might look at him and feel sorry for him. I couldn't chance it. I didn't want Duke getting up, throat flapping open from ear to ear where I cut at it and him not dead. Ain't no telling what he might do, bleeding like that, bubbling and shouting. He'd kill me for sure. That's when I knew James Terry would have to shoot him."

"I had to. You heard her."

"Hold on," Oletta Crews shouted. "Don't rush ahead. I got out of the bathroom, and they finished the dishes and came in and sat down, and James Terry said, 'Duke's been telling me about all the good times they had in the work camp. He liked it there.' And I said, 'If he liked it so much, why didn't he stay? Why come around here bothering us?' And then Duke says, 'What's on TV?' And I say, 'Nothing.' And he says, 'They got Monday Night Football.' And I say, 'I don't watch it. I don't know the rules.' And he says, 'What about you, old dad?'—speaking to my husband, James Terry Crews."

"I told him I don't watch it either, and he said, 'Why not? You don't know the rules?' And I said, 'I know them. I just don't watch it.'" He glanced at his wife. "It's too rough."

"That's right," Oletta Crews said. "I told him that game's all right for the work camp. I said, 'Rough men done worse than that to each other every day of their lives, but it ain't all right for women and children. It's too rough. Besides which,' I told him, 'it ain't Monday night.' And he said, 'Not Monday?' And I said, 'That's right. Yesterday was Monday. This is Tuesday.' And he laughed and said, 'Lord God,' and grinned like he just ate something he shouldn't."

"He had this kind of shit-eating grin," James Terry Crews explained.

"It was attractive, I don't mean that," Oletta Crews said. "And he said, 'I can keep up with it in the work camp. It's when I get out, that's when I lose track.' And I said, 'How many times you get out?' And he said every chance he got. That and Monday Night Football's his only pleasure, he said. That and beating up on folks to get in the work camp in the first place. 'And grinning,' I said. 'You left out grinning.' And he laughed and said, 'That's right, momma. That's the only pleasure I got, that and being here with you. What about going to bed?' And I thought, This is when the raping commences. And I said, 'Not me. I don't go to bed and get raped.' And you know what he did? He laughed. He fell on the floor like he couldn't stand up and kicked his feet in the air pretending. Looked like the devil come up through the floor from hell. And he said, 'Momma, you ever think you going to get raped, you know what I'd do?' But I didn't answer. I was too ashamed. And he laughed and said he'd stay up instead. 'I'd stay up all night before I'd go to bed and get raped,' and so on like that. But I didn't look at him. I heard him scrabbling around down there, but I didn't dare cast my eyes on him to see what nasty thing he was doing."

"He was getting up," James Terry Crews explained.

"I didn't want to see what it was for fear it might be something I didn't want to. That's how he was. He didn't care. Then I felt him lean over me, grinning and mocking, and say what he meant was for me to go to one bed and him to another and sleep this time, if that was all right with me. And that's when I knew there wasn't no way. Even if I could have saved him before, I knew I couldn't after that. I was a prisoner in my own house."

"He trusted us," James Terry Crews explained. "He said, 'I sleep light, but I trust you anyway, old dad. I know you don't want me to go back to the work camp for nine more years.' And he said to Mrs. Crews, 'Wake me for breakfast, you hear me, momma? Don't let me oversleep my welcome. I'm just going to rest a minute. Then I'm going to have to leave you, much as you hate to see me go.'"

"And I thought, To California. He's going to California without me," Oletta Crews shouted, "and leave me alone and take all the money. And that's when I told James Terry to kill him. I said, 'Go get your gun.'"

"I got this single-barrel shotgun," James Terry Crews said. "First gun I ever owned."

"They don't want to hear about that."

But James Terry Crews turned on her. "Let me talk," he said. "This is interesting. I got that gun in Fayetteville when I was a boy. Walked in and slapped down seven dollars and said, 'I'll take that Stevens single-barrel.' And Mr. Robert reached up and got it out of the cradle—had this cradle made out of deer hoofs—and he said, 'This squirrel gun?' And I said, 'Squirrel gun? I could bring you down with it if I had some buckshot.' That's the way I was then. I didn't take no smart talk from nobody. I said, 'This gun cost too much to waste on squirrels.' And he said, 'What you fixing to shoot with it, if you don't shoot me?' And I said, 'I don't know,' like I was still thinking about it. I said, 'I ain't made up my mind yet.' And then I said, 'Give me some buckshot,' and looked right at him. That got his attention. Buckshot'll blow a hole in a man big as a melon. I was a man when I was fourteen, when I first went to work for the sawmill. I worked there till I hurt myself and moved to Atlanta and got married and went to painting. But I kept that gun. I had others, but it was my favorite. It reminded me."

"That's beside the point," Oletta Crews said. "The point is I could say, 'Go in there and do it,' and James Terry would go in there, and I'd feel it shake where he shot at him—once, twice, three times maybe—in the head or in the back, wherever it hit him. But what then? He was laying in my bed, and he'd bleed on it and ruin the mattress."

"Not to mention the shot," James Terry Crews said. "She didn't even think about that. I had to tell her. I said, 'Blood ain't nothing. Blood washes off. But buckshot—buckshot'll blow a hole in a man as big as a melon, right through him and the mattress both. Might even blow a hole in the floor.'" His face lit up. "I ever tell you about the time we were moving, and there was a copperhead in the house, and I had the gun, but the shells were packed up somewhere in boxes?"

"Don't be an idiot."

"I shot a hole in the floor," James Terry Crews shouted, hurrying to the end. "I found the shells and shot the floor clean out. Snake with it." He looked at his wife. "Ever see buckshot hit a melon?"

"Hush up," Oletta Crews said. "You're talking too much."

"It explodes," James Terry Crews said. "You can't even find the pieces. It just lifts and disappears. Same way with heads."

"I knew I'd smell it," Oletta Crews said. "Whenever I put my face to it, I knew I'd smell it in my sleep no matter how good I washed it. The police would come and take off the body, but they'd leave all the blood in the mattress and on the sheets and on the rug across the floor where it runs out when they carry him off, and I'd have to clean it up. He can't clean," indicating her husband. "All he can do is paint."

"I say paint it. If it's dirty enough to wash it, it's dirty enough to paint it, I say."

"Only trouble is, you can't paint sheets and mattresses where all the blood ran out." She leaned forward and spoke confidentially. "If it wasn't drinking, it was talking. All his life. He'd get to painting a house and talk himself right off the job. Couldn't even climb the ladder or mix the paint, he talked so much. Folks don't like that. They run him off. And it wasn't even drinking sometimes. It's what he calls high spirits."

James Terry Crews looked at her balefully. "High spirits," he said.

"Besides which, I thought of something else," Oletta Crews said, rocking forward. "What about Q. B. Farris?" She bugged her eyes as someone else might simulate fright. "Where was his gun? And then I thought about the money. What if he had it in his pocket and James Terry shot it all full of holes? Would they still take it? What do they do with money like that?"

"They don't do nothing," James Terry Crews replied. "Because it blows away just like a melon. If he had that money in his pocket, you couldn't even find the pieces."

"That's what I thought. Besides which, he can't even see in the daytime let alone in the dark at night. He might point it at his head and hit the wrong place, where the money is, and just wound him, and he'd come crawling out at me."

"That's why I picked up two other loads," James Terry Crews explained. "In case I missed. I ain't never shot a man before."

"He said he might miss the first but not the second. But I told him, 'No. It's too dangerous. There's some other way.' And he said, 'I can't think of it.' And I said, 'I know. I wasn't expecting you to. Give me a minute.'" She paused and then spoke in an altered voice. "'Even though I walk through the valley of the shadow of death, I fear no evil, for thou art with me.' And then it said, 'It ain't your death. That's why it's a shadow. If it was your death, it'd be real. But killing him's only a shadow.' And as soon as I heard that, I knew who it was and all my fear fell off me like sweat, and I dried up, it's like I was reborn. I knew what was promised. And I said to James Terry, 'Let it go. Don't shoot him now. Wait till later.' And he said, 'When?' And I said, 'When he's fixing to kill us.'"

"And I said, 'What if it's too late? What if he beats me to it?' And she said, 'Then you don't have to worry. You'll already be dead by then.' That don't make no sense to me."

"And I said, 'It won't come to that. Just get it loaded. I'll give you a sign—like this.'" She winked her eye and waved her hand.

"And I said, 'What if I'm tying my shoe and don't see you do it?'" James Terry Crews said. "'What if I get up and go to the bathroom?'"

"We heard him rattling around in there," Oletta Crews said. "And I said, 'Get ready. He's fixing to kill us.' And James Terry said, 'What do I do?' And I said, "'Sit here.'" She patted the cushion beside her. "'Sit down here and hide the gun under the sofa where you can get at it.'"

"And I said, 'That's too slow. He'll shoot us both before I get to it.' And she said, 'That's good. In that case you don't got nothing to worry about.'"

"All my fear dried up like sweat," Oletta Crews said.

"And I cocked it and put it under the sofa. There ain't no safety on a single-barrel Stevens," James Terry Crews started to say, but his wife interrupted him.

"They don't want to hear about that. We were sitting on the sofa waiting."

"Not me. I was thinking about what if he kills me. That worried me. I knew what she said, but it still worried me."

"And always will. That's what's wrong with you." She paused suddenly.

"We heard him stirring and singing, and then he came in tucking James Terry's shirt in his pants where he hid the gun and stopped and fell back all of a sudden like he was surprised and said, 'I didn't see you sitting there. You almost scared me to death, sitting there side by side. You know what you look like?' But I ignored him. And he said, 'Two cats. You look like two cats, lined up waiting for dinner. Ever see that?'—grinning and laughing to show he was lying. He tried to hug me, but I pushed him off. And then he said, 'I got to go, much as I hate to leave you, momma.'"

"And I said, 'Why don't you stay then? What's your hurry?'" James Terry Crews said. "I didn't mind him so much. He wasn't too bad except he might kill us. He had a good heart. Then I saw her look at me, and I felt my bowels tighten up. They were feeling loose . . ."

Oletta Crews ignored him. "And then Duke said, 'I'd sure like to stay, old dad. It feels just like home.' And I said, 'Home? It ain't your home. I don't want children. I never had them.' And he laughed at that and said, 'I know. I'd have guessed it at how you kept your figure even if you hadn't told me about it. You sure look good for a woman your age'—laughing and grinning so I didn't know if he meant it or not. And I tried to hit him. I said, 'Go on. Don't talk like that, my husband sitting right here beside me.'"

"And I said, 'Don't mind me. I think she's pretty good-looking my-self.'"

"And then he said, 'They'll be along directly looking for me. Don't tell them I been here. I'd rather be dead than go back to the work camp the rest of my life. How would you like it?' And I said, 'I wouldn't. But I wouldn't deserve to.' That straightened him up. And he said, 'Well, I got to go. Much obliged for the company. It ain't often I get to have such high old times.'"

"And I said, 'Me neither,'" James Terry Crews said. "'I enjoyed it,' I said. 'Come back. You ever get where they ain't looking for you, come back. You know where it's at. Come back and stay. We'd like to have you. You're good company.'"

"I didn't say nothing," Oletta Crews said. "And he said, 'How about you? You want me to come back too, momma?' And I said, 'I won't be here. I'm fixing to go to California.' Then his face fell, and he looked old. He said, 'I sure do wish you luck,' reaching over to shake James Terry by the hand. And he said to me, 'I know how you feel, wanting to go someplace like that, even if it's only to go there and die. That's one thing I learned in the work camp.'"

"Then he slapped me on the shoulder," James Terry Crews said, "and hugged me like that and backed off and said, 'I might buy this place myself if I had the time.'"

"That's how I knew he had the money," Oletta Crews said. "He wasn't lying."

"He'd have done it if he had the time."

"And the money," Oletta Crews said. "That's when I told him I might see him out there. And he said, 'Where?' And I said, 'California.' And he grinned and said, 'You might do it.' Then he looked at me. He looked me right in the eye and said, 'I'll see you in California, momma.' And I knew then I was right. He's fixing to walk right out that door and shut it behind him and stomp his feet down the steps like he's going somewhere, and then creep back when we're sitting here side by side on the sofa thinking he's gone now, the danger is over, our lives are safe in our own hands again, praising God and weeping for joy we ain't dead, he didn't kill us, when all of a sudden the door flings open, and there he is standing there grinning and laughing like a devil from hell, because it's a joke, don't you see, pretending to leave and then coming back and shooting us both right on the sofa side by side, one after the other—bang, bang, bang—till it wasn't even a sofa no more, just a hole in the floor and us in it, bits and pieces mixed with the stuffing."

"That's a shotgun," James Terry Crews explained. "You're talking about a twelve-gauge shotgun."

"That was his plan," Oletta Crews said. "I saw it as clear as I'm seeing you, and I knew I was right. It's just like him, I thought to myself—kill us like we were some kind of joke. You ain't got no will if you're a hostage. It's like you get tired. You can't even move. You got to sit there and wait."

"Unless you kill him first. That's right, ain't it, Letta?"

"It's like you can't move. You ain't got no will of your own."

"That's what I mean. That's why I killed him. No matter how good a heart he had, he was conceited."

"Listen to this," Oletta Crews shouted. "I said, 'Ain't you scared?' And he said, 'What for?' I didn't know if he was joking or not. I said, 'There's a posse of police out there waiting.' And he said, 'What for?'—like he didn't know what I was talking about—and went to the door and stuck his head out like he was trying to see who was out there. And I said, 'Because you don't care. You joke too much. You ain't serious.'"

"He was conceited. I could see that."

"I made the sign. And James Terry reached under and got the shotgun, and Duke turned around and looked at James Terry, and James Terry looked at Duke, and then his head lifted off. If it weren't for the roaring in my ears and the light and the smoke and the shaking on the sofa beside me where James Terry shot it off, I'd have thought it busted or something, like a balloon. One minute it was Duke Farris, the next minute it was gone like it went out the door. It was still raining, and I thought to myself, It ain't there. It ain't out there. You can look all you want to, but there ain't even bits and pieces. It lifted clean off. That head exploded."

She paused. "I was glad the door was open. That way it went right out. It didn't blow a hole in the wall, and there wasn't nothing left to clean up. I said, 'Here. Help me up.' But he didn't move. I got up and went over there, and you know what he had in his pockets? A ring snap off an aluminum can. He didn't even have a wallet. If he was hit by a car on the highway and killed on the spot, you wouldn't have even known who he was. I searched everywhere, and I told my husband, I said, 'James Terry, I can't find the money.' I couldn't believe it. And he said, 'What money?' He didn't even know what I was talking about. And I said, 'That money he's going to California with. The money he hid and come out to dig up.' And James Terry said, 'Where is it?' And I said, 'I don't know. You shot him too soon.'"

"He didn't even have a gun," James Terry Crews explained.

"He didn't have nothing except a ring snap off an aluminum can. But how was I to know that? The police said, 'Don't worry. You shot him on your own property.' And I said, 'My own property? I shot him in my own house. How was I to know?' And they said, 'No way. He might have had a gun to kill you.'"

"That's probably even my ring snap off an aluminum can," James Terry Crews said. "He had on my trousers. There wasn't nothing in his at all."

"Police said it was self-defense. Said, 'You killed him to save yourself. That's only natural.'"

"Ain't a jury in the land convict you of that."

"I couldn't move it," Oletta Crews said. "I sat down on the floor beside it and tried to push it out with my feet. I wanted to close the door. It was still raining. I said to James Terry, 'I can't move it by myself. Get up and help.' And he got up. Then I saw him lift an arm and start to drag him out. A leg slid by me and then a foot, and then I was free. The door was open, and I looked out and saw the rain. The floodlight was still on. It went out in the yard like a room and lit up the rain. I could see it coming down like knives. It was all silver, and in the tree it was all silver like ice—like the whole world turned to ice. And James Terry started to come in, and I said, 'Get the light.' And he got the light, and it was dark. It was dark out there as far as the eye could see, and I could still hear it raining. It was like it was moving, like a great wind lifting and heaving. And I said to James Terry, 'Close the door. Close the door on it.' And he closed the door."

"He wasn't so bad," James Terry Crews said, as though in eulogy. "I don't care what they say he done. He had a good heart. Lots of folks rob banks got better hearts than the people that own them. He was what you might call a godsend. I thought that. I thought to myself, Q. B. Farris— Duke—you're what you might call some kind of godsend."

"We were hostages," Oletta Crews shouted. "He took our will."

"I mean before that."

"There wasn't no before that. As soon as he came and knocked at that door, he took our will."

"I mean when we were doing the dishes. I thought to myself, He's some kind of godsend. I wouldn't be here laughing and talking and cutting the fool if he wasn't here. I'm grateful to him. I'm grateful he's here. He reminded me of when I was working." He paused. "Robbing banks . . . Robbing banks ain't so bad. I might have done that myself if I hadn't got hurt and moved to Atlanta and got married. It's a whole other way of doing—a whole other kind of life."

"Listen to me," Oletta Crews shouted. "I know about godsend. As soon as I heard that knock on the door, I felt it knocking in my heart, and I said to myself, It's God knocking at the door of my heart, asking me to open up and let him come in and change me, change my whole life." She paused. "There's a better place than this, and I thought I was going. But I know better now, even if he don't," indicating James Terry Crews. She lowered her voice, increasing its intensity. It sounded like someone else speaking inside her: "'For even Satan disguises himself as an angel of light. His end shall be according to his deeds.' And his end shows that," Oletta Crews said—"when James Terry shot him and there wasn't no money."

"And no gun."

"And nothing to show except mockery. All my hopes mocked and bleeding half in and half out the door where I couldn't even shut it myself, and he dragged it out where it'd been killed, I felt like something inside me was dead."

"Me too. It felt like something inside me was dead too. I didn't know what it was."

"I did. I sat on the floor where I'd been looking for money, and I thought to myself, You can't serve two masters. Satan appeared as an angel of light and killed all my hopes—took my will and killed all my hopes. But I'm still alive. I ain't dead, and I ain't changed. I'm just like I was."

The Concisest Tenant

She thought it was her husband scratching the headboard in a fragment of dream she could not remember, and then she was awake hearing the same sound. It was over her head. She lay in bed and looked at it and saw nothing but darkness and the sound coming from it like the sound of her own thoughts. "The rat is the concisest tenant," she thought, the words rising up unbidden. "It pays no rent." She thought of it as a secret presence.

She struck her husband on the arm. "Get up," she said. "There's a rat in the house."

He stirred beside her, and she struck him again.

"What happened?" he said.

"Listen."

They listened to the sound on the slope of the roof over their heads.

"Squirrels on the roof," her husband said, and turned over to go to sleep. She smelled the whiskey. It was inside the bed like the smell of something under the covers. She thought of their marriage. That's what it smelled like. She struck him again and kept striking him until he sat up.

"What's the matter?" he asked. He had already forgotten.

"It's night," she said. "Squirrels sleep at night."

"So what?"

She got up and turned on the light and saw what it was and ran out of the house into the yard. The noises of insects exploded around her. They seemed like the stars. Every individual voice she heard was like the sound of a star. Her heart rose up in her throat. It was as though she had never been outdoors at night, had never seen stars or heard the myriad voices singing. There were so many. She had never known there were so many.

Then her husband came out and said, "Bat. It's flying all over."

She saw that he had propped open the screen door with a paddle and was taking a screen out of a window, and she said, "What are you doing? You crazy or what? I'd rather have bats. What you think you're letting in there?"—thinking of all the sounds she was hearing, each with a different kind of body.

"Get the screen back," she told her husband. "I'll get the front door," and she ran and kicked out the paddle and slammed the door after her. It was only then that she realized that she had not locked it out. She had closed herself up with it. The bat came reeling across the ceiling. She ducked behind a chair just as her husband came in, saw it staggering toward him, and immediately backed out.

"What are we going to do?" he asked from the other side of the door, and she thought, He's still drunk.

Looking back, she realized it was the moment her whole life had changed. She knew she could not rely on him. He was too drunk. He was always too drunk.

"We can't just leave the house," she heard her husband say through the screen. And then it came to her.

"Get in the bedroom and turn off the light," she said. Her husband had turned on all the lights in the house.

"What good does that do?" her husband asked. And then he said, "I know. I'll hit it."

"What with?"

"A shovel."

"What?"

"A broom. A broom will kill it."

"Not in my house you won't."

"A motel then. Go to a motel and call the exterminator."

And she said, "Get in the bedroom and close the door so it can't get in there." And he got in the bedroom, and she crept about the house as under an invisible ceiling two or three feet from the floor. The bat dipped and fluttered in the air space over her, herded from room to room as she turned out the lights behind it and closed the doors, driving it forward, the bat always leaving the darkened room seeking the light ahead as though guided by a tropism, until they ended up in the kitchen.

The door was closed. She turned out the light. In the dark the bat could be anywhere. She slid on her rump across the tiles, keeping her head down for fear it would seek out her hair as bats are said to do, having a mysterious affinity for human hair, particularly the hair of a woman. Bats are covered with lice and vermin. If it ever touched her, she would never get clean. She would have to shave her head and wash it with kerosene. Besides getting rabies. She would foam at the mouth and die slowly in spasms.

Then she was at the white hulk of the refrigerator. It looked like a marble sarcophagus. She reached up for the handle and flung the door open. The room filled with color and light and the odor of cold. She was momentarily comforted by it. Then she felt the bat sweep past her, the wings in her ear like leather gloves rubbing together, scraping and squeaking. Then it was inside the refrigerator, seeking the light, and she slammed the door on it.

She rose to her full height and went into the bedroom. Her husband had already fallen asleep. He stirred when she got in bed beside him and asked what had happened. She said, "I froze it," but he was too drunk and too sleepy to know what that meant. She lay beside him listening to him breathe. Her eyes were open, and she could see in the dark. She was thinking not of the bat but of the rest of her life. The two seemed related.

The next morning she got up while her husband still slept. He looked like something deposited in her bed by a truck. She went into the kitchen and stood beside the refrigerator listening. Then she eased the door open a crack. It was still dark. She opened it a little more. The light came on, and she quickly closed it. This was not at all what she had imagined. She imagined something clean and painless, swift as a scalpel to the throat, innocent as poison gas. She leaned her head against the door and thought of never opening it again. She would go in the bedroom and get dressed, take whatever money they had, and get in the car and go somewhere, as far away as she could, and change her name and get a job and start a new life.

She opened the door to look again. The bat was on its side on the grill beside a bowl of green beans. A number of containers had been knocked over, and beans and maraschino cherries were scattered about like garbage, some under the bat and some on top. Its shoulders were hunched. One wing was folded under its body. The other was partially extended. She saw the delicate membranes, more delicate than the web of flesh between her own fingers. The skin was pink and covered with a thin coating of down. It was fawn-colored and matted in places where its fur was wet. The veins were blue and thin as a spider web. The cherries looked like gobbets of blood. There was juice everywhere.

She closed the door, thinking of never opening it again. She would have them take it away and buy a new refrigerator. Then she went and got the Scott towels. She opened the door and picked up the bat with a triple layer of towels. She took it in the bathroom and flushed it down the toilet. That seemed more fitting than throwing it out in the garbage. She would not bury it, but she acknowledged that it had been something more than green beans or maraschino cherries. Then she got a garbage can. It was half full, and she lined it with a plastic bag and began emptying out the refrigerator—the leftover meals and the food yet uneaten, the unbroken eggs, the unopened packages and jars. All of it was tainted, even the fruits and vegetables. It had all been touched and polluted. Her whole life. It was not just the bat.

She began weeping and humming a tune to herself. When she finished filling the garbage can, she tried to lift it, but it was too heavy. She put a throw rug under it and dragged it across the floor, rolling it on its rim over the threshold out on the back porch. She closed the door on it and began washing out the inside of the refrigerator, knowing that she would never be through. It filled with pink suds. She rinsed it. The suds were still pink.

She kept rinsing it. Then she scrubbed it with Lysol, washed it again, and scrubbed it with Pinesol.

She heard her husband flush the toilet. Then she heard his heavy tread. She thought of getting inside the refrigerator and closing the door, but she knew that was futile. She was already that hollow herself. She began humming again and forced herself across the room to the breakfast table. She sat down at one of the places she had set the night before. The plate in front of her was empty. It shone dully in the light. I will sit here the rest of my life, the woman thought. I will starve to death.

We do not know how to pray for what we need, but it is the spirit itself that intercedes for us with inexpressible groanings.

An Errand of Mercy

"It's closed," Ruby Upchurch said.

"Push on through, then," Ora Belle Ivey shouted. "We're on an errand of mercy, ain't we?"

Ruby Upchurch tentatively lifted her hand and touched the metal plate on the door as if testing its reality. "What if he ain't there?" she asked.

"He's there all right. I asked the nurse. I said, 'He in there?' And she said, 'That new resident?' And I said, 'Yes.' And she said, 'Of course. He don't ever leave.' And I said, 'Not even to go to the nurses' station?' And she said, 'Not even to do his business. And not only that, he can't talk.'"

"Can't talk?"

"That's what I hear. The nurse said he can't make a sound. Opens his mouth, nothing comes out but air. And I said, 'What's he do if he can't talk?' And she said, 'Rolls about in bed and watches TV.' And I said, 'How old is he?' And she said, 'Your age.' And I just looked at her. This is Miss Hawkins I'm talking about. Taught her and all her sisters when they couldn't even wipe their nose, let alone the rest of it. And I told her, 'I take that as a personal insult. What you mean, my age?' And she rushed up and patted me. You know how she does. She's one of them touchers, always touching. Tell you something, she'll touch your elbow or pat your shoulder or squeeze your arm like words ain't enough for her. She got to touch and make sure."

"Make sure of what?"

Ora Belle Ivey pulled up short. It seemed for a moment she did not know the answer. Then she pushed on. "Make sure it's sinking in," she said. "It's like squeezing and touching is part of it."

"John was like that," Ruby Upchurch said. "He'd tell me something, his hands were all over, talking and touching. That's what I miss. I can't remember the sound of his voice. Ain't that funny? But I remember the way he touched me. That's what I miss the most."

"Let the dead bury the dead," Ora Belle Ivey shouted. "Meanwhile I was telling you something. I said, 'What you mean, my age? I take that as a personal insult,' and she said, 'Mrs. Ivey, I didn't mean nothing'—hands lighting all over like flies. 'I mean he's young,' she said. 'He's too young to be in here. He's nothing like as old as the others.'"

"You mean he's afflicted?" Ruby Upchurch said in sudden sympathy. "You mean he was born that way?"

"That's what I wanted to know. But she said, 'No, he had a stroke.' Wiped him clean."

"What you mean, wiped him clean?"

"Ever seen a rag on a blackboard? It's time to go home, and you take a wet rag and wipe it clean? That's what I mean. It blurs out and runs together, and then little by little it's gone. That's how it is with strokes. Some are partial and some are complete. The partial ones, it all runs together; and when it's complete, it wipes you clean."

"You mean he's like a vegetable? Ain't that awful?"

"It's awful, all right. But not as bad as it might have been. There's always something worse off than you are. Thank God for that. Even vegetables, they got that to be thankful for."

"What's worse than vegetables?"

"There's always something. You can be sure of that. It's what they call God's infinite mercy. Now push on through," and she shouldered Ruby Upchurch aside. "The errand of mercy is about to commence."

The door swung inward with the weight of Ora Belle Ivey behind it. Ruby Upchurch peered over her shoulder. The room was in darkness except for the blue light of a television set screwed to the wall. Opposite it stood the rectangular plane of the bed, white against the darker floor. In the bed was a figure no larger than a child or small ape dressed in a hospital gown and ski cap. The only other object in the room was a metal chair that served as a table. It was piled high with personal effects. On top of the pile was a blue towel. The rest of the room seemed to extend indefinitely into the shadows. The impression was one of immense sparsity and emptiness, not threatening, but featureless—a sense of sameness, boredom: one of the more subtle forms of despair.

"There he is," Ora Belle Ivey said. "But you can't hardly make him out, it's so dark in here. Turn on the light. No wonder he had a stroke and turned into a vegetable, laying in the dark all day."

Ruby Upchurch found the switch, and the room was suddenly filled with light. It was as though it emanated from them, just as angels are said to descend to earth in an aura of light, their shapes defining themselves within it.

"That's better," Ora Belle Ivey said. "And turn off that TV. He don't need that now he got us."

Ruby Upchurch looked toward the bed. "There he is," she said. The figure was rolling from hip to hip.

Ora Belle Ivey surveyed the bed. "What's it say his name is?"

"What?"

"That bracelet he got on his wrist so they know who he is if he dies, what's it say?"

"I don't know."

"Go see."

"Not me," Ruby Upchurch said levelly. "I couldn't do it."

Ora Belle Ivey walked toward the bed and lifted the wrist. "Ray Burgess," she said, letting the arm fall from her hand. It hit the edge of the mattress and bounced.

"Ray Burgess," Ora Belle Ivey shouted, as into a deep well.

"You reckon he hears us?" Ruby Upchurch asked.

"That's what we don't know," Ora Belle Ivey said. "That's the trouble. How you going to do an errand of mercy if the one you're doing it to don't know you're doing it? How you going to cheer him up that way?" She paused as though gathering her thoughts. "One thing is, he can't talk. We know that for a fact."

"That don't mean he can't hear."

Ray Burgess had stopped rolling back and forth. His eyes followed the conversation, shifting from one woman to the other.

"Look it there," Ruby Upchurch said. "He got his eyes open. Look at him looking."

Ora Belle Ivey looked at Ray Burgess. "That's awful, ain't it, the way he's looking? You see that?"

"I saw it as soon as we came in," Ruby Upchurch said. "One time John and I went to the zoo . . ."

"Let the dead bury the dead," Ora Belle Ivey shouted. "You got problems enough right here. We know he can't talk . . . ," she began again.

"But he can see."

"That don't mean he can hear. The question is, does he know what we're saying?" She turned to Ray Burgess. "Your name is Ray Burgess." She shouted louder than usual, the way some people try to converse with the deaf or with foreigners. "Your name is Ray Burgess. R-A-Y B-U-R-G-E-S-S," she said, enunciating every syllable as distinctly as possible.

Ray Burgess did not respond.

"He don't look so old, does he?" Ora Belle Ivey asked.

"Don't talk about him till you're sure he can't hear us," Ruby Upchurch said delicately. "You might say something you wished you hadn't."

"There ain't nothing wrong with not looking too old. I just meant he don't look as old as the rest of them, and I'd say that to him no matter if he could hear me or not. Ray Burgess," she shouted. "I'm Miss Ora Belle Ivey, and this beside me is Mrs. Ruby Upchurch, widow of Mr. John Upchurch, lately deceased. You might have read about it in the papers—if you can read," she said, glancing significantly at Ruby Upchurch. "But even if you can't, it don't matter. We're here on an errand of mercy on behalf of the New Harmony Baptist Association, to cheer you up and let you know there's something out there besides the nurses' station. We're here to fellowship you and help you forget them that cared so little about you they put you in here to die by yourself. You die, we'll be right here beside you, holding your hand. And I don't mean Jesus. I mean me. That give you comfort."

Ora Belle Ivey paused to let the significance of what she had said sink in, if not to Ray Burgess, who might or might not have been able to hear, then at least to Ruby Upchurch, who was a new member of the New Harmony Baptist Association, having joined shortly after her husband's death cast her on the world alone with nothing to do and no one to reach out and make sure she was there. She thought volunteer work at the nursing home would give her the human affection she missed. She was prepared to give all she had, knowing that what she would reap in the harvest was more than was sown.

She was a tentative woman, younger than Ora Belle Ivey (but not by much), slimmer, wearing clothes that were curiously dated and looked like they'd been worn for years but only on special occasions. She seemed eager to make a good impression, but uncertain of how to go about it. She had no public manner, having led a rich emotional life at home in a close circle of friends and family. To everyone else she was hidden, unknown, never at ease, never fully herself. Now, after forty years of relative isolation, she was like a woman returning to work after raising a family. She was not only inexperienced, she was trusting and childlike. The only difference between her and a child was that she knew what she was.

Ora Belle Ivey, on the other hand, knew almost nothing about herself. She was a large, busty woman with stout shoes like a man's, hair cropped short, ruddy complexion. She looked like an androgynous farmer. Her voice was loud with assurance, and as she spoke she tended to shout, not because she was hard of hearing, but because she was certain of her own rectitude and the justness of her opinions, which were not just biblical, but based for the most part on the Book of Revelation and the prophetic description of the last days. She carried herself like one of the elect given a white suffrage. Compared with her, Ruby Upchurch was like one of the poor souls in purgatory, suffering for all the venial sins of her life. She was infinitely well meaning and willing to do good—if only she knew what it was. Ora Belle Ivey knew. She was born knowing.

"So that's what we're here for," Ora Belle Ivey shouted. But before she could continue with the rest of the speech she had prepared for new residents, telling them what they might expect by way of earthly and heavenly comfort from the ladies of the New Harmony Baptist Association, she heard Ruby Upchurch cry, "Watch out, Ora Belle. He got something under the covers. He's pulling it out."

Ora Belle Ivey knew what that meant. She had seen it often enough—respectable men and women both, flaunting themselves. She lowered her eyes toward the covers, but instead of what she expected, she saw him draw out what looked at first like a bed slat, then a food tray.

"Look out," Ruby Upchurch cried. "He might want to hit you."

"Why would he do that?" Ora Belle Ivey shouted. "I'm here on an errand of mercy. I got angels guarding my feet lest I dash them against a stone."

Ray Burgess beckoned her toward him, and Ora Belle Ivey strode forth.

"It's some kind of board with writing on it," she reported to Ruby Upchurch. "An alphabet from A to Z. And numbers, it got numbers underneath, one to ten. And one side says, YES, and the other side, NO. And then his name, RAY BURGESS, in big letters across the top."

"A ouija board!" Ruby Upchurch said. "He got a ouija board in his bed!"

"What's that supposed to mean?"

"We had one when the children were little. You talk on it to the other side."

"The other side of what?"

"The other side of life. You talk to the dead."

"The dead?"

"You ask them questions, spell out what you want to know, and somebody comes, one of the dead, sometimes a loved one." Her voice sounded distant. "Sometimes the one you loved the most, if they've gone before and they want to reach out and touch you again, you can talk to them." Her voice trailed off, and then more brightly, remembering: "Sometimes they say it's an Indian. The directions say it could be an Indian, or a Chinese.

They might be dead a thousand years—Romans, Egyptians, one of them."

"What about the apostles of Christ?"

"The directions didn't say nothing about them."

"They're dead, ain't they? If it calls up the dead, they qualify, don't they? But it didn't say nothing about them, and I'll tell you why. The dead don't talk. Saul drove forth the witches from the land of Canaan, and Jesus himself cast out devils."

"And he rose up Lazarus from the dead," Ruby Upchurch said, surprising herself. Her voice seemed to be saying one thing while her mind thought something else. "He was dead in the tomb I don't know how long, and Jesus came in his infinite mercy and gave him back his life again, and he got up and walked out of that place of death into the light, and he saw his wife, and she knew he was living, that God in his infinite mercy gave him back to her."

"That's different," Ora Belle Ivey said. "That's something entirely different. We ain't talking about miracles here. We're talking about something you hide in the bed and slip up under the covers, like it was something nasty you got."

"It's just a game." Ruby Upchurch sounded embarrassed. "John used to say he only knew two things about it."

"What's that?"

"One was that someone was there."

"What you mean?" Ora Belle Ivey was quick as a bird.

"That you talk to someone."

"That right? What's the other?"

"The other is it always lied."

"That's because it's the father of lies."

Ruby Upchurch laughed. "It ain't all that serious," she said. "The children got it one Christmas. They used to talk to little children."

"You mean dead children?"

"Well, yes. But it wasn't like that. It was more like talking on the telephone. And the funny thing was," her face brightened when she thought of it, "the children they talked to couldn't spell. They mostly got children, and they couldn't spell. Ain't that something?"

"Most of them can't," Ora Belle Ivey said. "That's been my experience. Watch out," she cried suddenly, and moved as quickly as she could away from the bed. "Look it there," she said, drawing up beside Ruby Upchurch. "Look there. He's doing it."

Ray Burgess was holding the board sideways with one hand, as though displaying it to the two women. The other he used as a pointer, his index finger, thin as a chicken's toe, indicating the letters almost at random—first this one and then that. His eyes had what looked like intelligence in them.

"Look at him," Ora Belle Ivey said. "Ain't that awful? You reckon he knows what he's doing?" She watched Ray Burgess's hand move in patterns. "Is that how you do it?"

"No," Ruby Upchurch said. "That's what's so funny. It takes two. You work it together, and it flows between you."

"What flows between you?"

"The current that calls up the dead." Ruby Upchurch had spoken before she knew what she was saying, certainly before she knew what she meant. She had never thought of it as a current before. A current? What does that mean?

"He's calling you forth," Ora Belle Ivey said. "He knows I won't go. My feet are too guarded with angels from all the errands of mercy I been on. But you're new. You ain't been tested. Besides which, you had one of them before, and he knows it. The devil remembers. You called up dead children at Christmas. Look it there." She touched Ruby Upchurch on the arm as though to restrain her. "Don't go," she said. "Stand here with me and harden your heart. Resist him like I do."

Ora Belle Ivey glared at Ray Burgess. Ray Burgess glared back at her while his hands described motions of their own against the board. Each function was separate. He was saying one thing to Ora Belle Ivey with his eyes and another with his hands.

"Wait a minute," Ruby Upchurch cried. Ray Burgess turned toward her. "He's telling us something."

"Who is? That's what I want to know. Who's he got on the other side?"

"What other side?"

"*The* other side," Ora Belle Ivey reminded her. "You said it, not me.

Who's he got there behind that board working it with him we can't see? That's what I want to know. What kind of current's flowing between them?"

As Ora Belle Ivey spoke, Ruby Upchurch suddenly had a vision of the other side of a planet or perhaps a coin—two-dimensional like a geometric plane. There were no features, no landscape. There was not even darkness. Her husband was there. She sensed his presence. It was as though he had risen like Lazarus and had come forth to the other side and was waiting to speak. A current flowed between them. She kept hearing or seeing—she was uncertain which. It seemed like a murmuring in her ear saying over and over, "A LBUM, A LBUM, A LBUM." And it was John's voice. His eyes were like light, and the voice was like darkness.

"He's spelling something," Ruby Upchurch said suddenly. "Can't you see that?"

"I see it all," Ora Belle Ivey said. "And I tell you what, he ain't spelling. You know why? He can't talk, that's why. And as far as you know, he can't hear, and he got his eyes open, but you ain't certain he can see. And if he can't talk and can't hear and can't see, there ain't no way he can spell. That stands to reason." She paused suddenly, struck by light. "Unless it ain't him," she said. "Unless it's something else doing the spelling."

"See there," Ruby Upchurch said. "Watch his hand." Ray Burgess's hand described a pattern, and the word A LBUM appeared on the board.

"I been seeing that," Ora Belle Ivey said, barely concealing the contempt in her voice. "That don't mean nothing." She paused as though slowly filling with light. "Unless he's speaking in some foreign tongue." She paused again, brain churning. "It may not even be English. Ever think of that? It may not be nothing in no tongue known to man."

"No tongue known to man," Ruby Upchurch repeated, awed not so much by the phrase itself as by what it conjured up—the distance her husband had gone from her and what lay between them. It was like a tongue not known to man. She knew she could not remember his voice, but she had not considered that she might not be able to understand him if he should call to her. She still spoke like she always did because she was still living. But he was dead. She thought of being dead. Being dead was like a tongue not known to man.

"Look now, he's pointing!" Ora Belle Ivey said. "Oh God, he's pointing."

Ray Burgess had dropped the board on his lap and was pointing toward the chair in the corner.

"He wants you to sit down," Ora Belle Ivey said, putting out a hand to restrain Ruby Upchurch. "He wants you to get the junk off that chair and draw it up and set that evil thing in your lap and work it with him. That's what it means, that thing he was saying. Must mean that chair in some foreign tongue."

"No. Look there, he's spelling something. T-O. TO something, and then the rest."

"What's the rest?"

"W. See there? And there—E-L. WEL," she repeated. "TO WEL." She watched Ray Burgess's hand. It sounded like the thud of her heart. It was not just excitement. She felt him there with her. And then suddenly she understood.

"Towel," she said, laughing. It was so simple. "Towel. He's saying 'towel.'"

"I know that," Ora Belle Ivey said. "But what's it mean? That's what I want to know. What we need is a translator like they got in the Pentecostals. One of them gets to talking in tongues and the other will be right there beside her translating whatever it is."

"We don't need a translator," Ruby Upchurch said. "Don't you see? He's saying 'towel,'" and she rushed to the chair and lifted the blue towel. "You mean this?" she asked Ray Burgess. He nodded his head and started rolling from hip to hip.

"Look at him," Ora Belle Ivey said. "Look at him. That's disgusting—going from side to side like that. Ain't no telling what he's doing."

But Ruby Upchurch was too excited to listen. She was waving the towel like a banner. "Album," she said, "that's what he meant. Under the towel, here's the album." She picked up a book with PHOTOGRAPHS written across the front. "It's a photograph album."

Ray Burgess's hand was flickering across the board as she spoke. YES, the hand said. YES, YES, moving back and forth to the corner where the word YES was written.

"See there," Ruby Upchurch said. "He's saying yes. Don't you see that?"

"Unless it's just twitching," Ora Belle Ivey said.

"Do you want the album?" Ruby Upchurch asked Ray Burgess. His hand gestured YES, and he nodded his head.

Ruby Upchurch picked up the album and put the blue towel down in its place. Then she carried the album to Ray Burgess, who opened it in his lap and gestured toward her. LOOK, his hand said, moving across the board.

"He wants us to look," Ruby Upchurch said.

"Do what?" Ora Belle Ivey's mind had been far away, watching the simple, familiar gestures—picking the book up, putting the towel down, carrying the book to Ray Burgess. It seemed so natural and . . . Ora Belle Ivey cast about for a term to describe it . . . intimate. That's what it was. Like they were married. They moved so easy together. She felt like an intruder.

"Come look," she heard Ruby Upchurch say. "He wants us to see his picture album. Come stand here beside me."

Ora Belle Ivey stepped forward.

"You can't see from there. Come in closer."

Ora Belle Ivey shifted her bulk.

"There," Ruby Upchurch said. "That's better," and she turned to Ray Burgess. "We're ready," she said. "What you got there?"—as though she had known him forty years. She had the gift of intimacy.

Ray Burgess smiled and opened the book.

"It's a cat," Ora Belle Ivey shouted. "I knew it. Look there, he got a picture of a cat. A whole page of them."

There were five photographs positioned neatly in a quincunx on the first page of the album. All the photographs were of a Siamese cat.

"Oh God, it got blue eyes," Ora Belle Ivey shouted, "just like a baby."

Ray Burgess's hand flew over the board. SIAMESE.

"Siamese," Ruby Upchurch said. "He says it's Siamese."

"Blue eyes on a cat's unnatural," Ora Belle Ivey said. "That shows where it came from."

Ray Burgess described a word.

"Newark," Ruby Upchurch said.

"New what?"

Ray Burgess spoke again.

"N J," Ruby Upchurch said. Then her face lighted. "New Jersey," she said. "Newark, New Jersey. That's where you got the cat, is that right?"

YES, YES.

"That's what he says," Ora Belle Ivey said. "There ain't but one place blue-eyed cats come from, and it ain't Newark, New Jersey. God never made a blue-eyed animal. That means that cat came from a human."

"What do you mean?"

"They mate with them," Ora Belle Ivey explained. "Men, devils. I don't know what all. Cats and people—all mixed together."

NO, NO, Ray Burgess said.

"What's your cat's name?" Ruby Upchurch asked. "Sure is pretty."

OPEL.

Ruby Upchurch said, "Its name is Opel."

"That's some kind of car, ain't it? What's Opel mean?"

JEWEL.

"He says it means jewel. Opel means some kind of jewel."

FIRE, Ray Burgess said.

"He says it got fire in it. He says that jewel's full of fire just like his cat. That's why you called her Opel, ain't it, because of that fire?"

YES, YES.

"Look it there," Ruby Upchurch said, pointing to the album. "Look at that cat. See how she's laying there in that chair? Look at her feet."

"That's disgusting," Ora Belle Ivey said. "You or me sit in a chair like that, they'd put us in jail."

But Ruby Upchurch ignored her. "Look at that one," she said, pointing to another picture. "That cat's flat as a piece of paper. And there you are," speaking to Ray Burgess. "Look there. Don't he look handsome standing there holding that cat?"

Ray Burgess smiled. Ora Belle Ivey slit her eyes.

"That cat goes with you," Ruby Upchurch said to Ray Burgess. "You can tell how much she loves you the way she's laying there on her back. Cats don't do that unless they trust you. Look at her, look at that Opel just laying there in Abraham's bosom. Look how she goes with that suit you got on. You're both the same color—kind of brown-gray I'd call it."

MATCH.

"He matched it," Ruby Upchurch said. "Ain't that clever? He bought a suit to go with his cat." She turned to Ray Burgess. "And it shows, the trouble you took. Anybody looking at that picture would say, 'That man looks just like that cat.'" She laughed at her own joke.

Ray Burgess smiled and nodded and shook the bed, glancing at Ruby Upchurch as at a great light he could not bear to look at directly.

"What happened to it?" Ora Belle Ivey asked.

CANCER.

"It died of cancer," Ruby Upchurch said. "Oh. You poor man." She thought of her husband and the pain of living after he died. And she thought of his pain.

"My husband died of cancer," she said. "I remember standing beside the bed. He didn't even know I was there. He'd cry out and break my heart. The drugs couldn't touch it. I didn't want him to suffer, but I couldn't bear to let him go. It felt like I'd lose him. Then he died, and I felt better after that."

"Of course you did," Ora Belle Ivey said. "That's why he's buried, so you can forget him. Two weeks ago, wasn't it? It couldn't have been two weeks ago he died and was buried."

"Fifty-eight days. It was fifty-eight days ago."

NO, NO, Ray Burgess said.

"You sure about that?" Ora Belle Ivey waved at Ray Burgess as though to get him to stop distracting her. "Are you certain? I could have sworn it was two weeks ago." Without waiting for an answer she said to Ray Burgess, "Stop that. I can't think of what I'm saying with you jiggling like that."

Ruby Upchurch quieted his hand.

"That's why we got her to come out with me," Ora Belle Ivey explained to Ray Burgess. "We figured she might not feel so sorry for herself if she got to see cases like you, laying in bed the rest of their life with a stroke, scrabbling words on some kind of board. That's why we're here. This is the first time she's been out of the house in fifty-eight days."

Ruby Upchurch started to protest, but Ora Belle Ivey held up her hand. "I mean on a social visit." She turned back to Ray Burgess. "They say her husband was awful sick. He died for months. Eat up with cancer."

"What's this?" Ruby Upchurch said, changing the subject. "Look at that picture." She pointed to a picture of Opel the cat in a beige and white living room, all rug and not much furniture, with the edge of what looked like a brick hearth showing in the corner. "Ever see a room like that? It's all beige and white."

"Let me see," Ora Belle Ivey shouted, shouldering Ruby Upchurch aside. "Beige and white. Must be hard to keep clean."

"Look at that white rug," Ruby Upchurch said. "I never did see a white rug before."

"Looks like a bedsheet," Ora Belle Ivey said. "How long your cat live?"

Ray Burgess's finger stabbed at the number three and stopped there, pointing.

"That ain't very long," Ora Belle Ivey said. "Most cats live longer than that unless they get hit by a car or somebody poisons them. Yours died quick."

"Look it there," Ruby Upchurch said, turning the page. "Look at that baby."

"Let me see." Ora Belle Ivey snatched at the book. There were two full pages of a child. Some showed the child as a baby on the off-white rug in the same barren living room, some as a two- or three-year-old surrounded by Christmas wrappings, some at a party in a party hat, others in what looked like an Easter dress—pink, with patent leather shoes. In every picture the child was smiling the same smile. The photographs caught the moment and froze it in picture after picture. It was like looking at her immortal soul.

"I like how she's smiling," Ora Belle Ivey said. "She got a smile on her face like she just woke up and said hello to herself in a mirror. Looks like somebody glued it on her."

"Let's turn the page," Ruby Upchurch said.

There were more pictures of the child, always older, always smiling—not at the person holding the camera, but secretly, to herself. In one picture she was shown with a large, heavy-set man in a white shirt that looked to be stained where his stomach protruded. The man looked grim and stared straight ahead. The girl was looking at the man and smiling at something beyond him.

"I always did like a smiler like that," Ora Belle Ivey said. "Ain't a picture there she ain't smiling. She must have had a happy childhood. Makes me feel good just to see her looking so happy. There's time enough for grief later on when all the smiling dries up on your face like froth."

"She grew up to be a pretty woman," Ruby Upchurch said, turning another page showing the girl as a young woman, still smiling with the sure knowledge that she was the possessor of her own heart.

LISA.

"Lisa," Ruby Upchurch said. "I wish my name was Lisa. Don't you wish you had a lovely name like Lisa?" she asked Ora Belle Ivey.

"No, I don't. I always liked Ora Belle for a woman and Gilmer for a man. Gilmer was my daddy's name."

"And Ora Belle was your momma's?"

"No. I was named for a maiden aunt, never would marry. It runs in the family. Lots of Iveys ain't interested in that."

"Lisa married or she still live with your wife or what?" Ruby Upchurch asked Ray Burgess.

ZIMMERMAN, Ray Burgess said.

"She lives with his wife," Ruby Upchurch said.

"How you know that?" Ora Belle Ivey shouted. "You some kind of mind reader?"

"That's his wife's maiden name," Ruby Upchurch explained. "Lisa Zimmerman. They named the baby after her."

NO, NO, Ray Burgess said. ROSE.

"I was wrong," Ruby Upchurch said. "Her name ain't Lisa. It's Rose like mine."

"Your name ain't Rose."

"I mean—like Ruby. It means something. It ain't just a name."

Ray Burgess looked upset. NO, NO, he said. GEORGE.

"He says he wished his name was George," Ora Belle Ivey said. "I wouldn't want it. Not if I could have Gilmer I wouldn't."

ZIMMERMAN.

"That your wife's brother?" Ruby Upchurch asked. Then she knew. The man in the picture with Lisa, the one in the white shirt stained in the stomach, that was George. She flipped the page and pointed. "Is that George?"

YES, YES, Ray Burgess said. FATHER.

"He ain't your father." Ora Belle Ivey was disgusted. "Don't lie to Mrs. Upchurch, come out of a house of mourning with a dead husband in it not even two weeks ago and drug herself down here just to see you and cheer you up and let in some fresh air on the dying, and that's how you treat her. Ain't you ashamed?"

Ray Burgess's hand began to tremble. Ruby Upchurch reached out and touched it. "He didn't mean that," she said. "He meant the man in the picture is Lisa's daddy. Ain't that right?"

YES, YES.

"She ain't your daughter at all is she?"

NO, NO. MINE.

"See there," Ora Belle Ivey shouted. "Sometimes I think I'm wasting my time coming down here. They can't talk. They can't hear. They can't spell. They can't even think straight like real folks. Sometimes I wonder. And then they'll be someone that comes up and says they sure are happy to see you. They shake your hand or kiss your cheek and tell you how pretty you look. Say, 'Your cheeks as clear as the clear blue sky, and your breath smells like flowers.' And you start to go, they say, 'Don't go,' and play like they're crying. 'Don't go,' they say. 'I don't want you to leave me.' Well I tell you, when I hear that, it makes it almost seem like it's worth it." She turned back to Ray Burgess. "She ain't your baby if she's George's baby in the picture."

"He means he loved her like she was his, don't you?"

YES.

"And Rose Zimmerman was her momma."

YES.

"And you were their friend."

MORE.

"More? What's more?" Ora Belle Ivey shouted. "Stop lying. There ain't no more unless you're some kind of kin or something."

MORE, MORE.

"You're more than a friend?" Ruby Upchurch asked.

LOVEDS.

"You loved them? You loved the Zimmermans?"

FAMILY.

"They were your family?" Ruby Upchurch asked. And then it was as though someone spoke and called her by name. "You lived with them," she said. "You lived in their house, and they were your family. You never married."

YES.

"This was your family, and Lisa was your little girl, and George was your brother, and Rose . . ." Ruby Upchurch paused, leaving the sentence unfinished. "And Rose was your sister," she continued. "How long you live with them?"

Ray Burgess's finger stabbed the number one and then the number six.

"Sixteen years. You lived with them for sixteen years. What a long time." She thought of sixteen years. How short their time together seemed and how long it had been since he had died. The years seemed like days, and the days seemed like years.

"You pay them money to live there, or what?" Ora Belle Ivey asked suspiciously.

YES, Ray Burgess said. MORE.

"It was the love, not the money," Ruby Upchurch said. "At first it may have been the money, and then they were like your own family. You got to see Lisa grow up."

YES, YES.

"She must have loved you just like a daddy. Wasn't she lucky? She had two daddies."

"One was enough for me," Ora Bella Ivey said. "I loved my daddy. I wouldn't want another."

OPEL LOVED.

"Yes, she must have," Ruby Upchurch said. "That's why you put her first in the book. I knew you loved her as soon as I saw it."

"That's why it's such a pity she died," Ora Belle Ivey said. "I never would have me a pet, and that's why. Pets of all sorts are bad about dying. Three years ain't no time. I bet you just got where you loved her, and then she was gone. That's the way it is with pets. They're short livers."

Ruby Upchurch thought of years, not knowing what they were. They were still inside her, all the years she had ever lived, and yet she could not call them forth any more than she could remember the sound of his voice. There could never be enough. She wanted it to last forever. And then when he died, it was as nothing. Three years, forty years, what did it matter? She wanted to call him again. She wanted him to come and not speak, but reach out and touch her. She remembered leaving him that first night and how she went home and got in bed and thought of him lying there under the ground with all that dirt on him and how cold it was and what happens there, and she couldn't even cry out and call him. All she could do was mourn for him. She knew she would always mourn for him, even as she felt the body approaching, nearing the surface like something forgotten. Ever since she had been with Ray Burgess she knew it was coming. She waited in expectation.

"What you doing in Newark, New Jersey, all by yourself?" Ora Belle Ivey asked. "Why didn't you stay home like I did?"

JOB.

"He was poor. He needed a job," Ruby Upchurch explained.

"So what? So were lots of folks. Even me. I was poor and needed a job. But I didn't go off to Newark, New Jersey. I stayed right here and helped myself. And now look at the difference. There you are laying there and here I am, come to visit. Newark, New Jersey's a sick place to work, I hear. Lots of folks go to work there come down with strokes and can't even move. Lay all day looking at a spot on the ceiling."

ELECTRICIAN.

"Look at that," Ruby Upchurch said. "He was an electrician. Ain't that a coincidence? My husband was an electrician. You love your work?"

YES.

"That's what he said. He used to try to tell me about it." She remembered the touch. When he came to where he told about light, he'd squeeze her arm. He'd say, "Light," and his fingers'd contract, and it was like light. "We lived together so long," she said, "I knew what he meant before he even knew it himself."

"That's a lie," Ora Belle shouted. "Folks don't know what other folks're thinking. That's my observation. What other folks think's a mystery. You take my momma. When she got like him"—she pointed to Ray Burgess— "laying in bed waiting to die, ain't no telling what she was thinking. She was laying there with her eyes wide open, staring at a spot on the ceiling. And I'd say, 'Momma, momma, what you thinking about, staring at that spot all day? Don't you get tired?' Things like that to cheer her up. I used to sit there and watch her. It wasn't like him," indicating Ray Burgess. "Her mind was clear as a bell, and she could talk if she wanted to. But she didn't want to. Momma never did say a word, and I never did figure out what she was thinking about, staring at the ceiling like that. She died with the mystery still in her mouth before she could figure out what it meant."

"What mystery?"

"Her whole life. Like when you drown you see your whole life flash before you, like a great light, and there it is from beginning to end before you slip under and die in the waves."

Ruby Upchurch saw the body approaching, the electrified light like a living thing moving on the surface above it. The shores of light.

"After I got home from the funeral," Ora Belle Ivey said quietly, "I went up in the room where she died, and I was alone. My momma and daddy both were gone, and the wind was blowing, and the house was creaking, and I thought it was somebody coming up the stairs from the dark at the bottom, creaking across the floor. And then it was like it came in the room. I looked around and said, 'Who's there?' But nobody answered. And all of a sudden it was like some kind of blessing in there. And I heard this voice say, 'Ora Belle, you weren't able to help your momma. She died staring at a spot on the ceiling thinking something you don't even know what, like she was somewhere in some far-off land. But what about the rest of them? There're lots of others dying right now, this very minute. Old folks home's full of them, dying right and left. What about them? And that's where I first got the idea—the idea of the errand of mercy. It's like somebody walked in the room and whispered it to me, except there wasn't nobody there." She stopped abruptly and looked about as though adjusting her eyes to an excess of light.

"Well, I swear." She sounded surprised. "Listen to that. I swear, you all must be good company to get me to talking like that. I'm usually the quiet type. My daddy used to say, 'You're the quiet type, Ora Belle. That's why you ain't married.' But it wasn't that." She fell silent again, glaring about her as though in anger.

I WANT OUT, Ray Burgess said.

"You see that?"

Ruby Upchurch glanced about her, thinking he had come at last. She almost cried out, "Where is he?"

"Look it there."

I WANT OUT.

"See what I mean?" Ora Belle Ivey said. "Ain't that awful? All they want to do is die."

"Die? He didn't say he wanted to die."

"He says he wants out. What you think that means?"

"No," Ruby Upchurch protested. "No. No." It was as though the pain had come back. She couldn't let him die again. "That ain't what it means. He wants to live. He wants to get well and get out of here and go back to Newark, New Jersey, and take up his job he loves so much and get him a new cat he can call Ruby."

"That's your name."

"Or Ora Belle. That's a lovely name for a cat. Ora Belle. Don't it sound rich?" She turned to Ray Burgess. "Wouldn't you love a new cat in Newark, New Jersey? You could call it Ruby or Ora Belle?"

Ray Burgess looked at her.

"A tiger cat, a gray and striped tiger. Then you get you a sport coat. My husband has one just be perfect. Black and gray tweed. Match that cat perfect. And you could get dressed up on Sunday and ride to church with the Zimmermans."

"They're all Jews," Ora Belle Ivey shouted.

"They ain't Jews. They go to church every Sunday. George and Rose and Lisa and her husband and babies. They're all Methodists and get in the car and go to the Methodist church all together."

DEAD, Ray Burgess said.

"Dead? What you mean, dead?"

ZIMMERMANS.

"The Zimmermans are dead?" Ruby Upchurch was amazed.

It was a universe of death. In the album in Ray Burgess's lap the Zimmermans were still alive, fleshy and bright in their colorful clothes, in their beige living room, on the green grass of the lawn where they stood staring out at eternity as carefree and young as the day they first married, except for his voice, beyond recall, and the touch of his hand. She felt the world slipping away. There were more now on the other side than stood here in the light beside her. All her friends and loved ones gone. All the Zimmermans. They were all dead.

"What happened?" Ruby Upchurch cried. It was like learning of a disaster, some extraordinary act of nature or a horrible, unexpected accident. She refused to believe that the Zimmermans were dead. They were so healthy, staring at her with such assurance. Their eyes were not wasted. They still had their hair. They looked out of the frame of the photos as out of the windows of their own house. They were not in the terrible place John had died.

"What happened?" she said. "What could have happened?"

AUTO.

Ora Belle Ivey patted his arm. "There, there," she said. "Don't cry. You're too old and sick to be crying. Besides which, think of God's mercy. Auto accidents are fast. You get in one of them, you're dead before you even know it. One minute you're saying, 'Hold on, hold on there,' and the next minute you're laying on the pavement bleeding from the side of the mouth where your head's crushed in by the door knob in back. And I say, thank God. Thank God for that. Better that than what he got," she said to Ruby Upchurch. "Watching TV and getting bedsores."

But Ruby Upchurch was thinking of Lisa, broken against the back of the seat, one arm fallen out the door, palm up on the pavement. Gone. She was gone. She would never return, except as the body rose toward the light. She looked at the tears on Ray Burgess's face and knew what he was crying for. It was as though John whispered it to her and touched her shoulder to make sure she understood. They were both dead, he and Ray Burgess. Their lives were over except for what was stored up in memory, from which separate, inconsequential events stared forth as from a book of photographs—a piece of lawn, Rose Zimmerman's thick lip, a stupid glance, a smile like a light turned on. She knew how lonely they were in that strange place where it was all darkness except for the blue light of the TV, the flickering black-and-white images, not of life, but its ghostly reflection.

"Lisa died too?" she heard herself cry. It was more a statement than a question, a cry of the heart in grief and mourning for all the dead.

"Of course she did," Ora Belle Ivey explained. "All them Zimmermans died at once, all in the same car on the highway."

NO. CA, Ray Burgess said.

"What?"

ALIVE CA.

"She's alive," Ruby Upchurch cried. "Oh thank God. You mean she's alive?"

YES, YES. ALIVE CA.

"She's in California!" Ruby Upchurch said, suddenly understanding. "Oh, thank God. Lisa Zimmerman's alive in California!" It was like Lazarus come back from the dead, the body rising in the dark until the light smashed in on all sides, breaking into flesh and color, surging and pounding like words in her blood. ALIVE, ALIVE, it said, coming toward her.

"She married, or what?" Ora Belle Ivey asked suspiciously. "How she get out there?"

NO, NO, Ray Burgess said.

Ora Belle Ivey looked at his hand moving back and forth as she would at something singularly distasteful. "Whatever that means," she said to Ruby Upchurch. "Maybe *you* know." She was being sarcastic: Ora Belle Ivey could not conceive of anyone else's knowing anything she did not already know or had not at least already considered. She attributed her wisdom to her years and to her considerable experience as a teacher of the home-bound, traveling up and down every road in Gilmer, Pickens, and Fannin counties without ever having an accident, though she always believed that God in his infinite mercy would call her to him in that fashion, swift and clean as a knife to the throat with her mind still clear as a bell. And she thanked God for it every time she got in the car to proceed on an errand of mercy. At least she wouldn't be like them, the ones she would visit, lingering out her life in pain and sorrow. It was like being one of the elect. It carried the same sense of certitude and assurance as the seal on the forehead of the righteous spoken of in the Book of Revelation. The Book of Revelation had always been Ora Belle Ivey's favorite book of the Bible ever since she was old enough to read. She was especially partial to the seven-headed beast that swept the stars from the sky with its tail; the white suffrage, which in her mind had become associated with the state of virginity, which Ora Belle Ivey still technically enjoyed; and the plague of locusts that rose up like dust, obscuring the sun and biting the unrighteous on the forehead, piercing their brainpans at precisely the point where the seals protected the righteous. She imagined the seals to be something like her own clear thoughts. That's why she always knew what to do. She considered herself a woman of action.

"Let's go," Ora Belle Ivey shouted. "Time to go." Her own clear thoughts had spoken inside her. She knew she was right the same way a mathematician knows when the answer has come, when the equation is balanced and the problem solved. It was the sword that cut the knot. As soon as she thought of Revelation, her mind grew calm and cold as chrysolite, straightforward and reasonable as marble. God's elect had more to do than stand there and be confused. "We're wasting our time," she shouted. "There's many another needs cheering up. This ain't the only one in the poor house. Think of the others laying there waiting to kiss our hand and thank us for coming. And quit that scribble scrabble," she said to Ray Burgess. "Nobody likes that scribble scrabble, guess what they're saying. That's distracting. It gets in the way of cheering you up."

"Why don't Lisa come and get you?" Ruby Upchurch asked Ray Burgess. "She could take you home to her in California."

NO, NO.

"You're like her daddy. She'd love to have you." She thought of the girl in the photographs—the heartless smile, the self-possession. "She loves you, don't she?"

Ray Burgess looked at her. DEAD, he said.

"Let's go," Ora Belle Ivey shouted. "See there. It's time to go, he gets talking like that."

But Ruby Upchurch understood. "She don't want you," she said. "She don't love you. She don't love nobody. She loves herself. I can see how she smiles—like in a mirror."

Ray Burgess began to cry.

"There, there," Ora Belle Ivey shouted, moving toward the bed again and patting his shoulder. "Ain't no need to get upset about somebody in California may not even be alive. We don't know if she is or not," she explained to Ruby Upchurch. "It's all mixed up. She's dead, she's alive. Who knows what it means? But it don't matter." She turned back to Ray Burgess. "Don't worry about it. You still got us standing right here ready to fetch whatever you want or call somebody to get it for you if we're too dressed up to do it ourselves. Here, hold my hand." She reached over the edge of the bed as into the zone of another dimension and grasped his free hand, pinning it in hers. "How you feeling?" she shouted, assuming a professional manner. "You eating good?"

Ruby Upchurch watched while Ora Belle Ivey grasped the ouija board with her free hand and wrenched it loose from Ray Burgess. "There," she said when she had a firm grip on it. "That's better. That way he won't get so upset. The way he has to talk he gets tired."

"Yes," Ruby Upchurch said without knowing she had spoken. She was thinking of pain and how it hurt to feel it again—like walking on the stumps of feet that had gone to sleep, feeling the blood prickling like needles, the dead flesh that felt like another's revealing itself to be her own. Like Lazarus come back from the dead.

"Listen," she said to Ora Belle Ivey. "You know that story about your momma and how you heard the house creaking and you thought it was her coming back?"

"Of course I do. Who you think you heard it from—him?" She gestured at Ray Burgess.

But Ruby Upchurch ignored her. "As soon as I came in this room," she said, "I heard the footsteps on the stairs."

"What stairs?"

"The stairs of my heart. I said to myself, 'Here it comes. I hear it creaking.' I could feel it coming closer. And then it was in the room with me. I could almost reach out and touch it. I kept waiting for it to speak. I figured it was like some kind of message, it was so close—like something on the tip of my tongue I almost forgot. Except it wasn't words."

"It wasn't words with me either."

"It's like he reached out and touched me, put his hand on me and touched me. And there are no words, only mercy. I feel flooded with infinite mercy. And I say, thank God. Thank God, Ray Burgess. Thank God you're alive. Thank God, thank God, Ora Belle Ivey. Thank God, Lisa Zimmerman. Thank God you ain't dead in that accident. Thank God I still love him." She broke off. "I got so much mercy. I got infinite mercy. It died and was buried and now it's come back."

"That right?" Ora Belle Ivey said. "Then that ain't it. That ain't the same thing at all. Something really happened to me. I felt this kind of infinite mercy, and it changed my life. It changed my whole life. I ain't like I was."

She glared about triumphantly, like the Antichrist. "You ready?" she shouted. "We got to go. Errands of mercy don't last forever. There're too many needy crying out for teeth and eyeglasses, not to mention cheering them up, giving them something to think about besides being old and dying of cancer unless they're too far gone already, in which case we generally give them some candy. That makes them happy."

Ruby Upchurch pushed past her and stood beside Ray Burgess. "Don't go," she said, and she touched his arm as John had touched hers. She patted his shoulder telling him something, though she did not know what it was any more than John had known what it was. That was why he had come back from the dead, to give her that gift and comfort her. She touched Ray Burgess with infinite mercy. It flowed from her beyond comprehension. She felt her hand tremble.

"Don't cry," Ora Belle Ivey shouted. "You look like my momma."

Ruby Upchurch had not known she was crying. It was like joy. She was crying because of what she had been given.

"My momma cried like that all day at the end, and I couldn't stop her. That's why I can't stand it."

"I ain't crying," Ruby Upchurch said. "It's because I'm so happy." She turned to Ray Burgess. "Stay here with me. No need to go to California. I got a big house needs rewiring."

"Might as well," Ora Belle Ivey said. "That Lisa out there's dead already. She don't want you." She looked down and saw she was still holding the ouija board. It was like discovering she had absentmindedly picked up a piece of dried dog turd. She thrust it from her. "Here," she said to Ruby Upchurch. But Ruby Upchurch was too far away, so she put it down on the foot of the bed.

Ruby Upchurch picked it up and started to give it back to Ray Burgess when she noticed he was still holding the photograph album. She took the album from him. "Here," she said, "you won't need this. I'll put it over here," and she lifted the blue towel and put the album back under it.

"All them old times are gone," Ora Belle Ivey said. "You hear that? Most of them dead. Nothing but pictures. So what you got to do is forget it. Listen to me."

Ray Burgess looked at her.

"Get out your glasses and read the paper. That'll give you something of interest to do. There're lots of good times in that, you get to reading the paper and quit staring at the ceiling." She turned to Ruby Upchurch. "You reckon he can read?"

"Why don't you ask him," Ruby Upchurch said, handing Ray Burgess back the ouija board. He took it from her and slipped it under the covers.

"Him?" Ora Belle Ivey narrowed her eyes. "He can work that board," she said aloud, thinking it through, "but he can't talk. It's like hash in there." She paused a moment. "He can't read. We're wasting our time.

Let's go. Here," she said to Ray Burgess. "Here's you some candy. Suck on that." And she took from her purse a peppermint candy cane, the kind made for Christmas. "Here, give him this," she said to Ruby Upchurch, passing it to her. "That'll keep him busy till we come back."

Ruby Upchurch gave it to him and squeezed his arm and patted his shoulder. "I'm coming back," she said to Ray Burgess. "I'm coming back every day."

"So am I," Ora Belle Ivey shouted. "Wild horses couldn't keep me, not if they tied me to them. I'd drag them after to get to this room."

"So would I," Ruby Upchurch said.

"Who wouldn't?" Ora Belle Ivey shouted. "Let's go," and she pushed out into the hallway. "Suck on that candy till you get your teeth," she called back over her shoulder. "Cut that light off," she shouted to Ruby Upchurch, who was just leaving the room.

At the end of the hallway, past the nurses' station, the sunlight was blinding.

The Baptism of Water

She stirred in her sleep, rolling over on her left side. Her feet were sticking out from under the covers. They were so white in the moonlight they looked artificial, the toes running up them like scars. She pulled them back inside the covers. The motion was slow and hydraulic. They disappeared just about the same time she dreamed that it was last winter, when the faucet outside her window had run for an hour before she woke up enough to realize that it was not the washing machine or the toilet still flushing. She had gotten up and looked and saw the driveway was covered with ice. She had thought then of the ocean. The ice in the driveway was like the still part in the distance where it came to end at the sky. Then she thought of God.

The next morning she had heard on the news that twenty people had died overnight, most of them men in overcoats sleeping in vacant buildings. The police were still finding them days after the snow had melted. It was the worst cold in twenty years. No one was prepared. She remembered looking through the steam of the window at the cars spinning their wheels and dragging a knot of people behind them and then later seeing the ice where someone had released the water and the air fell on it like a blow. Nothing moved except the water turning to ice. It was filling the world with silence. Something had come that filled her with fear.

She was awake now.

Someone had come and turned on the faucet again.

She got out of bed and went to the window. Behind the burglar bars, trapped in the branches of a tree, the moon was full. Then she saw the man, standing the moonlight beside an outdoor water faucet so thick it looked like the barrel of a cannon. He had on what looked like two pair of trousers—dark on one side, light on the other. The dark leg was the one closest to the faucet. The water was turned on so hard it splashed like a fountain six feet in all directions at once. The water looked silver. She surprised herself by thinking how beautiful it was. It flashed through the air like knives. Then she thought of the violation. It was not only wasting her water and flooding her yard and costing her money, it was violating her. She rapped on the window. The man did not look up. She rapped until her knuckles hurt. Then she went over to the table beside the bed and got an alabaster bookend and rapped the window with it so hard she was afraid she might break the glass, but she still could not get his attention. She opened the window, and the night air filled her with rapture. It smelled like honeysuckle or hay or the sweetest of flowers. She thought of ghosts manifesting themselves in pools of cold air. It was like that, only more lovely.

"What are you doing?" she said to the man. He was a few feet below her. "Turn off that water."

The man looked around as though searching for the voice. He kept looking up toward the roofs of the houses or the tops of the trees, trying to locate it.

"I said turn it off."

The man just stood there.

"You hear me?"

"Not until you let me in."

"Let you in?" She was truly surprised. "Turn off that water."

There was no answer. The man suddenly seemed to notice his leg was getting wet. He shook it like a dog and moved a foot or so away so that most of the water fell on his shoe. He had on running shoes, white and some other color that registered in the moonlight only as dark. His trousers looked wrinkled, and he wore a white shirt that even from that distance she knew was dirty. The man lifted the foot that was getting wet and stomped it in the grass as though to drive the water out. He kept stomping it, churning the grass into mud.

"Stop that," the woman said. "You're ruining my lawn. Get out of here."

"Not until you let me in."

It was like fear. She remembered how her husband would come home like that and call her to help him, standing in the yard and shouting. He'd lost his keys. The steps were gone. The door wouldn't open. He couldn't find it. They'd taken his money. He'd hurt his hand. He couldn't walk. Something had happened. He was hit by a car, cut by a knife. The neighbors would hear. The children would wake and see him like that. And she let him in.

"I'm not fixing to let you in," she said to the man. "Get away. I'm calling the police. Turn off that water."

The man was still stomping his foot, and she knew she would have to do it herself.

She took the robe from the foot of the bed and went to the front door. She eased off the deadbolt and stepped out so quietly she did not even hear it herself. She was out of the house, down the steps, and across to the faucet before the man even knew she had come.

"Now leave it off," she said after she had finished, "or I'm going to have to call the police." She went in the house and got back into bed.

It's just like a dream, she thought—the sudden apparition, the running water, someone wanting to get into the house. And she remembered once when she was a girl a woman had appeared and rung the doorbell. She had come in a taxi, and as soon as she opened the door, the woman pushed past her into the living room. Her mother stood up as the woman sat down and said, "Who are you?" and the woman waved at her as though she were deaf and dumb, then put her head down on the wing of the chair and slept. "She's drunk," her mother said. "How'd she get in here?" They found an address in the woman's bag and took her home. Her husband accepted her at the door like a package sent to the wrong address.

Suddenly the porch trembled. Then she heard the doorbell ring. She leaped as though at the cry of a baby waking her from sleep. The second time the doorbell rang she was prepared. It kept on ringing every four seconds. She timed the intervals. At first it was annoying. Then disturbing. The sense of personal violation returned. What right did he have to do this to her? She put her mouth to the crack at the side of the door and said, "Quit that. Quit ringing that doorbell. Get out of here."

"I turned off the water."

The woman was shocked. What a liar. She could never tolerate a liar. That's why she had always hated her husband. It wasn't just the drinking. It was the lying and the deception.

"*I* turned off that water," the woman said. "Don't lie about it. You crazy or what?"

There was no answer. Then the man said, "Let me in."

"Get out of here," the woman shouted. "I already told you. I'm not fixing to let you in."

The man rang the doorbell again. He kept on ringing it at four-second intervals.

"Listen to me," the woman said. "You're disturbing my rest. This is my house you're breaking and entering. That's my water you spilled on the ground. That's my doorbell. You're wearing it out. Electric and water cost me money. I'm not fixing to let you in."

The doorbell stopped.

"Why not?"

Why not? The question was so unexpected she hardly knew where to begin. She would not let him in because he did not deserve to be let in. That was the answer.

"Because you might rape me," the woman said, her mind darting in different directions at once, "then cut me up in little pieces and flush me down the toilet, and the sewer gets stopped up, and you have to call the plumber, and he comes and smells human flesh, and they get you for murder, but that doesn't matter, I'm dead anyway." It was the story of a mass murder she had heard on the evening news.

Then it came to her.

"Why should I let you in?" As soon as she said it, she knew there was no answer. There was no reason why she should let him in.

"Because I live here."

The woman was stunned. She stepped back from the door and inspected it. Just then the doorbell rang, and she rushed to the crack and cried, "I'm calling the police. If you aren't out of here in three seconds, I'm calling the police, and don't think I won't do it. I called the police on better than you many a time." The sound of her voice was urgent, persuasive, breaking every now and then like a cracked mirror. The door in front of her was silent. She looked at it as though it might explode. Then she tiptoed across the room to the window that looked out on the porch. She drew the curtain aside so stealthily it barely moved and saw the man leaning against the screen door. He was bending over taking off his pants. She saw him remove one leg and then lose his balance. The belt buckle clattered on the porch, and she thought of calling the police at once. She rushed to the phone, then hesitated and returned to the window.

She watched as the man unbuttoned his shirt. Then he removed his socks, his shirt, his jockey shorts. They lay in a pile like detritus, as if he had sloughed off his ancient skin and revealed himself as he truly was. His flesh looked like marble. A racial memory of such visitations stirred in her loins. She had never heard the names, but she recognized the thing before her.

The porch shook as he walked across it down the steps toward the street until she could no longer see him. Then she heard the sound again—the running of water. She ran to the window in her bedroom. "What are you doing?" she cried.

"Taking a shower."

"Turn off that water. I'm calling the police."

A second later he turned off the water. She was afraid to look, hoping that if she didn't see him he might go away, the same way children cover their eyes to make themselves invisible. She imagined him walking down the street turning on every faucet in town. And then it came to her. He was taking a shower because he lived there. That's why he was naked. The god revealed a human face just as she heard a rap on the window.

"Let me in."

He pounded on the wall of the house and scratched at the door like a dog.

"Get your clothes on," she said into the crack at the door. "Aren't you ashamed of yourself looking like that?"

"Like what?"

"Like you look."

"I can't help it."

"Then cover it up. That's what I do."

"I'm getting tired."

"You're getting tired." It seemed like a joke. "It's 2:30 in the morning, and you're getting tired? What you think I'm doing?"

"Keeping me up. If it wasn't for you I'd be in bed."

"Whose bed? That's the question. You stay right there."

"What for?"

"I'm calling the police. You haven't got enough sense to keep your clothes on. I want them to see it. They're going to think that's something, they see you looking all streaked like that."

"Streaked?"

"All that hair." In the moonlight the surface of his skin was striped. The hair swirled across him in patterns. It looked solid and thick as fur—like animal markings. "They see that, they say what is it, man or beast?"

"Man," the man said.

"I know it," the woman said, perceiving his interest. "You want them to see you looking like that?"

There was no answer. Then something crashed against the door.

The woman ran to the window and looked. He was trying to put his shirt on his legs. For a moment she thought of helping him, then realized her danger and rushed to the door. "You getting dressed?"

"I was," the man said. "But I'm too tired. Let me in. I got to get to work in the morning."

"Work?" the woman said. "You're working right now." She meant that she could not conceive of him as a person. He was like something from the sea or something webbed that had fallen from the sky.

He's trying to rape me, she thought. That's why he took off his clothes. The shower was just a trick. She thought of the men who lure children with candy just to get them in the car.

"Thanks for the shower," the man said, and she felt the house stir beneath him.

She rushed to the window. The porch was empty. She ran back to the door and put her mouth against the crack and shouted, "Where are you? You go or what?" Oh dear God, she thought, don't let him go. How are the police going to know where he's at?

"You want a cookie?" she said. It was the first thing that came to mind. "You like candy?"

"No ma'am," he murmured. His mouth was right beside hers at the door. She could almost feel his breath.

"You got a marijuana cigarette?"

"A marijuana cigarette? Of course not."

The worst shock was feeling his mouth next to hers and sensing something more than his presence.

"What would I do with a marijuana cigarette?"

"Give it to me."

"I got more things to do with my time than stand here at 2:30 in the morning and give out marijuana cigarettes."

"You got any candy?"

"Of course I got candy." She had candy in every room in the house—jars of peppermints and caramels, Indian corn and Hershey kisses. She had as much candy as she had cigarettes and cigarette lighters. The cigarettes were for herself in case she might need one. The candy was for her son-in-law when he came to visit and started to roam about the house getting restless. The candy kept him busy while she talked to her daughter.

"What kind of candy you like?" she asked. But he was not there. The connection was lost.

"What's your name?" she cried. "What they call you?" She ran to the window and looked out. She thought she saw him go down the steps, but she was not certain. It may have been wind moving a shadow. The moon was still bright against the street, the housetops across the road a wilderness of geometry, like ice floes tilted at angles. Every one of them was white—so white as to be almost phosphorescent. She looked at the pile of clothes in front of the door. Thank God for that anyway. Even the shoes. He couldn't get far without the shoes, and she ran to the phone, got out the book, and dialed the number.

"Sixth precinct." It was a woman, a black woman. Young from the sound of the voice. Too young and innocent for that sort of work.

"Who is this?" the woman asked.

"Police," the voice said, accenting the first syllable.

"How old are you?" the woman asked. "You underage?"

The phone went dead. She dialed again.

"Sixth precinct."

"We were cut off," the woman said.

"You got some business?"

She was controlled by the firmness of tone. The voice said it was busy. It did not have time to waste.

"I want to report a drug fiend," the woman said. "He's high on something, asking for drugs, and I told him I just smoke cigarettes. That's drugs enough at my time of life. And he said, 'What time is that?' And I said, 'The sere and yellow leaf.'" It was a quotation she remembered from high school. The conversation was one she had had with her daughter, who was concerned about her smoking.

The voice at the other end cut in. "You got something to report?"

"Of course I have. That's what I'm trying to tell you about." The woman was shocked. It made more sense to talk to a drug fiend out on the porch than it did to the police. At least he'd listen.

"You think I'd call you up just to talk?" the woman shouted, and she hung up before she knew what had happened.

She looked at the phone, stunned at what she had done. Then she heard it again—the sound of footsteps on the porch. She ran to the window. The man was sitting on the bannister putting on a shoe. Oh my God, she thought. He's taking his clothes and leaving. How could she report him now? Who would believe her? It was like having witnessed a miracle all by yourself. Everyone would think you were crazy.

"Stop that," the woman cried. She rapped at the window. The man swung his head up like a horse. He was distracted, but not very interested.

"Stop that putting on your shoe. I just called the police. They say stay where you are. Don't do anything. They'll be here in a minute." And she rushed to the phone.

"Hello," she said, "I want to report an accident." She spoke before the operator had a chance to say "sixth precinct."

"What you say?" It was the same young black voice. The conversation seemed to be over before she had realized it had begun.

"I want to report an accident," the woman said, trying to disguise her voice. "We didn't touch a thing."

"Name?"

"I don't know," the woman said. Then she realized she'd better answer. "Wilbur Roach." It was the first name that occurred to her.

"Address?"

But the woman was not finished with the name. "*His* name is Wilbur Roach," she explained. "He's on the porch. I wouldn't let him in because he's naked. My name's Macbeth." As soon as she said it, she knew the source of the quotation.

"Why is he naked?" the policewoman asked. All of a sudden she seemed interested.

"That's the accident," the woman said.

That was sufficient for the police.

"Address?" The policewoman asked the routine question with the same routine indifference as before.

The woman gave her address and directions on how to get there in case they got lost and her telephone number. The policewoman said they'd have a patrol car out there in a minute.

"You need an ambulance?" she asked.

The woman's first thought was to say yes whether she needed one or not. Then she realized what had happened. "It's not that kind of accident," she said. "Much obliged." And hung up.

She tiptoed to the window and peeked out. He had on his shoes and trousers. The socks were a puzzle. He had them in his hand, inspecting them.

"What's your name?" she asked, thinking to keep him talking until the police arrived. He seemed to be able to do only one thing at a time.

"Wilbur Roach."

The woman looked behind her. The action was quick, spontaneous, almost a reflex. It was as though she had expected to see someone there. Then she whirled around again.

"How you know that?"

"What?"

"Your name."

"My name?"

"I just made it up."

"Wilbur Roach."

"I know that. I just made it up."

"What accident?"

Oh thank God, the woman thought. He overheard me.

"Those are socks," she said, tapping on the glass so he would be sure to know what she was talking about. If he knew they were socks, he would have to take his shoes off and then put his socks on and then the shoes again, and by that time the police would be here.

The man put the socks over the toe of each shoe and walked toward her across the porch. He put his face to hers at the window. "Let me in," he said. "I live here."

She could not bear to look at him. He was too homeless, too forlorn. She had no sons, only the one she baited with candy, and he didn't count. She never thought of him as a son. Except for her daughter she was all alone. All she ever wanted was peace and quiet.

She looked at the face outside the window. It was like a baby left on her doorstep. She would never let it in.

The man turned and walked across the porch and started ringing the doorbell. As long as he's ringing I know where he's at, the woman thought. Just then the room filled with blue light like the inside of an icebox. There was a brief blast of a siren. She ran to the window. The lights of the patrol car blinded her. Someone was shining a flashlight onto the porch. It picked up the man and moved up and down him. Then the light searched out the house. It finally picked her out at the window, and she shielded her eyes, then ran to the door, opened the deadbolt, and flung it open.

"Come in, officer," she said, and the man turned and stepped forward.

"Not you," the woman cried, slamming the door. She heard new footsteps on the porch and opened the door again.

The man came at her. He was inside the screen door and halfway across the threshold before she even had the presence of mind to scream.

"Good God, what happened?" the policeman shouted.

"He's trying to get in!" the woman said. "What are you standing there for? Grab him!"

The man turned and looked at the policeman as though he had already forgotten he was there. The policeman's face was thin and edged like a hatchet. It was mostly all moustache. He was neither black nor white—the usual categories—but some kind of foreigner.

"What you think you're doing?" he said to the man.

"I live here," the man said.

It suddenly occurred to her to take action. She pushed the man in the small of the back. He leaped forward at the policeman, and she slammed the door shut. She heard them scuffling on the other side.

"Good God," the policeman shouted. "You almost got killed."

"He doesn't live here," she yelled at the crack. "That's the whole reason I called you. He's trying to get in. I don't know why. He's some kind of dope fiend."

She heard low voices. "What you talking about?" she yelled at the door. "I can't hear a thing you're saying. Speak up."

"Open the door," the policeman said, "if you want to register a complaint."

"He was naked," the woman said. "I was so scared." She eased the door open and peeked out. They were both on the other side of the screen. She reached out tentatively and put on the latch. Then she opened the door fully and stood in the entrance. She felt naked as though she were standing in front of a great light. They could see right through her gown, up her organs. Her whole house was exposed. Again the sense of violation returned.

"You going to arrest him?" she asked.

"He says he lives here," the policeman said.

"And I say he doesn't. It's my house."

"He says you're the landlady. He says he was taking a shower, that's how come he was naked."

"Taking a shower!" the woman said. "You know where he was taking a shower?" But before she could explain what had happened the man turned and walked away. He was already down the steps.

"Hey, buddy," the policeman yelled and went after him.

The woman unlatched the screen door and followed. "That's how he does," she said.

She was standing on the top of the steps looking down at them in the yard. The policeman jerked the man around and drew his hands behind his back. It looked like a Red Cross illustration of the Heimlich maneuver.

"That's how he's been doing all night," the woman said. "Coming and going and acting crazy. He's out of his mind."

"I'm going to book him," the policeman said, breathing heavily. "Son of a bitch resisting arrest."

They were still clinging to each other. Then the policeman pushed him away as though they had done something together—some brutal act— and now they were finished and he loathed himself for doing it. The man's arms were still twisted behind his back. She saw the glint of metal at the wrists and realized they were handcuffed. Thank God for that, she thought. He can't ring the doorbell.

"Where's your partner?" she asked the policeman. She suddenly realized they were alone.

"Partner?" the policeman said. "You got to be kidding."

"I thought you had partners. One gets shot and the other one's always there to protect him."

"You're thinking of TV," the policeman said. "We got short staff. We got niggers, that's what we got. Niggers for mayor, niggers for the chief of police. What you expect? *They* going to protect you?" He sounded angry.

"Who's going to protect *you*?"

"Me? I'm the policeman."

"He might kill us both," the woman said. She was enjoying the conversation. He seemed like such a nice young man, even if he talked like a Yankee and looked like one too.

"You must be a brave young man," she began, launching a conversation she felt would be at least as expansive as her mood.

She noticed the policeman was groveling about the man's feet doing something. Then he began feeling his legs. The man started to walk away like a cow or horse undergoing some sort of treatment, not knowing what its master intended. The policeman tried to follow, still squatting, still patting the man's legs.

"You might have to tie him up," the woman advised him. "He doesn't look like he's standing still."

The policeman rose and jerked the man's arms. "Goddamn it, stay there. You're under search."

The man stood there like a horse. If it had been raining, the steam would have risen from his clothes. At least he's docile, the woman thought. He lifted his face and looked at her, and she felt the same pity she had felt at the window. Why had he come? She did not want him. He seemed so lonely and forlorn standing there waiting for the policeman to finish. There was something infinitely sad about him—some primitive sadness that rose up like a racial memory. She felt the same thing in herself. It was like grief, but she did not know what she was grieving for or why. It was part of her existence, as familiar to her as lungs or eyes. It was present in everything she did. No matter how joyous or happy she was, it always seemed superficial, like lights on the ocean. The other moved beneath the surface like a great fish. She looked at the man and felt great fins. They swirled around her and billowed like wind. The great hulk slid past, moving in her mind like a shadow.

"I figured he might hurt himself," the woman said, uncertain if it was true or not. She couldn't remember. It sounded likely.

"Son of a bitch going to get hurt, he doesn't stand still," the policeman said.

"I mean with him crazy," the woman continued. "He might have something happen."

"He already did."

"I mean something bad. He might hurt himself. That's why I called you. When I saw him naked, I figured there wasn't no telling what might happen to him looking like that. I wanted to save him."

"Look at him," the policeman said. "Looks harmless, don't he? I seen them look like that, they kick your nuts out." He looked up quickly. "Excuse me, lady."

The woman ignored him. "He might have set himself on fire. Or fallen down a manhole. I couldn't trust him. That's why I called—to get him protection. At least you wouldn't rob him and beat him. At least you're going to take care of him, see he doesn't do any harm to himself until you find out what's the matter."

"What's the *matter*?"

"If he's drunk or crazy," the woman said. She saw something out of the corner of her eye beside the porch bannister, a piece of white cloth—circular, indefinite. She checked the man's feet. The socks were still on the toes of his shoes, and he had his shirt on.

"He left his underpants," the woman said.

The policeman did not answer.

"I said his underpants are still on the porch."

"He don't need them."

"I don't want them on my porch."

"Yes ma'am." The policeman took the man by the arm as though preparing to leave. The sound of a siren rose and fell coming toward them down the hill, proceeding hysterically in surges. She could see the red light flashing.

"I said get his things off my porch. I don't want to have to see them." She spoke the same way she had spoken to her husband whenever he was drunk. She had trained herself to authority. Nothing else would get his attention.

The policeman stopped and turned. He came up the steps and bent over the underpants as though inspecting something dead.

"You want a stick?"

The policeman looked at her, but did not reply. She sensed something move, a flurry of white like a flock of birds, a blur on her right. She turned to see the man begin running. He rolled and waddled like a duck, hands clasped behind his back.

"Let him go," the policeman said unnecessarily. "He can't get far with them on his hands."

"He's not running on his hands!" She thought, Oh God, don't let him loose—he'll come back tomorrow. She imagined him turning on the faucet. She would wake from sleep to go to the window and see him standing there in the yard like a nightmare. Or whatever it was. She was not certain what to call it—a visitation of some sort, a call. She imagined it occurring night after night until something happened.

"Go get him!" she shouted, and the policeman moved past her down the steps.

The yard was shallow, no more than fifty or sixty feet to the sidewalk. On one side was the patrol car, parked in the driveway. The door on the driver's side gaped open, and the headlights were still on. On the other side was a strip of grass and a curved walk leading to the sidewalk. The man headed down the walk, then veered suddenly across the lawn and went straight for the car. If it had been moving, it would have killed him. The siren came closer and began to slow down. The wailing turned into a mechanical moan, losing its fine edge of hysteria.

The policeman had already stopped at the sidewalk. "You call an ambulance?" he shouted.

She couldn't remember. "I think so," she said. "I told them it was an accident. He might have been hurt."

Then she saw the man again. He was running up the street toward the ambulance. The lights picked him up like an animal on the side of the road, then lost him again in the shadow of a car parked at the curb, then picked him up and lost him again. It was as if someone kept turning the light on and off. The policeman turned and ran after him just as he cut in front of a parked car and leaped out into the headlights. She thought for a moment they would just miss him. Then she saw him on the grill. It looked as though he was trying to climb up on the hood. Then he seemed to fling himself off. It was dark where he hit. She could not see him, but she heard the sound. It was like a melon she had dropped. Even above the moaning of the siren she remembered the sound of the watermelon slipping from her soapy hands and falling at her feet in the kitchen. The sound was the sound of its splitting open. The seeds rattled across the floor, scurrying like bugs.

The policeman seemed to be saying something. She could see him turn and gesture. She heard the shout, but the sound was indistinct. Then he was running again. The lights of the ambulance were still coming. Then they stopped. The siren was silent, and she knew he was dead. Before they even opened the door to ask what had happened, she knew he was dead.

Toward morning, after they had taken her statement and gone, she lay in bed waiting for sleep. It never came, and she imagined herself lying there the rest of her life, night after night waiting for sleep, eyes open in the dark, thinking. It was like looking out at the ocean.

She remembered the first time she saw the ocean. It was in Florida. She and her husband had traveled three days on bad roads in a borrowed car to top the dunes and cut off the engine and look. It was moving back and forth. That was the first thing she noticed. It was like some kind of animal breathing, the gills of a fish opening and closing. At the edge was a dribble of seaweed and trash, and the beach was littered with boards and cow shit. In the distance were the cows, moving ahead of them as though herded. They had driven up the beach on the hard sand beside the ocean. She tried not to look at it, but she could still see it out of the corner of her eye. It heaved on itself as though swelling with passion. She kept her eyes on the cows, and when they turned off into the shrub, she insisted that they turn off and follow them up a sand road through what looked like a jungle. The cows kept looking back and trotting, and her husband kept saying they were going to end up in Mexico. "The only way them cows are going is away from the car." But she was looking for the highway, and when they found it she had insisted they keep on going until they got back to Georgia. It was to have been their honeymoon. The year was 1948.

She thought about God and how the ocean was like Him breathing and how it was an ambulance that killed him and what he was doing there and who sent him, and she thought, I don't want to have anything to do with Him the rest of my life if that's how it is. I'd just as soon stay here and never move, never get up, just lay here and stare at the ceiling if that's what it takes. I may not sleep, but I ain't going to think about it.

The next night she read until her eyes tired. Then she turned off the light and propped herself up on the pillows. It was like looking down a well. At the bottom there was a glint of something or other. At first she thought it was the reflection of her own face. Then she dropped a rock and heard the faint sound of water cast back with the echo. Without knowing, she had drifted off to sleep, head lolling on the pillows, and she heard the sound of water running. It was rising everywhere. It had already taken the street, and the cars were gone. The yard was gone, the driveway, the walk. It covered the steps, the foundation plantings. It had risen over the porch and was seeping under the threshold like blood. She waited for what she knew would come next.

The man had been sent by God. Soon she would get up and let him in.

Chicamauga

It was not a voice. It did not speak or call him by name or touch him on the arm or shoulder to get his attention. It was more like breath. Like suddenly feeling his own breath and waking at two o'clock in the morning to find his mouth pressed in the crook of his arm, breathing the smell of his own skin, or pressed against Forest's bare back, breathing the same smell. He turned suddenly, and there it was, standing beside him—a man his own age or older.

"The blue ones say 'Go,' and the red ones say 'Stop,'" the man was saying.

"What blue ones?"

"The blue ones and the red ones," the man said, pointing to the Plexiglas map of the Battle of Chickamauga on the wall beside him. The map was so big it looked like a billboard. The Union forces were depicted by blue arrows moving south. The Confederates met them in red. The arrows swept and swirled like sickles—broken edges and fragments of circles moving toward a vortex. Except for the implicit motion, the suggestion of something out of control, the map was almost pleasant to look at, it was so neat and orderly. It had nothing to do with what actually happened there.

"Fucking arrows," the man said, smiling. The smile was disturbing. It didn't fit. Something was wrong. He seemed to be sending two different, contradictory messages at once. Ventris Tidwell checked him out. Nondescript. Middle height, middle weight, middle aged. Madras shirt, blue trousers. Thinning hair. The only odd thing about him was the smell. It was too strong for after-shave. It was more like a woman's perfume. The man was rank with it.

French, Ventris Tidwell decided. Or Welsh. He himself was a little of both—French on his mother's side, Welsh on his father's. The man beside him looked vaguely familiar, like one of his uncles. He not only smelled like a whore, he talked like one too. And besides that, he lisped. Ventris Tidwell did not say "shit" and "fuck" in ordinary conversation and was never comfortable with those who did, not even in the army. It was like child pornography, hearing someone lisp like that and say things like "fuck" and "shit." He expected "shit" any minute.

"I can see, but I can't read," the man said.

Ventris Tidwell hardly heard him over the lisp. It roared in his ears, and he kept straining for another "fuck," the same way a pianist reaches ahead for a difficult passage and misses the next note.

"You can't read."

"I can't read," the man agreed. "I told them that in the army. And they said, 'We'll test him. See if that fucker can read or not.'"

There it was. The "fucker" fell on Ventris Tidwell's ear like grace. It was all he wished for, all he ever expected. He hardly heard the man continue.

"They set me down in this room they got," the man said. "Squeezed me in, and they started buzzing."

"Buzzing?"

"Buzzing like fuckers," the man said gaily. The smile came on again like a great light. His entire appearance changed. Before he had seemed abstracted as though he was plugged in, listening to distant music on a Sony Walkman. Now he was focused the way a magnifying glass is focused. The smile felt like heat on his face, and Ventris Tidwell suddenly realized he was angry. He felt the blood pound in his head. The language upset him.

"This is a National Battlefield," he heard himself say. He noticed he was speaking in a stage whisper. It seemed to go with the polished floors and the clean windows and the shine on the freshly painted woodwork of the museum.

"It's like church. You don't say things like that in church."

The man ignored him. "I stood that shit as long as I could. Then I got up and walked around, and one of them fuckers said, 'Sit down,' and I stepped out the window."

"You stepped out the window?" He couldn't believe it. "What's your name?"

"U. S."

"U. S. what?"

"U. S. Hightower. My momma said, 'Call him Sonny.' "

"Listen," Ventris Tidwell said. "You stepped out the window?" He felt his heart lift again as soon as he said it.

It was the first grade, the first week of school. A nun had locked him up in the cloakroom, and he leaned against the wall among the hats and coats feeling like something hung up in there until he couldn't stand it anymore, and he climbed out the window and went home. They came looking for him a few hours later, and his mother hid him under the table. He heard them shouting in the other room—his mother asking what sort of women they thought they were, if they *were* women. She would never think of locking a baby up in a cloakroom, because she had one of her own. Speaking of him like he wasn't even hers, like he was some foreign baby in some far-off land where things like that were supposed to happen: dead bodies stacked up like cordwood beside the twisted tracks of the railroad.

Sonny Hightower smiled like a picture of a drunken Dutchman, radiant in his own confusion. Suddenly it all seemed all right—as normal as the National Park Service.

"I saw the window," Sonny Hightower said, "and stepped out, and they yelled, 'Go get him,' and one of them got me and took me in this other place and said, 'Here, read this, you say you can't read.' And I said, 'I can't read.' And they said, 'Read it. This is a test.' So I buzzed at it, and they said, 'Out loud. Read it out loud.' And I said, 'What the hell you call this, fucker?' and they said, 'Read it where I can hear it and tell if you can read or not.' So I buzzed at it louder, and they said, 'Hell, that ain't reading,' and I said, 'Hell no, I told you that, fucker.' And they said, 'He can't read. This guy's a moron.' And I said, 'That's what I been trying to tell you.' If I could read, I'd be in the army." He gestured at the glass cases full of the burnished relics of war.

"What you mean, you retarded or something?"

"Damn right."

"Is that your real name?"

"What?"

"U. S. You named for Ulysses S. Grant, or what?" It seemed appropriate at Chickamauga, a moron named Ulysses S. Grant.

Sonny Hightower ignored him. "Looks like a red light. You know how to drive?"

"What looks like a red light?"

Sonny Hightower pointed at the map of the battle. The red and blue arrows. It looked like a complicated traffic pattern, a cloverleaf on the interstate. Red for stop. Green for go. Then it came to him. Green for go? The arrows on the map were blue.

He was about to say something about it when Sonny Hightower asked if he had a sword.

"What? A sword?"

Sonny Hightower nodded his head. "You got a sword?"

"No."

"Me neither."

They fell silent, contemplating the map again. Ventris Tidwell thought of the time when he drove the interstate all the way to Dalton before he realized where he was going. It was like a river. He was carried by the current far past his destination. The cloverleaf shuttled the traffic, and the traffic moved on it wherever it went, going to its destination. Without the pattern, it would all gridlock. Same thing with wars.

"You ever kill anybody?" Sonny Hightower asked.

He did not know if he had killed anybody or not. It was a question he was careful never to ask.

"What you mean, 'kill anybody'?"

"When you were in the army."

"How did you know I was in the army?"

"The way you look," Sonny Hightower said. "What's your name?"

"Ventris."

"Ventris what?"

"Ventris Tidwell."

"Ventris Tidwell." He spoke as though he was testing it. "Don't sound like a name to me."

"My mother's maiden name." As soon as he said it, he knew that was no explanation. Names were not supposed to mean anything, but *Ventris* always seemed to contain some sort of suggestion of meaning. He never knew what.

"Sounds like it means something to me," Sonny Hightower said.

"That right?"

"Sounds like it's somebody knocked on the door waiting to get in, to me."

Ventris Tidwell nodded his head. He knew what he meant.

"Sounds like U. S. to me."

"What?" Ventris Tidwell was quick as a rat in the wall. "What you mean, U. S.?" And then he knew. "Well, shit. Who was Ulysses S. Grant?" he asked.

"What you mean, who was Ulysses S. Grant?"

"I mean, who was Ulysses S. Grant, you named for him like you say you are?"

"Who gives a shit?"

"That's what I figured."

"Look here." He went over to one of the display cases and tapped on the glass.

"U. S. Look at those canteens. U. S. This is a National Monument." The initials were everywhere in the room—on the belt buckles and rifles, the wallpaper, the maps and displays. They were carved on the lintels and woven in obscure red-and-blue patterns on the drapery shrouding the windows. "That ain't your real name. You just made it up."

Sonny Hightower began moving his hand in front of his face, slowly at first, then faster and faster, staring at the map of the battle. Ventris Tidwell did not know what he was doing. He looked at the face moving through the arc of the hand and fell into the same rhythm himself. It was like looking through the blades of a chopper and seeing the landscape split into fragments, mismatched circles spinning out of the sound of the engine, the gunships awkward as great beasts—buffalo or rhinos—lifting off like his own name in a thrusting of wind, the trees bending to the vortex, circling where they said was a village, burning the trees like flesh off a body, the face lifting, turning toward him, features burned beyond recognition.

"I don't know if I killed anybody or not," Ventris Tidwell said. "I was in Nam."

"Nam what?" Sonny Hightower asked. He had quit doing whatever it was he was doing.

"Nam what?" Ventris Tidwell asked. "Goddamn." He took two vicious steps and returned. "Vietnam," he said, pronouncing it to rhyme with *jam*. He looked at Sonny Hightower. It was like looking in a mirror and seeing himself not as he was but as he used to be, and he thought of an advertisement on TV. A politician walking down the corridor of a prison. Bars on either side painted green. The whole place painted green. All of a sudden he stops in front of a cell and turns to the camera. "When I'm president," he says, grinning like he got a mouth full of shit, "I'm going to put all the criminals in jail and keep them there." All of a sudden a guard rushes up and slams the door on him. It makes a loud noise, clanging and banging. Fucker's inside. They finally got the son of a bitch, Ventris Tidwell said to himself whenever he saw it. He was not innocent.

"Listen," he said to Sonny Hightower. "The army took me, but I wish they hadn't. They liked to've killed me."

"That's what they're supposed to do, ain't it?"

"I don't mean *them*," Ventris Tidwell said. "I mean *me*. They liked to've killed *me*."

"What's the difference?"

"What's the difference?" Ventris Tidwell couldn't believe it. "Listen," he said. "They killed my brother."

"Who killed him?"

"His own men." He spoke in confidence, lowering his voice and leaning forward. Sonny Hightower leaned back in the opposite direction. "The Americans," Ventris Tidwell said almost in a whisper. Sonny Hightower was too far away to hear.

"Who?"

"His own men," Ventris Tidwell said. "Our own army. Americans. They thought he was somebody else."

"Who they think he was?"

"How the hell do I know?" Ventris Tidwell shouted. He was angry. "What does that matter?"

"He's dead, ain't he?"

"What you mean? Of course he's dead. I just told you he was dead. His own fucking men killed him."

"That's why it matters."

"Yes."

"If they knew who he was they might not have killed him. They know he was your brother?"

"Listen," Ventris Tidwell said. "What the shit does it matter whose fucking brother they thought he was?" He stopped suddenly. "They thought he was the Viet Cong."

"The Viet Cong," Sonny Hightower said. He sounded amazed, as though he had just learned that Forest Tidwell was believed to be a Coca-Cola bottle.

"You know what I mean?"

"What?"

"The Viet Cong. You know what I mean?"

Sonny Hightower looked about the room as though searching for something.

"Shit," Ventris Tidwell said. "They thought he was the enemy."

Sonny Hightower looked like someone had put him in neutral.

"I mean the Americans," Ventris Tidwell said. "They thought he was the fucking enemy. His own men. They killed him." The words rose up like apparitions. "There wasn't even a body inside the coffin. They sealed it up and covered it with an American flag, and we didn't even know what was in there, it was so light."

"You mean there wasn't nothing there?"

"They said, 'Don't open it. These are remains. He was burned beyond recognition.'"

"You mean you didn't even get to see him? How'd you know who it was?"

Ventris Tidwell did not reply.

"I said, how'd you know who it was, you didn't even get to see him. It might have been the wrong one."

"Yes."

"What?"

"It was the wrong one."

"They killed my brother with a car," Sonny Hightower said. "They buried him, I knew who it was. I kissed his face, and they closed the lid, and I knew he was in there. That's how we're different."

"That's one way," Ventris Tidwell said.

"What are the others?"

"What others?"

"The other ways we're so different."

"We ain't so different."

"Yours didn't die right. That's one way. You got an empty box. Mine was full. I know what I got."

Ventris Tidwell nodded and started to leave.

"What about reading?" Sonny Hightower said. He looked suspicious. "Can you read?"

"Yes."

"Read that." He pointed to a large display on the wall.

"It was a haunted land," Ventris Tidwell began, and then stopped. "How's that?" It was a test.

"Don't stop now!" Sonny Hightower said. "Keep on going. Read it out loud where I can hear it."

"It was a haunted land," Ventris Tidwell began again. It did not occur to him to pick up where he had left off. He read all the *A*'s as *A*'s and all the *The*'s as *The*'s.

Chickamauga Creek was larger than most rivers in Europe. It flowed out of the mountains of North Georgia toward the lowlands of Tennessee through a rough and broken country, a sparsely settled region of gloomy woods and lonely cabins. It had been given its name by the Indians—Chickamauga, the River of Death. For the early settlers who lived on its banks it still retained that meaning, flowing in the heart of nature, eroding the edges of their fields, and then suddenly rising up wild and uncontrollable, sweeping away their loved ones and all their possessions. But the soldiers who arrived on its banks and began their blind, bitter struggle gave it new meaning, baptizing it afresh with their blood. Marching, the armies sang the words of the old hymn, "There Is a Fountain Filled with Blood." Chickamauga was that place.

"Don't stop!" Sonny Hightower said. He seemed to be charmed by the words as snakes are said to be charmed by music. "You ain't come to the end of it yet." He walked up to the display and peered at it. The type rose up over his head like a sign warning of a disaster.

"That's it," Ventris Tidwell said. "That's all it says."

"Well, shit," Sonny Hightower said. He walked along the base of the wall as though looking for a way out.

"What about that one?" He pointed to another display. It looked like the tombstone of a wealthy banker. "What's that say?"

"The Battle of Chickamauga went to nobody's plan."

"Go on," Sonny Hightower said. "Read the fucker. Don't just stand there."

A Brigadier General in the Union army summed it up perfectly when he wrote that Chickamauga was a "mad, irregular battle, very much resembling guerilla warfare on a vast scale in which one army was bushwhacking the other and wherein all the science and art of war went for nothing." The country was full of trees and underbrush with little clearings here and there; nobody could see much of his enemy's position, it was almost impossible to move artillery along the narrow country lanes, both armies were sodden with weariness, drinking water was hard to find, casualties were extremely heavy, and by nightfall all anyone could be sure of was that there had been a terrible fight and that it would be worse tomorrow. They were the two bloodiest days of American Military History. More than a quarter of the 124,000 men engaged were killed, wounded, or missing; in some units casualties exceeded 80 percent.   *Bruce Catton*

"What?"

"Bruce Catton."

"What's that mean?"

"I don't know. Man's name that wrote it. Some kind of general."

"That's what I figured. Why didn't you tell me before you started?"

"What? His name? How the hell am I supposed to know that? I don't read backwards."

"Well, shit," Sonny Hightower said, leaning forward to inspect it more closely. The light on the surface was dazzling. "Don't ever do it again, you hear me?" He walked on past a cluster of flags and came to the next major display. He stood in front of it as though praying or expecting to absorb the message without reading it but simply by remaining there in its presence. Ventris Tidwell joined him. It looked like an enormous telegram so outsized it would have taken two men to carry it.

"Son of a bitch," Sonny Hightower said. He leaned forward and inspected the grain of the print as one might inspect the brush strokes of a painting.

"What's it say?"

William S. Rosecrans, Major General, U.S.A., Commanding, The Army of Tennessee, Chattanooga, Tennessee, to Henry W. Halleck, Major General, U.S.A., General in Chief of the Armies, War Office, Washington, D.C., 21 September 1863.

"Washington, D.C.," Sonny Hightower repeated.

WE HAVE MET WITH A SERIOUS DISASTER.

"We have met with a serious disaster," Sonny Hightower said. He sounded delighted.

EXTENT NOT YET ASCERTAINED. ENEMY OVERWHELMED US. DROVE OUR RIGHT, PIERCED OUR CENTER, AND SCATTERED TROOPS THERE. EVERY AVAILABLE RESERVE WAS USED WHEN THE MEN STAMPEDED. CHICKAMAUGA IS AS FATAL A NAME IN OUR HISTORY AS BULL RUN.

"Goddamn," Sonny Hightower said. The whole thing conformed to what it was saying. "Look how it looks. See that?"

"Yes."

"Looks like a train whistle. You know how to drive?"

"Yes."

"Me too. I ain't forgot it. My brother taught me. They don't give you a license for driving unless you can read."

"I heard about that."

"I reckon so. Most folks have." He waddled on down the wall like a rat moving along its base.

Ventris Tidwell was reminded of a wall he had seen in the *National Geographic* with all these pictures of men leaning their heads on it and sticking flowers in it or pieces of paper with messages on them. The wall was black. It was covered with names. On the other side of the wall was nothing. It was just a wall, and the men cried to it for help in their lives and pity and mercy on their souls.

Sonny Hightower kept on going and stopped at the end. There in the corner was the last message.

"What about that one?" Sonny Hightower asked. "What's that fucker looking like that for?"

He was pointing at a grainy blowup of a young man with a round face and slick hair that looked as though he had just combed it with water. He was wearing a bow tie and an open coat with large brass buttons running obliquely down his chest like bullet holes. His clothes looked rumpled as though he had been sleeping in them. His face was plump and well fed. In the crook of his left arm was a felt campaign hat with a large brass H on the front above the brim. The fingers holding the hat were tense.

Ventris Tidwell read the caption. "Sam R. Watkins, High Private, Company H, First Tennessee Regiment, Confederate States of America." Underneath that was a quotation.

"What's it say?" Sonny Hightower asked.

I got a piece of cold corn dodger, laid my piece of the rat on it, eat a little piece of bread, and raised the piece of rat to my mouth.   *Sam R. Watkins*

"Piece of rat. Well, shit. Looks like you, don't it?" He pointed at Sam Watkins.

"Like me?" There was no resemblance.

"Read what it says."

We remained on the battlefield of Chickamauga all night. Everything had fallen into our hands. We had captured a great many prisoners and small arms, and many pieces of artillery and wagons and provisions. The Confederate and Federal dead, wounded and dying, were everywhere scattered over the battlefield. Men were lying where they fell, shot in every conceivable part of the body. Some with their entrails torn out and still hanging to them and piled up on the ground beside them, and they still alive.

"That's all," Sonny Hightower said. "I know all about that"—waving his hand in front of his face like the blades of a chopper.

> Some with their underjaw torn off and hanging by a fragment of skin to their cheeks, with their tongues lolling from their mouth.

Sonny Hightower touched his arm. Ventris Tidwell looked at him.

> Some with both eyes shot out, with one eye hanging down on their cheek. In fact, you might walk over the battlefield and find men shot from the crown of the head to the tip end of the toe. . . . Dying on the field of battle and glory is about the easiest duty a soldier had to undergo. It is the living, marching, fighting, shooting, soldier that has the hardships of war to carry.

Sonny Hightower was still holding his arm when he finished. They looked at each other for a moment. Then Sonny Hightower detached himself and wandered among the display cases.

"Look at this," Sonny Hightower said.

"What is it?"

"I don't know."

"What's it look like?"

"I don't know."

Ventris Tidwell went over and looked.

"Canteens."

They came in all shapes and sizes. Those still wrapped in cloth reminded him of dead bodies piled on one another in heaps until they no longer resembled individual human beings, not even dead ones. They were too piled. The piles were too neat. The piles looked like rows of canteens.

"Look at that," Sonny Hightower said.

Ventris Tidwell turned away in revulsion.

"Any more of them fuckers?" Sonny Hightower said, straightening up.

Ventris Tidwell looked around. The only other displays in the room were some photographs of Chattanooga and Lookout Mountain and the Moccasin Bend of the Tennessee River. On the opposite wall between two windows looking out over a sweep of lawn was a large blowup of a trench full of dead soldiers. He walked over to it. Northern or Southern—he couldn't tell. They were all jumbled up together. It looked like the remains of some great disaster, some great wind that swept down and lifted them up and then flung them down to lie there like that, sprawled obscenely on their backs. They looked sexually assaulted. The trench was muddy. It was full of pieces of paper, books, scraps of wood, logs, shoes, pots and pans, dead bodies.

Underneath the photograph was the word: "CHICKAMAUGA."

That's it, Ventris Tidwell thought. The place was healed over, the debris cleaned up, the bodies buried. Rotten and eaten now. Even the bones leached out in the wet soil. But it was still there.

Sonny Hightower was standing directly in front of the photograph. "What's it say?" he asked Ventris Tidwell.

"Chickamauga."

"What?"

"Chickamauga. The Battle of Chickamauga. This's where it's at."

"That ain't here," Sonny Hightower said.

"Yes it is. That's where we are."

"Not me," Sonny Hightower said. "That ain't where I am. Shit." He laughed. "You read them all?"

"Except for the windows."

"The windows?"

"A joke. I was making a joke."

"A joke?"

"Forget it."

"I mean that story," Sonny Hightower said. "Any more about that story?"

"What story?"

"The one you were reading."

"Just the maps."

"Read that," Sonny Hightower said. He walked over to one of the maps and pointed at a blue arrow. "What's that?"

"A map."

"What's it say?"

"Thomas's Corps."

"What?"

"Thomas's Corps."

"What's that mean?"

"It means where they went. The men in Thomas's command."

"Well, shit. Read it."

"I already have. 'Thomas's Corps.' That's what it says."

Sonny Hightower went closer and scrutinized it, tracing the arrow slicing south.

"That's all it says?"

"Listen," Ventris Tidwell said. "You don't read a map."

Sonny Hightower looked at him expectantly. He was like some sort of animal in a field—a mule or a horse or a cow.

"Maps show what happened," Ventris Tidwell started to say, and then stopped, knowing that was not it.

Sonny Hightower waited.

"They're like diagrams," Ventris Tidwell said. "They show the movement."

"The movement."

"Yes. This is Thomas's Corps"—tracing the blue arrow. "And this is Longstreet's."

"Longstreets."

"Yes."

"Where's that?"

"Here." He pointed at a red arrow.

"That's Longstreets."

"That's right."

"What's Longstreets?"

Ventris Tidwell did not answer.

"Read it," Sonny Hightower said.

"I can't," Ventris Tidwell shouted. It made him angry. He was so angry he wanted to kill somebody.

"Listen," he said. "You don't know why you came here, and I don't know why I came here." He broke off.

It was like blind, lumbering armies marching around in the woods all day on and off the roads. They met at a place called Chickamauga, and the men whose lives made up those armies died there or lived through the fighting to die somewhere else. Like his great-grandfather, who was born and raised in Chattanooga and fought in all the battles around there on the wrong side, in the Union army, and came home after the war and went into the hardware business and had a family and lost his business and retired and lived with his only daughter until she died and then with her daughter until he died himself of old age or a bad heart or indignation or despair sitting in a chair in the side yard under a Yeats apple tree. And there was a reason. He was not killed at Chickamauga, and there was a reason. There was a pattern that guided men's lives. He could not explain it or say what it was, but he felt its wings. He felt the cold air of its wings.

"Damn right," Sonny Hightower said. "That all you got?"

Ventris Tidwell nodded his head.

"Then I'm obligated to you," Sonny Hightower said. "You gave me the information I needed, and I'm much obliged."

Ventris Tidwell was touched by the speech. It reminded him of the elaborate courtesy of people he had known when he was a boy. They adopted it in all their relationships with one another, even with their loved ones at home. There were still a few of them left in Chattanooga, on the heights overlooking the city, and in some of the wood-frame houses in the flats along the river.

Whoever took care of Sonny Hightower took care of him well. They kept him clean and had taught him his manners. He was like an elderly pet or a well-loved child. He was trusting with strangers. He knew no fear.

"You're welcome," Ventris Tidwell said, assuming the same serious air.

Sonny Hightower stood there waiting. He seemed about to say something. Then he turned and walked across the room. There were two doors. One was marked EXIT. The other said MAINTENANCE. KEEP OUT. They were side by side, with only a small display case between them. Both were paneled, both painted the same Williamsburg blue. Sonny Hightower was just at the point of having to choose between them when he turned and looked at Ventris Tidwell.

"The one on the left," Ventris Tidwell said.

But Sonny Hightower did not open the door. He turned instead and waved goodbye the same way children wave goodbye with their whole arm. Ventris Tidwell waved back.

Sonny Hightower stood there a moment. Then he came back across the room.

Oh shit, Ventris Tidwell thought. Sonny Hightower was on him like a dog.

"Now it's my turn to tell *you* a tale," Sonny Hightower said. He marched toward the center of the room, arms stiff at his side like an automaton. When he reached the middle he stopped and turned.

"Attention!" Sonny Hightower shouted. The sound filled the room like an explosion. "Attention! This is the captain. We're going down." He made an elaborate sinking motion with his hand. "Who knows how to pray?" He paused, waiting dramatically, then turned to Ventris Tidwell. "None of them know how to pray."

"Keep your voice down," Ventris Tidwell said. "Don't shout so loud." What would he say if someone came in and asked what was happening? He did not know what was happening.

"No one could pray," Sonny Hightower said. He had stepped out of the joke or story or whatever it was and stopped as though it was over. Silence seeped into the room like water. Ventris Tidwell felt like praying. But not for himself. It was such a crazy, useless story. It was not even a joke. It was nothing.

"That's some story," Ventris Tidwell said.

Sonny Hightower just stood there, eyes shut, arms rigid at his side. He seemed to have fallen into a trance.

Then all of a sudden Sonny Hightower shouted, "All right. No one can pray. We'll take up an offering. You got a hat?"

Ventris Tidwell did not know what to say. He had fallen down the rabbit hole.

"We took up the offering," Sonny Hightower said and made as though someone gave him a hat full of money. He stuck his face into it as into a mirror.

"This is the captain," he said, straightening up. "We're going down. Then the ship sunk," he said. "They all died." He gestured with his hand. It fell through the air like a leaf. "Now I told you a tale." His eyes were still closed. He still stood at attention.

"Much obliged," Ventris Tidwell said. Then he realized he was angry. He was so angry he wanted to kill him.

"What kind of story is that?" he shouted. "What you mean telling me something like that for? What's it mean?"

Sonny Hightower did not reply.

"It wasn't money. That what you mean?" He stopped abruptly. What was he talking about? Sonny Hightower was a moron.

But what was he doing here? What did he want? For there are no accidents. Ventris Tidwell was certain of that. His breath flowed out of him and returned. It filled the world like a balloon. And that was no accident. Sonny Hightower had come here today. He felt his breath coming and going. And that was no accident. There are no mistakes. Invisible pathways lead through the earth, currents of the air and sea beyond our means of comprehension. It all made sense now, just for a moment, until he looked at Sonny Hightower and realized there was no message. He was a moron. That was the message.

Sonny Hightower was still standing at attention, arms stiff, jammed down beside his legs like stripes on a convict. His fists were clenched as though he was about to hit somebody. The cordons and tendons of his neck were twisted like rope. His face was flushed. Ventris Tidwell watched as his mouth pulled back into his neck, baring his teeth. The whole body was like a muscle undergoing a massive contraction. A low sound rose from it as though forced out by the tremendous pressure. It was not the sound of a voice. It was the sound of the tissues themselves contracting.

Ventris Tidwell became alarmed. He glanced at the door to see who was coming. What could he say? He rushed over to Sonny Hightower.

"Keep it down!" Ventris Tidwell said. He began to shake him. "Shut up, goddamn it! Somebody's coming. They're going to hear you. What are you doing?"

Sonny Hightower fell over backwards and hit a display case. Ventris Tidwell expected to see it overturn or slide across the room and smash into something, but it was too heavy to move, and Sonny Hightower slid off and scuttled around on the floor as though he was trying to creep under it. His arms and legs were moving in different directions. The heels of his shoes struck the floor in an irregular rhythm. His arms flailed, and his head started to beat on the floor. The moans were increasing. The volume was louder.

Ventris Tidwell began to run. He was halfway across the room before he turned to see what had happened. He remembered something about biting one's tongue and ran over to the registration desk, got a few brochures, folded them lengthwise, and tried to force them into Sonny Hightower's mouth. The teeth were clenched. The head flung itself about in his arms like an animal seeking release. Then it was done, and he allowed the teeth to close on it. They snapped shut, and he thought of a turtle he had caught once in the Tennessee River. He remembered teasing it with a stick as big around as his arm. The turtle had seized hold of it with its beak and was still holding on when he cut off its head. He looked at Sonny Hightower's eyes. They were still open, but the irises had rolled back in his head. He looked like a fish.

That was it. Ventris Tidwell got up from the floor and started to leave. Someone would find him. He would come to sooner or later. His tongue was fixed where he couldn't bite it and drown in his own blood. Ventris Tidwell owed him nothing.

The paint on the door had such a high gloss that it reflected his image like asphalt after a rain. He pulled it open, and instead of the steps and the parking lot, the sweep of lawn leading up the hill that overlooked the battlefield, there was only a wall and a darkened room. It might have been his own heart.

Inside the room were obscure shapes such as he had seen in Southeast Asia, the clothes they were buried in rotted half off them. Some were on shelves. Others were hung up by hooks at the back, shoulders hunched over their ears. Skulls gleamed like plastic jugs.

He slammed the door and stumbled back. The light was like grace. It fell on him so suddenly that he was not only disoriented, he was completely bewildered. He had already closed the door and read the sign before he realized what it meant. The sign said MAINTENANCE. KEEP OUT. Inside were buffers, electric cords, coveralls hanging on hooks.

"Oh God," Ventris Tidwell said. "Oh God." He started laughing.

He walked over to the other door. A red and white arrow above it said EXIT. He wondered how he could ever have missed it. The doorknob in his hand was brass, part of a massive rim-lock set. He noticed how cold it was to the touch. All he had to do was open it.

Then he turned and went back, the noise of his heels coming after him like a shadow. Sonny Hightower's feet were sticking out from under a case of bayonets. Every so often they would move as though he was trying to pull them in after him.

Ventris Tidwell dropped to his knees and looked in under the case. Sonny Hightower had worked himself all the way to the back and was sprawled with his head and shoulders propped against the wall.

"What are you doing?" Sonny Hightower asked.

It seemed like the perfect question. Ventris Tidwell did not know what he was doing.

"I don't know," Ventris Tidwell said.

"I do."

"What?"

"Looking at me."

Ventris Tidwell laughed. "That's right. I came back to see how you're doing."

"Back from where?"

"I don't know. Nowhere. How are you feeling?"

"Fine as wine. How are you?"

"Fine as wine."

"What happened?"

Ventris Tidwell did not know what had happened. "An accident," he said.

"Where am I?"

"Under the table. You want to get out?"

"Sure."

"Give me your leg." Ventris Tidwell started to pull him out by the leg at the same time that Sonny Hightower kicked him away and tried to stand up by himself. He kept hitting the case with his back.

"I can't stand up!" Sonny Hightower shouted. "It's all over me. I can't move!"

Ventris Tidwell dropped to his knees, crawled under the case, and wrestled Sonny Hightower to the floor.

"Kneel down," Ventris Tidwell said. "Look here, like this." He crawled out. A few moments later Sonny Hightower crawled out after him. He continued to crawl until Ventris Tidwell put his hand on his shoulder and stopped him.

"Can you stand up?" Ventris Tidwell asked.

"I don't know."

"You want to try? You want me to help you?"

"Sure. Who are you?"

Ventris Tidwell did not know what to say. "A friend," he said finally.

"A friend. Where am I?"

"Chickamauga."

"What?"

"Chickamauga. Where they had the Battle of Chickamauga."

"I already been," Sonny Hightower said.

Ventris Tidwell laughed. "You look like you been."

"Fucker already read it to me. You ready to go? Let's go."

Ventris Tidwell was not certain what he meant.

"Take my arm," Sonny Hightower said. "You going to help me, that's how you do it. You carry my arm."

Ventris Tidwell carried his arm.

"My pins ain't steady," Sonny Hightower said.

"Your pins?"

"The pins on my feet. They're coming loose. My feet feel like they're wobbling off."

"You want to sit down?"

"Not yet. I got a tale to tell you about that."

"About what?"

"The pins on my feet. You want to hear it?"

"Not yet."

"It's too early," Sonny Hightower agreed.

They came to the set of doors, and Sonny Hightower headed straight for the wrong one.

"Not that one," Ventris Tidwell said.

"How you know?"

"I already been there."

"What's in it?"

"Nothing."

Sonny Hightower saw the arrow. "It got an arrow," he said. "This what we're supposed to do."

Ventris Tidwell knew that this was what they were supposed to do. The only problem was that he did not know why they were supposed to do it. The message said pray, and he had prayed all his life, but they were still going down. What do you pray to? The wall is nothing. On the other side is a vacant lot and another man praying.

"How you feeling?" he asked Sonny Hightower. It was as though he had just been given a gift but did not know yet what it was.

"Gooder than snuff," Sonny Hightower said. "How about you?"

"Gooder than snuff. You want to open the door?"

"Sure," Sonny Hightower said. He moved forward and tried to push it open with his hands, then with his shoulder. The door wouldn't open.

"Pull," Ventris Tidwell said.

The sunlight was blinding. Then his eyes focused, and Ventris Tidwell saw the whole world. The sky was endless as an ocean. It filled the horizon. There were no clouds. The air was like marble. The cars in the parking lot caught the light and sent it spinning, dazzling his eyes. The lines on the asphalt heaved in the heat as they walked across it arm in arm onto the grass and up the hill to the clump of oaks overlooking the battlefield and then down the other side to the row of trees in the far distance marking the place where the river flowed, the muddy Chickamauga, eroding the edges of the field and opening a way in the forest. Even now, here and there, he caught an occasional glint of light like something moving through the trees, a flash of something barely seen out of the corner of his eye. He thought of it as some kind of glory.

58 Babylon Dread Bean

It was like sitting beside a wall of dark glass. She tried to look out, but all she saw were the obscure shapes of what she suspected were trees moving past. They looked like forms of undersea life. If she got close enough and shaded the glass with her hand, she saw traffic, an occasional face, the large towers of buildings. Falling back in her seat, she saw the glare from the interior lights and projected against them her own reflection. She looked away. She had seen enough of that in the last week since her husband had died.

She turned to the woman beside her. "Do you ride Marta often?" she asked.

"Often as I have to," the woman said and stared straight ahead. She had just gotten on at the last stop. The only vacant seats in the bus were the one beside Margaret Winchell and one beside a man who was obviously drunk and muttering to himself. Margaret Winchell took it as no compliment that the woman sat beside her.

"How often is that?" Margaret Winchell insisted.

"Whenever I go to work," the woman replied.

She looked past Margaret Winchell into the glare of the glass.

Margaret Winchell followed her eyes. It was like looking into an aquarium. Dim shapes floated past. She caught the woman's eye as in a mirror and addressed her there. "You work as a maid?" she asked. The woman was black and middle-aged. What else could she do?

"The Gradies," the woman said.

"The Gradies?" Margaret Winchell cried. She turned and grasped the woman's knee. Grady Memorial Hospital was a municipal institution that served as the emergency medical facility for the city.

"That's its name ain't it?" the woman said.

Not quite, Margaret Winchell thought. She called it Grady, but all the blacks in town still referred to it as the Gradies. It was where most of them went to die in the charity wards. They were more familiar with its various faces, more intimate with its multiple units and departments. They also remembered the time when there were two separate institutions side by side—one for white, one for colored. Hence the use of the plural.

"I haven't heard it called the Gradies in years," Margaret Winchell said. It was like coming home. "I was born and raised right here, but I've been living out of town. My husband just died, and I brought him back to be buried at Oakland." Oakland was the oldest cemetery in town. All the old families were buried there, and since all the lots were bought up and most of them already filled, it was considered quite prestigious to be buried there behind the brick wall, below the arching water oaks.

Prestigious for who? Margaret Winchell thought. The dead don't care. They are too dead. She glanced at herself in the window and quickly looked away again. It was typical of the sort of thing that had been happening to her lately. Thoughts like that kept rising unbidden, like primitive forms of marine life. She wondered at times about her mind. It was not like her to be so cynical. She was the queen of the cruises. The Vicereine, her husband had called her. He was the Viceroy. Accent on vice.

"What did he die of?" the woman asked.

Margaret Winchell caught a sudden flare of attention, like a match in a dark room.

"Are you a nurse?" Margaret Winchell asked.

"Practical nurse."

Margaret Winchell suddenly felt frightened and lonely. That was why she had remained in town after the burial, to seek out her old friends and let them console her. But they were all dead or moved to Florida or the Caribbean or recovering from mastectomies or divorces or face-lifts or drug-abuse programs for multiple addiction at various psychiatric hospitals. Or they were just too old to do anything more than meet for lunch and drink Bloody Marys. The old times meant nothing to them. "That's because you moved out of town and got so rich," they told her. "You didn't live here like we did and let it wear off gracefully." And she asked them, "What?" And they said, "The dreams of youth." And she said it wasn't the dreams, it was the old places she missed, knowing it was not that. It was her life when she was a girl and the happy times before she was married. None of the exotic places she had visited in the last twenty years had ever compared with that. And they said, "Most of those old places are gone. This whole city is bright as a brand-new penny except downtown, and that's all high rise and offices. The malls," they said, "all the stores moved out to the malls," and then turned back to talk of their grandchildren or stare at the wall, caught in the trough between hangover and the incoming effects of the first drink of the day.

"Practical nurse at the Gradies," Margaret Winchell cried. Even to her it sounded forced. She checked out the woman's clothes. Cheap, nondescript overcoat, brown, loose weave, and at the knees where the overcoat parted a triangle of starched white cotton so startling it looked like a vision of another world. She'll do, Margaret Winchell thought. She had not been able to tell any of her friends about the shame and horror of her husband's death, and none of his family would have been interested. They were all nephews and nieces and distant cousins with young children pulling at their arms to leave. They were too busy. And her friends were too old. They did not want to talk about dying. Time was a subject they were not interested in anymore, or rather they were so interested in it they spent all their time trying to avoid it, like a man with a morbid obsession.

"You ever been on a cruise?" Margaret Winchell began.

"A what?"

"A cruise. A vacation."

"I been on a vacation."

"Well we were cruising the Caribbean," Margaret Winchell began.

"What did your husband die of?" the woman interrupted.

"That's what I'm trying to tell you about," Margaret Winchell said. "It happened on a cruise."

"That ain't what he died of," the woman said. "I asked what he died of."

"And that's what I'm trying to tell you about." Margaret Winchell felt herself getting angry. It was the woman's duty to listen, just as it was hers to talk. "The cruise is part of it."

"I never knew nobody to die of a cruise," the woman said.

Margaret Winchell checked her out in the wall of glass. The woman's face was impassive. If she was being ironic, it did not show.

"It was one afternoon in our stateroom," she began. "It was the second largest stateroom on the ship."

"Who had the first?" the woman asked.

Margaret Winchell was sure she was being ironic.

"The chairman of the board of Stevens Textiles," she replied. "Robert J. Wilfing. He and his wife are old friends. We went on the cruise together. My husband was in textiles before he retired."

"And he got the first best, and you got the second?"

"In a manner of speaking. Actually, we gave it to them." She laughed her gayest silver laugh. "Noblesse oblige."

"When did he die?" the woman asked.

"I'm coming to that," Margaret Winchell said. "Actually, it was the largest cruise ship afloat. Our stateroom was enormous. We had just come in from walking. Speed walking," she said, correcting herself. "My husband always insisted on that."

"What?"

"Calling it speed walking. He said there's a world of difference. We do three miles a day, five days a week."

"Did," the woman said.

Did? She had forgotten. "I mean did," she said. "I was lying in the bed resting. All the furniture was gray and green and blue, only it was so subtle, the colors were so muted, you could hardly tell what they were."

"What did they look like?" the woman asked.

Margaret Winchell did not know. "Like lava," she said, suddenly inspired. "It looked like lava." She surprised herself. That's exactly what it looked like.

"That some kind of mud, or what?" the woman asked.

"Gray rock, like they have in Hawaii. And the furniture was soft sculpture."

"Soft sculpture?"

"Sort of like quilts, except it's free standing. Even the table tops were covered. It's very new."

"Sounds like it," the woman said.

"I was lying in the bed reading. There were two king-size beds, that's how big it was, and my husband was sitting in his chair. Wherever we go he always picks out his special chair. That way, he says, he never leaves home. This one was red." She remembered the chair. It was more fuchsia than red, more purple than fuchsia.

"It was an accent piece," she explained. She realized the woman probably did not know what that meant. "Like a specimen tree or shrub in the landscape, a point of interest, something to catch your eye and arrest it," Margaret Winchell explained. The woman's face was impassive. She looked as though she did not care if she never knew what an accent piece was.

"He was taking off his running shoes," Margaret Winchell continued.

"I thought you said walking."

"We walk in running shoes," Margaret Winchell said.

"Walked."

"Walked," Margaret Winchell said. "And he was sitting there taking them off, and he had one in his hand and the other on his foot, and he said, 'I feel funny,' and hiccoughed, and I didn't know whether to say anything or not. I was interested in what I was reading."

"What was that?" the woman asked. She sounded like a detective.

"I don't know. A magazine. I don't remember. About breast cancer."

"You got breast cancer?"

"No, of course not." Margaret Winchell was insulted.

The woman nodded her head as though she was fully satisfied at last. Margaret Winchell felt relieved. She appreciated the woman's approval. "I was interested in my husband's health," she explained, "but that didn't include hiccoughs and such as that. I'm interested in serious things like breast cancer and heart attacks."

"Me too," the woman said. "That's what I'm interested in."

Margaret Winchell looked out the window and saw herself and, behind her, in the background, unrecognizable shapes, appearing and disappearing. Where were all the familiar sights she had come there to revisit? That was the whole point of the trip. She had planned it as carefully as a tour. The new transportation system would carry her into the heart of the past, hurtling at ninety miles an hour through tunnels blasted in solid rock. She would sit at the window and watch all the familiar sights slide past, like blood in her own veins, and they would comfort her at the same time she was experiencing firsthand the challenge of the new. The subway system that had just been installed was an entirely new dimension to the city. If she meant to keep up, she would have to learn about it. Like computers—as soon as she got home, she intended to buy one and learn to play games.

"Which one did he die of?" the woman asked.

"What?"

"Cancer or heart attack?"

Margaret Winchell was suddenly angry. "Just a moment," she said. "I'm telling this." She paused. "Where was I?"

"Reading."

"Yes, and he said, 'I feel funny.' Did I tell you that? And hiccoughed. And I kept on reading, and then I heard this explosion of air, and he hiccoughed again."

"He was holding his breath," the woman said. "That's a good thing to do. That, and breathing into a bag."

"There were no bags," Margaret Winchell explained, "so I threw him a pillow and said, 'Here breathe into this.'"

"That's good," the woman said. "That's what I'd do."

Margaret Winchell again felt grateful for the approval, but at the same time she wondered why. It was so unearned, so inconsequential.

"Anyone would have done the same," she said.

"You'd be surprised," the woman said.

Margaret Winchell accepted that. Ever since her husband had died, the whole world seemed a surprise.

"I know some tore their lungs loose," the woman was saying. "You could hear them flapping inside."

"Tore their lungs loose?"

"From hiccoughing," the woman said. "It's a terrible sight."

"I'm sure it is," Margaret Winchell said, not knowing how to picture it.

"I'm talking about serious cases," the woman said, "where they been hiccoughing so long they can't remember when they started and can't stop and can't even eat or drink. Don't have time to chew it, that's why, and can't hold it down anyway even if they could. And then their lungs start coming loose, and they can't breathe, and they die of two or three things at once."

"That's horrible," Margaret Winchell said.

"I know it is," the woman said. "I seen it all. Any way you want to die, I seen them do it. Hiccoughing ain't nothing."

Margaret Winchell understood. "My husband did not die of hiccoughing," she explained.

"I never said he did." The woman was still staring straight ahead as though unwilling to acknowledge the fact that they were talking to each other.

"What was it, then?" the woman asked the head of the man in front of her. "What did he die of?"

"I'm coming to that," Margaret Winchell said. She refused to be hurried. It was necessary to understand all the details to realize how truly horrible it was. A fragment of verse came to mind, a snatch of song—the refrain of what she thought of as a medieval love poem. Something about woe never like this, referring to a woman's sorrow. She was that woman.

"After a while I said, 'How's it coming?'" Margaret Winchell began again, picking up the thread of her story. "But he didn't answer. He had put the pillow in his lap and bent over and buried his face in it. I said, 'That's right. Keep on breathing.' And then I thought about what it smelled like."

"What's that mean?"

"I mean the way the pillow smelled. I had a bunch of them propping me up in bed, and I could turn my head and smell them."

"What they smell like?"

The woman's interest seemed curious to Margaret Winchell until she suddenly realized that the woman probably thought the pillows were poisoned.

"The pillows weren't poisoned," Margaret Winchell said.

"Nobody said they were."

"They just smelled stale and dry like old furniture stuffed with Spanish moss, old cigarette smoke, mice, something like that." She thought of the dresser in the attic of her mother's house full of her maiden aunt's effects, awaiting her return from the private sanitorium where she was being treated for drug addiction. Inside were nests of old letters and dance programs shredded by mice and full of lint, corsages of flowers so old they looked like roots, and, what she found most fascinating, a group of photographs of girls on vacation, her aunt among them, riding goat carts and standing laughing, fully dressed, against what she imagined to be the ocean, though she was not certain. It might have been a pile of old mattresses. Or even soft sculpture, she now realized. It was shapeless and blurred like lava. What fascinated her was that the girls looked so young. They might have been her own age. In fact, they might have been any of her friends dressed up for a masquerade party wearing all the clothes in her maiden aunt's dresser. The photographs were yellow with age even then.

"It reminded me of the grave," Margaret Winchell said. "I thought to myself, That must be what it's like to be buried. You smell that smell."

"Except you're dead."

"What?"

"You're already dead," the woman said. "How are you going to smell it, unless they buried you alive? I've known them to do that. I've known them to do worse than that."

"I'm sure you have," Margaret Winchell said. She was not to be distracted. "I said, 'How are you doing?'"

"Who's that?" the woman asked.

Margaret Winchell wondered if she had been listening. "My husband," she said. "There was nobody else in the room."

"I thought somebody else might have come in."

"Don't rush me," Margaret Winchell said. "That was later."

The woman was looking at herself in the window. Her glasses reflected the glare. She was invisible behind them.

"I said, 'How are you doing?'" Margaret Winchell continued. "And he didn't answer, so I checked his breathing."

"That's right," the woman said.

Margaret Winchell felt relieved. She knew now what it was. It was guilt. She wanted someone in the medical profession to assure her that she had done everything for him she possibly could have under the circumstances.

"I check his breathing every morning as soon as I wake up," she assured the woman.

"How old was he?"

"Sixty-nine."

"That's a good idea," the woman nodded.

Margaret Winchell was grateful. "I was always afraid I'd wake up one morning and find out he was already dead lying there next to me all night long. I couldn't stand it." The only fear worse than that was to have him stall above her when they were making love. Margaret Winchell put the thought aside. At least it wasn't that. She wasn't entirely Job.

"He would have gone by himself in the night," Margaret Winchell said aloud, "and I wouldn't have heard him cry out for help."

"Sometimes they don't make a sound," the woman said. "What happened to the pillow?"

"It was still there, and he was still breathing into it, but I couldn't see him move. I watched for a while and then tried to read, but I couldn't concentrate. And then I said, 'Willie.'"

"That was his name," the woman said.

"His name was William. William T. Winchell. I called him Willie."

The woman waved her on. "And he was dead," she said. "What killed him?"

"He was dead," Margaret Winchell said. She did not tell about the moment she knew, sitting in the king-size bed propped up on a lava flow of pillows, reading an article on breast cancer. She looked at the figure slumped in the chair and realized that her husband was gone and she was left with something over there she did not even know what to do with. She remembered not moving. She sat on the bed and called his name, knowing that he would never answer. She thought if she kept it up long enough he might reply. Then she stopped and looked at him.

"I didn't know what to do," Margaret Winchell said aloud.

"Nothing *to* do," the woman said. "He was dead on arrival."

"What could I have done?" Margaret Winchell asked. "I was right there."

"You get his head out of the pillow?"

"Of course I did. As soon as I saw he was dead, I rushed over there and said, 'Willie, Willie, what happened?' and tried to lift him. But he was too heavy. He almost fell, and I had to push him with my hip, and his face went back into the pillow, and I touched the back of his neck and said, 'I can't lift you, honey. You wait there,' and I rang for the steward. I finally realized where I was."

"Where was that?"

"I mean aboard ship. Surely they would know what to do. I needed a doctor."

"Too late for doctors," the woman said. "You needed you an undertaker."

"I needed help," Margaret Winchell said. "I needed someone to deal with the body. I didn't know what to do. I thought of trying to get it in bed, but it was too heavy."

"Nice to meet you," the woman said and started to get up.

"What?" Margaret Winchell was confused. She did not know what was happening. It was like that ever since her husband had died. One moment he was complaining of hiccoughs, the next minute he was not only not there, he had left himself behind for her to do something with. And it was not even him. If it was, it might have been different. He could have helped. No wonder she was afraid.

"You can't leave now," she heard herself say. "Sit down." She reached out and touched the woman's thigh as though to restrain her.

"It's my stop," the woman said, and she started shifting her bulk to get up, pulling on the chrome plated bar on the back of the seat in front.

"I'm not finished," Margaret Winchell cried. "Sit down. I'll pay you. Ride with me, and I'll pay your fare."

"I already paid it," the woman said. "I got to get off," and she hoisted herself to her feet and lurched down the aisle. After a few seats she stopped and turned around and lurched back.

"I'm sorry about your husband," she said. "What was it? A heart attack?"

Margaret Winchell nodded her head. What did it matter? No one knew.

Maybe the pillow was poisoned. Maybe his lungs tore loose. The appalling part was what had happened. He was so changed.

"That's what I figured," the woman said and smiled. Her teeth were outlined in gold. Margaret Winchell noticed she had a mole on her face. It looked like a melanoma.

"Sure was good to talk to you," the woman was saying. "That's an interesting story about how it happened. There are all kinds of ways, and every one of them different. That's what makes it so interesting." She leaned over and spoke softly so as not to be heard more than five seats away. "I knew one of them died on the toilet. He was a relative of mine. Heart attack," she said, straightening up.

She turned and lurched back down the aisle. Margaret Winchell watched as she made her way out the door and disappeared behind the dark windows.

Margaret Winchell leaned forward and tried to look out. There were some buildings, very tall, cut off by the top of the window, and darker spaces between them that she assumed was sky. There were no people.

A truck blocked her view. She fell back in her seat, and her own face appeared beside her. She was alone. This was the city of her birth, and she didn't even know where she was. She couldn't even see out the window without seeing herself instead. Her first thought was to get up and rush out and catch a cab back to the hotel, but after a moment the panic subsided, and she decided to proceed as planned. She would ride the subway into the heart of the city and eat lunch at the most elegant restaurant in town and shop and be consoled. She would know where she was as soon as she got there.

The steward did not come, she remembered. She rang again and waited with her husband. What could she have done? She tried to take off his other shoe. Then she put on her slippers and went out of the room, leaving the door ajar. It seemed important to keep the door open. She did not want to leave him shut up in there alone. She found a maid with linen in her arms who said she would notify her supervisor.

What good would that do? Margaret Winchell thought. Above her she could hear the distant music of the tea dance she and her husband had planned to attend. They were playing the songs of her youth. To turn back to her room was like picking up a burden she had just put down. It was a long journey, and this was only the first stage. Inside the room she smoothed the bed and rearranged the pillows. She patted her husband's hair and rearranged his shirt collar. The one shoe he had removed she put out of sight beneath the chair. The other was still on his foot. She had not been able to lift his leg for fear of tipping him off balance. She had hardly finished tidying up when there was a soft knock on the door, and the doctor was there. A minute later he pronounced her husband dead.

That is what she would have told the woman. He was already dead. There was nothing she could have done.

They came with a table on wheels, and two men in mustard-colored uniforms lifted him and put him on it. The doctor went into the bathroom and got a towel and covered her husband's face.

"Are you all right?" the doctor asked her, and her only thought was no. She was not all right. "I'll send a chaplain," he said. She told him she was a Catholic, she wanted a priest. Then she thought of the last rites. Her husband was already dead. What good would they do? That would be the first question. The doctor said he was sorry. There were no priests on board, only a nondenominational minister. "What good would he do?" she asked. The doctor said, "You never can tell," and walked out behind the body.

She remembered the panic when the door shut. She was in there alone, and she rushed to open it. Instead of returning inside, she walked down the corridor and followed its turnings. She met a maid. The music was still playing in the distance, but it was too far away to recognize the name of the tune. It was the same maid. She smiled and paused as though she might speak, but then walked on. The carpet was so thick there was no sound except the vibration under her feet, the movement of a ship at sea. They were somewhere between Port-au-Prince and Cartagena. She remembered thinking that and thinking how it seemed important. Soon she would understand what had happened.

She felt the presence of someone behind her and turned to see a man approaching, moving sideways like a crab. He tacked from side to side and crept forward, and she knew just from looking at him that he was the preacher. He took her by the arm and led her winding back to the room. Once inside she sat on the edge of the bed, and he sat in her husband's chair. She refused to sit in it. "I'm comfortable here," she said, and he said, "Is this where it happened?" meaning the room. And she said, "Yes, you're sitting in it," and he jumped up and looked at the chair and then sat down again. She asked about the last rites, but he said he had come to console her, not argue about theology. Besides, he was nondenominational.

"I've come to pray," he said. Then he asked if they could pray together, and she said, "Not yet"—she had some questions. But he went right on. "Extemporaneous or scriptural?" he asked. She said, "What's the difference?" And he said, "In one case I make it up, and in the other I read it from scripture, unless you want a little of both."

It was as though she was already at the funeral. But she didn't know what to do with the body. She could imagine two possibilities. One was burial at sea. The other had no name. She imagined it wrapped in tin foil and put in the freezer. And then she thought of the rest of the cruise. What would she do at the candlelight dinners and carnivals, the shopping expeditions in port, the interminable card games and exercise programs?

She felt as though her husband had died of the plague and she was infected. Everywhere she went she would carry it with her.

The preacher was laughing. "My dear woman, my dear woman," he said when she told him her fears and asked what would happen to her husband. "I have never performed a burial at sea and never intend to. I find the thought of it quite . . ."—and he paused, groping for the proper word—"quite unbiblical."

She thought of Jesus walking on the water. She thought of him waking and calming the storm, and something like a prayer rose in her heart. Calm the storm, she prayed. Let him rise and walk on the water.

"Most of our guests are quite elderly," the chaplain explained. She thought of him as the man in the death chair. He laughed discreetly as though telling her a choice piece of gossip. "Few on board know this," he said, "but we carry as part of our standard equipment a complete stock of mortician supplies." She asked what that meant. And he said, "A room full of coffins. You choose your own." And she thought, If you aren't dead already. He laughed discreetly. "Not an item we advertise, of course, but very convenient, as I'm sure you'll agree. Your husband will be quite comfortable. Shall we pray?"

She never did know where they kept her husband. She imagined him inside the coffin stored in the freezer along with the meat and frozen vegetables. In Cartagena they left the ship and revels behind and flew back for the funeral, her husband in the baggage compartment, she in first class. The ship was continuing on to St. Kitts, Grenada, Barbados, the Yucatan—all the storied, legendary places. She felt as though her whole life had been interrupted.

"End of the line."

Someone was speaking.

"End of the line, lady."

It was the driver. He had turned around in his seat and was looking at her. She was the only one on the bus. Where were the others? She noticed the driver was black. Everyone she had met today was black. The entire city was black. She was not certain where she was.

"Where am I?" she asked the driver.

"End of the line, lady." And he named some familiar streets.

She did not mean that. She meant something entirely different.

"How do I get to Marta?" she asked.

"You're already on it," the driver said. "See that?" and he pointed through the windshield.

The reflection on the windshield revealed only the interior of the bus and what she imagined to be two wiper blades, cutting the windows like knives on an eyeball. She walked to the front of the bus.

"What do I do?"

"Just follow the people," the driver said. "You got your card?"

She showed him the piece of pasteboard he had given her.

"Just follow the people and put that in the machine."

But there were no people. She stepped out of the bus and stood on the sidewalk. The driver closed the doors and lit a cigarette. She expected to be flooded by sunlight and surrounded by all the old familiar sights, but she was somewhere underground or inside a building. The streets the driver had named were not there. Nothing was there except a sweep of concrete road behind her, leading down, and in front of her the same road, leading up. Opposite, on her left, was a concrete wall built in interlocking sections like the huge blocks of stone assembled by the Incas without mortar, such as she had seen in Cuzco. They fit perfectly. The surface of the wall was already beginning to sprout with graffiti, the patterns intricate as the swirlings of lichens. "58 Babylon Dread Bean," she read, and immediately knew what it meant. It was the name of the place she had come to. The streets of her youth were somewhere above her or beyond that wall. She was here now. On her right was a series of glass doors that held the bus in their reflection. Beyond them was the place she was seeking. She heard her own shoes click on the cement and looked behind her to see who was coming. No one was there. Inside the doors was a tiled tunnel. The tiles were beige. Oatmeal, her friends would have called it if they were choosing that color for the bathrooms in the new house they were building at the beach. And then she remembered. It was her house. She had chosen the tiles herself. She paused at the turnstiles and thrust her card into the slot. The machine tore it from her hand and opened the gate, through which she proceeded, descending the steps to the platform.

It was like being inside a *hamam*. She remembered the one at Çekirge, on the outskirts of Bursa. The baths had been there from the time of the Romans. The springs were thermal and flowed from the flank of the Mysian Olympus, the mountain rising above the town like a fist. She had gone immediately to the central pool and immersed herself to the neck in the water. Steam rose and obscured the air. At intervals along the marble walls were spigots where naked women crouched washing themselves.

She expected the angel to come stir the waters as at the pool of Bethesda, but there were no afflicted on pallets waiting for grace, there was no water, only the tiles to remind her of water and the silver tracks like a stream leading both ways through the tunnel. She sat on a seat and waited. Suddenly the platform began shaking, and the train appeared beside her, the doors open, the cars still swaying.

She stepped inside and found a seat beside the window. As the car jerked and lurched forward, the station lifted and flung away, leaving only her own reflection superimposed on the darkness. An occasional green or red light flashed past. She leaned forward and cupped her hand against the glass. Hurtling past were ledges of rock. And suddenly she knew where she was. It was not lava that stood behind her aunt in the photographs, lifting and heaving like the ocean. It was the same rock as outside the window. She forced herself to look away.

On the seat opposite were a pair of legs and beyond them a body. It sat in the corner and seemed detached from the rest of itself the same way the legs of a spider seem detached from the dot of its body. It was a boy, a young black boy. He was staring out the window and twitching his foot the way a cat will twitch its tail. He was in pieces—that was the dominant impression. When he gets up, Margaret Winchell thought, he will pick himself up in his arms and walk out.

"Sit up straight," she heard herself say.

The boy pulled himself together. The various pieces flew up and then reassembled themselves, legs folding under the rest like the legs on a grass-hopper.

"You talking to me?"

"Yes," Margaret Winchell said. "Tell me where we are."

"You don't know where you are?"

"I didn't say that," Margaret Winchell said. She knew where she was. She meant where she was in relation to the world above her. If she were back on earth again, where would she be?

"We ain't there yet," the boy said.

"Where?"

"Five Points."

"I mean where are we now?"

"Nowhere, lady. This ain't nowhere. We're on the train."

A red light flashed and disappeared.

"What are those red lights?" Margaret Winchell asked.

"Signal lights."

"Did you see the moisture?"

The boy looked at her but did not answer. Then he turned back to the window.

"On the rocks outside," Margaret Winchell said. "Some of them are dripping wet."

"That's underground rivers," the boy explained. "They got rivers inside the rocks. You can hear them in there running."

"How do you know?"

"I been in there."

"You mean in the tunnel?"

"Yes ma'am. I walked down it."

"What for?"

"See what was there."

"What's there?"

"Different things," the boy said. "Rats and men making coffee."

"Whatever for?" Margaret Winchell cried.

"They live there," the boy said. "There and under the viaducts too. You seen them."

Margaret Winchell had seen them. They were in every city she had ever visited. Men who slept in alleys and doorways, in cardboard boxes and long tunnels underground—alcoholics, derelicts, and drifters. They were all waiting. She thought of herself. They had nothing else to do.

"Sit up," Margaret Winchell said. The boy had scattered himself around again, depositing parts of himself on the seat beside him like packages. "That's bad for your posture. Your spine's still young and pliable. You'll get a set in it."

"You teach school, or what?" the boy said, pulling himself together.

"I'm a mother," Margaret Winchell replied. Her only child had died of a drug overdose in his second year at Yale almost twenty years ago, but she still loved children. She thought of it as her instinct for them. "And stay out of that tunnel. What do you mean going in there?" The dangers. She thought of the dangers. "A train might hit you," she said.

"They got places you can stand."

"Listen," Margaret Winchell said, and she got up to move over and sit next to him. The boy folded his legs like wings as she slipped into the seat beside him. "Some of those men, they like young boys." She did not have the heart to continue. His eyes were deeper brown than his face. They were like the pools at the Sheep Gate, Bethesda, in the early morning at dawn before the angel descended to stir them and cure the afflicted.

"Rats carry bubonic plague," she heard herself say, looking at him.

"What's that?" the boy asked.

"Some kind of disease. You get boils all over and turn black. Then you die." She realized he was already black.

"They have to bite you?"

"No. It's in their breath. They just have to breathe the same air you breathe."

"Them rivers," the boy said, "you can hear them if you put your ear to the rock."

Margaret Winchell was not surprised. "That rock's Stone Mountain," she told the boy.

Stone Mountain lies twenty miles northeast of town and is reported to be the world's largest piece of exposed granite. When Margaret Winchell was a girl, she and her friends could catch a trolley that ran on its own tracks alongside the road and ride out to the base of the mountain and have a picnic beside the ruined monument to the Confederacy carved on one of its sheer flanks.

"Stone Mountain?" the boy said. "That ain't nowhere near Stone Mountain."

"It runs underground," Margaret Winchell said. "Like Luckie Street. We might be under Luckie Street this very minute. Just because you don't see it, doesn't mean it isn't there. Luckie Street goes clear down, and if you're under it, that's where you are."

She had a sudden vision of the city spread out on a grid above her. If only she could locate herself on the grid, she would know where she was. The streets went straight down. Marta was the same as moving across town, except it was underground. The thought was consoling.

"Parts of Stone Mountain run everywhere," Margaret Winchell said. "Haven't you ever dug in the yard and hit Stone Mountain?" It underpinned everything in the city.

"I don't dig," the boy said.

"Don't dig?"

"What would I dig for? I got everything I need."

"You don't dig *for* anything," Margaret Winchell explained. And then she understood. "You mean treasure? You don't have to dig for treasure. You just dig. You make forts and things like that."

"I don't make things," the boy said.

The inertia on the train had shifted. She felt herself being lifted up as though by some force deep inside her. She pushed against the seat in front and resisted with all her might, knowing that force as the final cause drawing her to the wall of interlocking pieces of concrete that looked like a giant jigsaw puzzle and bore slashed across it the name of both the place itself and whatever it was that was leading her to it. This was not Five Points. Five Points was up there. This was 58 Babylon Dread Bean.

"This is Five Points," the boy announced and stepped over her, his long legs hardly touching. The car had come to a stop, the doors flung open. Before she could recover from the shock, he was already gone.

Margaret Winchell allowed herself to rise. She followed the people out of the door and found herself in the same place she had started from, except now it said "Five Points" in blue tile. The words ricocheted from wall to wall as though cast by mirrors.

But it was not Five Points. She knew Five Points. Her father had worked there in the Palmer Building, opposite the statue of her grandfather, clutching bronze papers in one fist and shaking the other in the air. "Orator and Statesman," the plaque had said. "Father of the New South." And she suddenly knew what was troubling her. It was the blacks. They infested the inner city like lice. She should never have ridden Marta. I will take a cab back, she thought, and immediately felt better. She was free to do whatever she wanted.

The only problem was what. And suddenly she was back in Turkey. On one side was the Byzantine Church of the Divine Peace. It was completely empty. All the marble had been stripped from the walls, all the gold and silver looted. There was not even an altar. Ahead were the walls of Topkapi Palace, with gates leading to the inner courtyards still guarded by soldiers. In the outer court where she stood the grass was untended. It was full of debris and waste paper. The whole place looked like parts of New York. She half expected to see rats eating orange peels on the paths or derelicts urinating in corners, rising from cardboard boxes or nests in the grass. But what she saw instead were chickens. They were everywhere, scratching the garbage, pecking at invisible scraps of food, grains of sand, shiny fragments of glass. They ran in all directions around her, scattering under her feet like explosions. And suddenly she was in the land of unlikeness. This was not history, her heart told her. It was the same place the boy on the train had been when he walked in the tunnel and put his ear to the rock and heard the distant rushing of rivers. She sensed some other ongoing life.

The people she followed knew the way. She proceeded up the stairs, guarding her feet, knowing that if she walked long enough she would eventually come to the surface. At the top of the stairs she came to another level. People were thrusting themselves at turnstiles, and Margaret Winchell followed them. The crowd narrowed and lifted her up. In front of her was a darker passage, and at the end a different sort of light. She began rushing, knowing that she would step into it, and there would be the knot of the city where all the roads come together at Five Points, from more directions than there were even points on the compass. All the different ways she had gone, all the different journeys taken would come together, and she would suddenly find herself back at the place she had begun.

She hurried forward almost running and emerged from the tunnel into the light. It fell from the sky above her as into the shaft of a well or a mine. She stood at the bottom and looked up. Above her she saw a cloud, the sky, the edge of a building. In front was a bank of escalators. They looked like a cliff, the black steps like ledges of rock. The escalators rumbled and rattled, rising and falling like something moving just beyond the limits of comprehension. People flowed past her on all sides, stepping forward and finding their places. Once there they never moved again, and yet she saw them lifted up until at the top they disappeared. From that angle it looked as though they stepped off the last step into sheer space. There was nothing around them but light, and they went out into it and were gone. Seeing them go, her heart filled with longing. "Rest of their bones"—the phrase occurred to her—"and soul's delivery." She knew she could never step forward and trust herself to rise like that, or if she did her fear would get loose halfway up, seize her by the throat like a demon, and fling her back down. It was too steep. She was too old.

And then it was given to her like a gift. She stepped out into the air as though stepping out of this world, and the escalator caught hold of her. She shuffled her feet and gripped the handrail, and the next thing she knew she was aloft, her heart soaring like a bird. She looked and saw the people around her ascending and descending. It reminded her of Jacob's ladder, feet fixed on earth, its top rung touching heaven, and on the ladder the angels of God coming and going. Behind her was a pit of darkness. Ahead there was nothing but light. Halfway up her heart burst. It seemed to leap about in her bosom like a hooked fish. Then came the pain. It hit like a hammer and spread up her neck to the jaws. She gripped it like something held in her teeth. Then it exploded, and she fell down at the same time the escalator caught her and lifted her up, transporting her beyond herself. The last thing she thought was how awesome it was. This is the house of God, she thought. This is 58 Babylon Dread Bean.

The Call of Nature

"Where we going?"

It was like the voice of God. Dortis Mulkey lost control. The car leaped out of his hands and swerved across the white line onto the yellow-striped loading zone of the Winn-Dixie Food Store. Then it straightened out and proceeded on through the Gateway Shopping Center.

"Where we going? You from the car wash?"

"Yes ma'am."

"What?"

"Yes ma'am!"

They had turned left on Highway 5 and were picking up speed. Dortis Mulkey looked in the rearview mirror. A figure of some sort against the light. Face black in shadows. Hair smoky, electrified. Old voice.

"I'd quit if I was you," it was saying. "What kind of future you think you got in a car wash, anyway? Young man like you. Deaf already. You can't hear a thing I'm saying. I have to shout, and that makes me tired."

"Yes ma'am!" Dortis Mulkey shouted.

"That's better. I can hear you better now. You hear what I say?"

"Yes ma'am."

"Well, then, why don't you?"

"Do what?"

"Quit the car wash," Lucille Arp said, leaning forward, her breath hot on Dortis Mulkey's neck. "I been looking for a young man like you."

Dortis Mulkey turned to look at her. The right wheel dropped off the pavement onto the shoulder of the road and shuddered before it righted again. She was older than he thought.

"I been wanting to go home," Lucille Arp said. "I been looking for a young man to drive me."

"This your car?"

"It's Hollis's car."

"Who's Hollis?"

"Charlene's husband. They gone shopping. You know how to get to Unadilla?"

"No ma'am," Dortis Mulkey lied. He was listening to the tires. The tires were saying, "Unadilla—kiss-my-ass. Unadilla—kiss-my-ass."

"Roll up the window and turn on the air. It's blowy back here," Lucille Arp said. "You're driving too fast. Now, listen. The way we get there is go to Macon. You on the Macon road?"

"Not yet." It was like being locked up with some kind of wild animal, the windows closed and the air conditioning on. His soul pounded against the panes the same way his heart beat against his ribs and his mind raced down the highway ahead of the car so fast it was already there trying to explain who the old lady was before they even got past the Burger King.

"Well, get on the Macon road," Lucille Arp said. "Go on through till you come to Perry. You know where that's at? Of course you do. Drivers know the Macon road. Young man like you. Been driving for two or three years, I reckon."

"I been driving since I was eight," Dortis Mulkey said, disgusted. "There ain't nothing I can't drive. Or fix it, either one." It was as though his professional competence had been called into question. He'd started driving a go-cart when he was eight, a Ford-Fergusson diesel at ten, a dune buggy at twelve, and lately whatever he stole in his business, any sort of heavy equipment—mostly farm tractors and bushhogs used by the State Highway Department to mow the right of way. Careening up the loading ramp, chaining them down, and driving off in less than two minutes. He was the best. Eighteen years old and already at the top of his chosen profession.

"Driving's my hobby," Dortis Mulkey said. "I purely love it."

"Me too. Homer too. He loved it too."

"There ain't nothing I like better than getting in a car and going."

"That's right. We used to go every Sunday after dinner down this road and that. I been down every road in Houston and Pulaski counties twenty-five times. You turn here?" There was a paved road to the left. "That one goes to Macon, don't it?"

"Talking Rock. That one goes to Talking Rock."

"Well, you know where it's at. Smart young man like you. Drive anything. I can't even drive. Old as I am, I never did know how. Homer got sick, and I couldn't drive him. I blame myself. I had him in my arms in the front seat. I got him that far. It takes a man for some things, I reckon, and driving is one. That's why I'm so glad I got you," she said, leaning forward to pat Dortis Mulkey's shoulder.

As soon as she touched him, he knew what to do. It was like a gift from God.

"What about the car wash?" he said. "Car's awful dirty. Besides which, they'll miss me"—his mind leaping ahead like a rabbit. What car wash? Where? And then he knew. Two or three miles ahead.

"Dirt don't hurt the running of it," Lucille Arp said. "That's one thing I know about cars. Hollis ain't clean. You know Hollis?"

"No ma'am," Dortis Mulkey said, thinking about what he would do when they got there.

"Speak up," Lucille Arp said. "Don't mumble like the rest of them. You're still a young man. Speak out crisply." It was a phrase she had often used in class. Speak out crisply, she told her students, and stand up beside your desk when you talk. "You meet him," she continued, reverting to Hollis, "that's all it takes. Shake his hand, you know all about him. Might as well shake the hem of my skirt. Got more starch in it."

"Yes ma'am."

"That's better. You're speaking up now. Ain't it strange the things that happen? I'm going home." Dortis Mulkey started to slow down. "Why are we stopping?"

"This's the car wash," Dortis Mulkey said. It was at the rear of a filling station, a long tunnel with red and white brushes and two or three large black women in rubber boots with rags in their hands.

"I thought you quit."

"Time to get out," Dortis Mulkey said, executing the plan perfectly. He reached back and freed the door.

"I ain't leaving," Lucille Arp said, pushing back in the imitation velvet upholstery. It was gray, and when Hollis first bought the car she would not ride in it until it became obvious that Hollis was prepared in that case to leave her. It reminded her of the sides of a coffin she had seen in the funeral home at Unadilla when she picked out Homer's. His was oak stained like walnut. The other was gray cloth that looked like automobile upholstery. No telling what was underneath it. "I'll wait here till you get done," Lucille Arp said. And then she stopped. "Rooster?" He was turned around in the seat facing her. "I didn't know you were Rooster."

"I ain't," Dortis Mulkey said.

"Thank God you came. You're going to drive me to Unadilla."

"As soon as you get out of the car so we can get it washed, I am."

Dortis Mulkey got out of the car and opened the back door. Lucille Arp screamed as though cleaved in the middle. The black women ran toward the car. Dortis Mulkey leaped back in and drove through the car wash, triggering the wash mechanism. It was still churning and squirting behind them as they broke into the sunlight again and fishtailed around the side of the service station onto the highway.

"That's better," Lucille Arp said. "What you say your name was?"

"Tar Baby."

"Tar Baby? What kind of name is that? What your folks call you?"

Dortis Mulkey was reminded of every year he had been in school. It even sounded the same, the questions peremptory as barks.

"Rickey," he said. "Rickey Mulkey."

"Rickey Mulkey." Lucille Arp rolled it around in her mouth, testing for taste. "I like it," she said. "I like that name. It ends on a high note."

"What's that supposed to mean?"

Dortis Mulkey had picked it out himself. Every year at school when he started a new grade and was asked his name, he had tried to create the new identity he felt straining within him, and every year the teacher had the old one written down on a card—the shameful Dortis, which was not a real name but the designation of a whole group of people he was related to on his mother's side. And every year the other students who knew him from birth said, "Bubba! His name's Bubba! It ain't Rickey. That's Bubba Mulkey." And the teacher said, "Hush up. That's baby talk. Bubba and Sissy and such as that. We don't use them." And she called him Dortis just like his grandma.

"What you mean, high note?" Dortis Mulkey asked.

"The way it sounds," Lucille Arp said. "I like it. Sounds like a scream."

"Scream?"

"Like somebody shouting pinned in the wreckage."

"Wreckage?"

"If they were in an accident from driving too fast."

Dortis Mulkey looked at the speedometer and immediately took his foot off the accelerator and touched the brake, scanning the rearview mirror for police.

"Rickey's all right," Lucille Arp said. "What's your momma call you?"

But Dortis Mulkey was no longer in school. "Rickey," he said. "That's my name, ain't it?"

"No it ain't." She knew his name was not Rickey without questioning or wondering why. "You got some kind of family name."

"Dortis," Dortis Mulkey said. He was touched in the heart with an icicle. His mouth opened and the name appeared. "How you know that?"

"No momma in her right mind would name a child of hers Rickey. That's one thing. Rickey ain't got no weight. Besides which, it's my gift."

"What gift is that?" Dortis Mulkey asked, checking the speed again. All he needed to do was get caught. He just realized it was not only theft by taking, it was kidnapping too, and if he crossed the state line it was probably rape.

"I got a special gift of God," Lucille Arp said.

The icicle pierced his heart again. The shivers went up his spine, and his soul was back at the windows trying to get out.

"I was born with a prophet's mantle. You know what that is?"

"No ma'am," Dortis Mulkey said—mind darting this way and that looking for a hole to crawl in.

"You're born with it like gauze on your face. Comes from God."

"What's it do?"

"Sees the future. I know what it is before it happens. I saw you coming."

"Me?" Dortis Mulkey said. He knew! He knew! That's why she'd suddenly risen up in the backseat burning with light like an apparition.

"I knew He wouldn't let me stay on with Hollis. I figure He loves me too much for that. I knew He was fixing to send a servant to drive me home, and then you got in. You know why that was?"

Dortis Mulkey locked his mind. He did not want to know.

"To free us both. You from the car wash and me from Hollis. And look at us now, driving like birds on the road to Macon, going south where the warm weather is. Going home."

The sign said "Snelville 10 miles." Dortis Mulkey expected the car to turn around of its own volition and start heading south to Unadilla. He had no control. Lucille Arp was looking out the window singing. The words drifted weightlessly inside the car. "Love lifted me!" she sang. It was the old hymn. Dortis Mulkey sang along with her silently.

> Love lifted me!
> When nothing else could help,
> Love lifted me.

"You ever been to Unadilla?" Lucille Arp asked.

"No ma'am," Dortis Mulkey said. He was still singing. "We're turning here." He pulled into a gravel parking lot in front of a trailer that had been transformed into a Bar-B-Q restaurant by the addition of an overhang. Under the overhang were two redwood picnic tables chained to a concrete slab. "We got turned around back there. This's the road to Snelville. It don't go to Unadilla."

"That's what I thought. Get on the road to Macon first. That's the one going to get you there."

"Yes ma'am."

"You're going to love it. I got me a house there painted white and a place for a garden and shade trees Homer planted when we were first married and a glider and spring chairs set under them. That's where you can sit and rest when you get done driving. Help me get set up. You hear me, Rooster?

You can sleep in your own room. I kept it for you just like it was," and she patted his shoulder.

Dortis Mulkey swerved at the touch. "Set up? Set up in what? Sounds to me like you're set up already."

"I am for living, but not for business. I mean for business."

"What business?"

"Reader adviser. Pull over here." She pointed with an arm that looked like a stick with a dead bird nailed to the end of it.

"What for?"

"The call of nature."

Oh God, Dortis Mulkey thought. He imagined Lucille Arp stepping out of the car and calling and nature responding—stars sweeping out of the sky as in the Book of Revelation, figuring forth the promised upheavals and cataclysms of the last days.

He pulled off the road and stopped beside a barbwire fence enclosing a pasture rank with overgrown grass and weeds and spotted with dark pines. In the distance, at the far edge of the field, was a line of darker pines, and inside them the darker woods. He cut off the engine and suddenly in the silence that followed he knew for certain. She would not call. He listened to the silence. There was something beyond the fence that would call from the darkness. That's what she meant.

"Not here," Lucille Arp said. "I ain't no man to go in the bushes. I mean down there," and she pointed down the road to a filling station.

Dortis Mulkey drove down the road to a metal door with a handwritten straggle of letters across the top saying LADIES, and under that, in the same broken, illiterate hand, WOMEN.

"There it is," Lucille Arp said. She struggled to free herself from the car. "Wait here." She flapped her elbow. Dortis Mulkey grasped it and lifted her into the daylight. She was frailer than he had imagined. Even chickens were stronger than she was, the sinews and muscles under their skin thrusting violently to get loose. Lucille Arp was more like a handful of kindling.

"Wait here," she said. "I won't be a minute."

Dortis Mulkey got in the car and prepared to leave. The filling station attendant would call the police sooner or later, and Hollis or Charlene would come and get her. She could have a Coca-Cola while she waited, and before she finished they would be there—no harm done—and he would be gone. He would drive up to Snelville in Hollis's car, and Sandy would say, "Where'd you get that? You got a new car." And he would say, "I borrowed it," and drive it a day or two and leave it somewhere.

He was still thinking about it when Lucille Arp appeared again, face wet and shining in the light.

"There ain't no towels," she said, sticking her head in the window. "My face is all wet." A drop of water dripped on his forearm. "Help me in. I feel a whole lot better now. There ain't but one thing better than washing your face."

"What's that?"

"Breathing. Let's get going," and she flung herself at the rear door before Dortis Mulkey could get out to help her.

"You're going to hurt yourself," he said, helping her in.

"You're too slow. We're wasting time. Get on to Macon, and I'll show you from there." The car picked up speed. They were heading south to Unadilla. She looked out the window and started to sing.

> Some glad morning when this life is o'er,
> I'll fly away;
> To a home on God's celestial shore,
> I'll fly away.

Dortis Mulkey joined in the chorus—tentatively at first, then with gusto.

They laughed when they finished. Dortis Mulkey beat on the steering wheel and honked the horn. He turned around to get a good look at her.

"What's your name?" he asked.

"Princess Mosak."

"Princess Mosak! That ain't your real name."

"Of course not, you ignorant boy. Princess Mosak's the name of my gift. Princess Mosak, Reader Adviser."

"What's that mean—reader adviser?"

"Reader means I read the signs. Adviser means I give advice. I was sitting in the glider one afternoon watching the yellow jackets eat a piece of watermelon Homer left when it came to me. Princess Mosak. Just like that. As soon as I heard it, I knew what it was." She leaned forward and touched him on the shoulder.

Dortis Mulkey's head shot sideways as though struck by an electrical current.

"Things'd come to me, I'd be washing the dishes," Lucille Arp said. "You think I'd go tell them about it? It's like good deeds—like loving gestures. You think about it, and then you don't do it. I don't know why. Time passes. It slips away. I'd finish the dishes and dry my hands and go out and sit with Homer and rock in the spring chair or swing in the glider, and then I'd forget it. I never even told Homer or Rooster. Not even what I saw at the end."

"Who's Rooster?"

"My only child. My loving baby. I never even told him."

"What about Hollis owns this car?"

"He ain't mine. He'd burn the house down and me in it if he had his own way. I told Charlene, he's going to set the house on fire. That which cometh to pass, if it ain't now, it will be, and if it has been, it may be in time to come. Charlene don't know about that."

"How come Rooster's your only child if you got a daughter named Charlene married to Hollis?"

"She came later, to take Rooster's place. Rooster died," she said simply. "It ate him inside and ate me too. It killed me for two years till I had Charlene, and I never even told him, or Homer either. We got to the hospital when the ambulance came, when Homer was too sick to teach me to drive. The pain was too strong. Doubled him up like he was bent over a rail. And we got to the hospital, they told me to wait, but I wouldn't do it. I waited for Rooster and look what happened. So I told them, 'No. I'm staying with him. He's all I got. This is all I love right here in this room.' So they said, 'Don't talk, then. Don't say nothing. Just hold his hand and watch that screen, and if it acts different, you come and call us.' And they went off to sleep on top of a table, and I did their business. Sat there and watched it. And that's when I saw him. The same one I saw with Rooster. I don't care how he was dressed."

"How was he dressed?"

"All in white—a black man all in white. Like somebody worked for the hospital. He stood in the doorway, and all you could see was his clothes. It was so dark and he was so black, it looked like there wasn't nobody in them except they just stood there."

"What you say to it?"

"What could I say? I knew who it was. But I never told Homer. I just held on to his hand. And then he was dead. He died in peace, but I could have warned him. I could have cried, 'Watch out!' All my life I had the gift and never did use it for good or evil. I let it rot like a rag in the water, sloshing this way and that, wearing itself out with the motion. I had a gift like a bright flame, and I took it and put it under a bushel. I buried it out in the side yard under the trees sitting with Homer instead of getting up and going about the Lord's business."

"The Lord's business! What's that?"

"Making them happy. Giving them warnings and advice. That's what I'm here for. The Lord sent me like a prophet of old. But I wouldn't tell them. I was too busy."

"What about me? You know what I'm fixing to do?"

"We're coming to that. Drive the car." She fell silent, looking out the window at the dark landscape fleeting past. "I knew you were coming," she said as though speaking to herself. "Ever since Homer died and Charlene wouldn't let me stay home alone, I knew you were coming to get me."

"You knew I was coming?"

"Of course I did. You or somebody else just like you. Whoever the good Lord saw fit to send and give him the talent."

"What talent?"

"The talent of driving and knowing the way."

"You knew I was coming." Dortis Mulkey repeated the words as though the judge had just pronounced sentence.

"That's right. If it hadn't been you, it'd been someone else, and if it hadn't been someone else, it'd been you."

"Why me?"

"You're the agent, that's why. I been redeemed. Pharaoh's chariots drown in the water, and I keep on going. My whole life has been redeemed. I get to start over and do it right this time."

"What about me?" It sounded like a cry of pain.

"You're free, ain't you? If it weren't for having to drive me home, you might spend the rest of your life washing cars. But look at you now. You don't even know where you're going. That's how free you are."

"Tell my fortune," Dortis Mulkey said, thrusting a hand over the back of the seat. His palm was turned up as though asking for alms. "What you see I'm fixing to do?"

"I wait for a sign," Lucille Arp said, pushing the hand aside. "Something tells me."

"Tells what?"

"This and that. Whatever comes to me. I ever tell you about the Unadilla girls' basketball team?"

Dortis Mulkey did not bother to reply.

"Won the state championship fifteen or twenty years ago. I had those girls in my class. They were all in the same class, looking this way and that like some kind of puzzle got lines going every which a way. Call on them, they'd look at the blackboard. I remember the day. I saw them looking, and then it came to me like somebody spoke."

"What?" Dortis Mulkey said, attention suddenly drawn like a magnet.

"The state championship. That's one thing I can be proud of. I got right up and went down the hall and told the coach, Mary Dewey. Skinny girl. Calves of her legs bunched like a man's. Ever see that?"

Dortis Mulkey was staring straight ahead at the farthest limit and point of the road. Lucille Arp punched him in the middle of the back. "Ever see a woman's leg bunched like a man's fist? That's how Mary Dewey's were. Mine are smooth. Always have been. Round as an egg. Hers looked like a bunch of grapes. Mary Dewey. Dead now. They're all dead. Gone into the sky like stars. I see the stars, I think of them shining."

"I never have."

"You're too young, that's why. All your loved ones ain't dead already. All except you," and she patted him on the shoulder. "You're still with me, ain't you, honey?"

Dortis Mulkey was not certain who she was talking to. "What about the state championship?" he asked, hoping to get her on track again.

"I told Mary Dewey. I said, 'You got a state championship sitting right there in study hall last period if you only knew it.' And she said, 'How's that?' Snippy-like, the way she talked—fast and snippy like she was busy going someplace and already late before she even got started. And I said, 'I saw them looking.' And I told her what it was, and she got them and trained them, and they won the state championship two years in a row. Every cross-eyed girl in town—all five of them. Natural-born basketball players. Look here and shoot there. Couldn't figure out which way they were going."

"That's good," Dortis Mulkey murmured. The more Lucille Arp talked about the Unadilla girls' basketball team, the more Rickey Mulkey reclaimed himself as one reclaims oneself from sleep. The sense of being chosen fell like a mantle from his shoulders.

"That's how signs are," Lucille Arp said. "Look one way and go the other. Took me to tell them or else they'd still be a bunch of ugly girls instead of a state championship basketball team bringing back glory. And you know what else? Every one of them girls got married within the year. How about that? I get the credit, that's what I figure. If it wasn't for me, nobody would have wanted to marry them. Sit on the porch waving at cars the rest of their life if it wasn't for me. Ugly girls got a hard life."

"Ugly boys too." Dortis Mulkey was sensitive about his acne, which covered the sides of his jaws and the back of his neck with red welts and intermittent whiteheads, which he scraped off as soon as he found them, thinking them less noticeable that way.

"I used to be ugly," Lucille Arp said, "but Homer married me anyway because he had good sense. All my life I had blessing on blessing as long as he lived. Someday you're going to get married too."

"No ma'am. I love girls. I purely love them. But I don't aim to marry one."

"What you aim to do with them then?"

"I aim to race. Girls don't like that."

"Why not? Ain't nothing wrong with athletics, even after you get out of school. Most girls don't mind."

"I mean cars," Dortis Mulkey said, wondering who he was talking to. "I don't mean athletics."

"You mean automobiles like this one?"

Dortis Mulkey could barely conceal his contempt. "I mean stock cars," he said. "Track racing. Special built."

"How fast you going? Check your speed." It was the same voice she used in class.

Dortis Mulkey obeyed without thinking.

"That's what I mean," he said as soon as he realized what he had done. "Women think you're going to get killed. That's why I don't plan to get married till after I retire. Women hold you back. You ain't free, you got a woman holding you back. Track racing's safer than highway driving." It sounded like part of an old argument.

"I don't doubt it," Lucille Arp said. "It ain't safe nowhere." She sounded disinterested. "You hungry?"

"Yes ma'am. They say I stay hungry."

"Who says that?"

"Everybody. I say it myself."

"You eat everything?"

Dortis Mulkey did not understand what she meant.

"Everything that's food," he said.

"I *mean* food. You think I meant seat upholstery?"

"No ma'am," Dortis Mulkey said, ashamed at having been caught out. It was just like being in school. She carried it with her like a disease.

"What you like best?"

It was as though he had not read the assignment. His mind went blank. "Hard-boiled eggs and cornbread." It was the first thing that occurred to him.

"You're kind of unusual in that. You like them together?"

"Yes ma'am," Dortis Mulkey lied. "I eat them for breakfast. That's my favorite breakfast food."

"I like oatmeal. That's all I eat—oatmeal and sugar cookies. Charlene worries. Says, 'Momma, eat something else or you're going to get hookworm.' And I say, 'Don't worry, honey. Hookworm don't come in at the mouth.'"

"You want you some oatmeal?" Dortis Mulkey peered in the rearview mirror to see what effect it would have on her. All he saw was her halo of hair frying in the light. The silence was filled with the hissing of wind and the sighing of the engine leading them on. He could almost hear her thinking. Then she took the bait.

"Why not? Why ever not? It didn't say, 'Hurry. Don't stop to eat.' Besides which, we're free, ain't we? We got the whole world to go where we want to. It might take a year or two, but who cares about that? As long as we get there sooner or later, we do what we want to. That's what means free, ain't it, Rooster?"

"That's right," Dortis Mulkey said. He would have agreed to anything.

"Where you get it?" She looked out the window. "Oatmeal ain't always easy to come by."

Dortis Mulkey struck. "Huddle House. I know where one's at. They make anything. Breakfast twenty-four hours a day. And that don't mean fried eggs and grits. That means oatmeal. Twenty-four hours a day."

"I missed my lunch," Lucille Arp said. "They hurried me so I had to leave before I could fix it or else they'd have left me. Where's it at? I could eat a whole bowlful."

"Me too," Dortis Mulkey lied. "I like oatmeal."

"You can have hard-boiled eggs and cornbread. You don't have to eat oatmeal. All that's behind us. We do what we want to," and she began singing again.

> I am living now in Canaan,
> Where the fruit so richly grows,
> Where the saints are all rejoicing,
> Where the milk and honey flows.

Dortis Mulkey sang along with her, not knowing what he was doing.

And suddenly there it was on the left. Dortis Mulkey slowed down to let a tractor-trailer pass, then turned left aross the highway. There were no cars in the parking lot. He drove slowly up to the building. The windows were blinding. The whole front wall was made of glass. It was like looking directly at the sun.

"You sure this got oatmeal?" Lucille Arp asked. "Looks too new for oatmeal."

"Yes ma'am," Dortis Mulkey said, suddenly panicked. On the roof above the windows was a red neon sign, pale in the daylight but glowing anyway, waiting for night. It said PIZZA HEAVEN. As soon as he saw it, Dortis Mulkey accelerated, heading straight toward the door. The sign withdrew across the roof.

"Here we are," he said, coming to a stop and turning around to face Lucille Arp all in the same motion. The engine was still running.

"You say they got oatmeal?" She sounded suspicious.

"I guarantee it," Dortis Mulkey said, getting out to open the door. He seized Lucille Arp by the elbow in order to extract her.

"Let go," Lucille Arp shouted. "You're pulling my arm off. I ain't got my weight under me yet," and she struck at him with her free hand. She looked about her. "Where are we at?"

"Pizza Heaven."

It was like someone else using his voice. It spoke before he knew who said it.

"I don't eat pizza," Lucille Arp said, settling back in the grave gray upholstery. "I seen it, but I don't eat it." She turned her head sideways like a chicken, inspecting him. Her eyes were ablaze with the glare of the glass.

The head of a woman suddenly appeared at the window. Seen through the sunlight and the reflection of trees from across the highway it looked supernatural, as though it had only partially materialized and was still half made of light and darkness. She was wearing a cloth or paper crown. The knowledge that they were being observed made Dortis Mulkey even more panicked. "What about the call of nature?" he asked. It was the same unknown voice. He had no idea it had spoken.

"I reckon I better as long as we're stopped. Help me up."

Dortis Mulkey lifted her out into the sunlight, aware once again of how frail she was. As soon as he got her on her feet, he steadied her, touching her shoulder to get her in balance. Then he ran to the front of the car, leaped in the front seat, and drove off without closing either of the doors. They gaped like explosions, the sound of the tires screeching across the parking lot onto the highway, and he was heading north again, beyond Snelville.

He fell into the rhythm of driving, taking whatever came as it came, except for something like little flashes of light, an image that kept coming and going: the last sight he had of Lucille Arp standing in front of the glassy light of Pizza Heaven with the other woman inside the window looking out like a ghost or a soul in another dimension and the desolation that spread out from it on all sides—the empty asphalt of the parking lot, the wasteland beyond that where the bulldozer had flattened half a hillside where nothing could grow, and the alien ground of the highway itself, possessed not by people but by cars. Lucille Arp stood in the midst of that utter desolation looking confused and out of place like someone in a photograph, a woman in a dress on the beach in Florida with the ocean lifting behind her and all around the flatness of the earth and sky. One wondered what she was doing there. She was utterly alone.

Dortis Mulkey pulled into the entrance of the Dixie Drive-in Theater, which had been closed for two years, the gravel already turned to grass. Then he turned around and drove back. He expected to find Lucille Arp still standing where he had left her, or maybe toppled over, having lost her balance. But she was gone. The desolation was even more desolate without her, the vitreous glare even more empty. He drew up to the building and circled it slowly. She was not there. He circled the building once again and almost ran into her. She was standing outside the restroom door near a Dempste Dumpster, directly in the path of the car, waving madly to flag him down. He slammed on the brakes and stopped close enough for her to pound on the fender.

"What took you so long?" she said. "I was done ten minutes ago and had a bottle of Coca-Cola while I was waiting. That comes to fifty cents."

Dortis Mulkey stared at her, not understanding. It was like a word problem in arithmetic. All he could think to do was get her back in the car. He did not know why, nor did he question it. She was his. He had been chosen.

Lucille Arp hung in the door of the backseat, gripping the frame on either side. Dortis Mulkey steered the small of her back, urging her forward like a pinball machine he was trying to keep from tilting.

Suddenly he felt a hand on his shoulder and was already in the front seat fumbling for the keys before he turned to see who it was. It looked like the woman in the window. She was saying, "Fifty cents. That'll be fifty cents for the Coca-Cola your momma drank while she was waiting. How come they call you Rooster?"

"This is Mildred Tuggle," Lucille Arp said from the dark of the backseat where she had clambered unaided and was now half sitting, half reclining, catching her breath. "Close the door, honey," she said to Mildred Tuggle. "I'm too old to reach it. Thank you." And the door slammed shut.

Mildred Tuggle's face hung in the window. "That's fifty cents," she said threateningly.

Dortis Mulkey fumbled in his pocket for change, finally understanding. He was responsible. Whatever Lucille Arp chose to do, he was responsible. When he drove back to get her, he had assumed her.

"I told her I don't carry no money," Lucille Arp said. "As soon as you drove off, she came out of that swinging door like she was tied on back of the car with a rope. Said, 'What happened? What happened?'—like it was some kind of wreck on the highway."

"I didn't know what happened," Mildred Tuggle explained.

"I know you didn't," Lucille Arp said, straightening herself and leaning out of the window so as to be heard better. "He already knows that. Don't repeat yourself. Stand up and speak out crisply."

Mildred Tuggle was twenty-eight years old. Nineteen of those years had been spent fighting with men. The result was two children. One had a name of its own. The other was called Mildred Tuggle. Her skin was beginning to harden like leather that had been left out in the rain too long. She was not to be intimidated.

"I ain't no celery," she said, looking levelly at Lucille Arp. "I talk like I want to."

"Then say something somebody wants to hear and don't keep on saying it over and over. Folks get tired of repeaters like you."

Mildred Tuggle was finished with her. She turned back to Dortis Mulkey. "That's fifty cents for the Coca-Cola," she said, "plus thirty cents for the extras."

"Extras!" Lucille Arp said. "What extras? There ain't no extras unless you count standing on the premises waiting."

"Ten cents tip and twenty cents for use of the service facilities."

Lucille Arp strained her neck out of the window like a chicken in a cage. "Don't pay! Don't tip her nothing."

"What's service facilities?" Dortis Mulkey asked.

"Bathroom," Mildred Tuggle said. "Over there." She gestured toward the Dempste Dumpster.

Dortis Mulkey followed the motion of her hand the same way he followed a curve. It came to a blue door set in a glass wall beyond the Dempste Dumpster.

"Employees' restroom," Mildred Tuggle said. "She wouldn't go to the one inside. Said she might miss you."

"I meant when you got back," Lucille Arp explained. "I didn't want to be somewhere you couldn't see me."

None of this had registered. Dortis Mulkey was still back at the bill of particulars. "What's service facilities?"

"Use of the bathroom," Mildred Tuggle said. "What are you, some kind of repeater?" She glanced back at Lucille Arp.

"Don't let her talk to you like that!" Lucille Arp shouted. "Drive off. You hear me?" and she pounded on the side of the car.

"You charge for the bathroom?" Dortis Mulkey asked.

Mildred Tuggle nodded.

"What for?" He still could not understand what was happening.

"Flushing," Mildred Tuggle said.

Then he knew. He looked at the money he had in his hand and started the car both in the same motion. Then he was gone, tires smoking, streaks on the asphalt moving across it as though coming up from inside.

Mildred Tuggle took two steps. "I got your number." She started to run after them. "EXR 545. You hear me? I'm going to call the State Patrol."

"That's the best thing I ever did see," Lucille Arp said, struggling to sit up. "You see how she looked?" She leaned forward to touch him again. "I'm proud of you, son." Her hand caressed the back of his neck. "You learn fast, old Rooster. Pretty soon you'll be like me."

Dortis Mulkey's heart was leaping about like a dog. "Where you want to go?" he shouted. "We're going anywhere you want to go."

"What about Unadilla?" She looked out the window and saw only her own reflection, like the woman inside the glass at Pizza Heaven, and beyond that the dark wall of trees she was being hurled against. "This is the road to Macon, ain't it?" It looked like anywhere in the state.

"Yes ma'am. We're going to Macon and anywhere else you want to go."

"Like where?"

"The whole world." Dortis Mulkey lifted his hand from the steering wheel and gestured at the road, the trees, the empty fields and pastures, the mailboxes and telephone poles lifting up and hurtling toward them, caught by the eye just for a second and then flinging past, disappearing behind them forever.

"The whole world," Lucille Arp repeated. The phrase was stirring, like something that moved deep inside. "I been to Indian Springs," she said, trying to find some way to understand what it meant. "Homer and I used to go there."

"What's it like?"

"Sat on the porch in the evening. They had these rockers on the veranda. Green floor. And you take the waters."

"Where you take them?"

"You drink them, you ignorant boy. What grade you in?"

"No grade," Dortis Mulkey said. "I quit." He was trying not to feel the end of the rope. "I drink waters too," he said boldly, "except I wouldn't go *there* to do it."

"These are special waters. Ain't you ever heard of Indian Springs?"

"No ma'am," Dortis Mulkey said, not caring. He had the whole world. Indian Springs was just a part.

"They had different kinds of water inside these houses."

"That right? What they got in them?"

"Different kinds of water, I said. Pay attention. Some smell like sulphur."

"You mean the water?" The information was galvanizing. The thought of water actually smelling had never occurred to him.

"Tastes like sulphur," Lucille Arp said. "Some taste like iron. And tomatoes. The iron one tasted like tomatoes to me."

"They got one tastes like squash?" Fried squash and onions were Dortis Mulkey's favorite vegetables.

Lucille Arp ignored him. "Across the road was the Indian house. Chief McIntosh. Had a stuffed horse in the bedroom."

"Had a what?"

"Had a stuffed horse in the bedroom."

"What for?"

"It died, and they stuffed it. I don't have to tell you what for. I ain't accountable for that."

"You want to go there?" Dortis Mulkey said. "That's one thing I'd love to see—a horse in a bedroom."

"We ain't got time," Lucille Arp said. "Burned down, anyway. Last summer we were there. Hotel burned, and the museum rotted."

"No sense going," Dortis Mulkey agreed. "Let's go to Six Flags over Georgia."

"I been."

She had gone one weekend with Hollis and Charlene and the children when she first went to live with them. They stayed in a motel across Interstate 20. Lucille Arp rode one ride called the Scream Machine, a roller coaster over water—humped trestles fragile as matchsticks. Then she made her way in what seemed like comparative safety back across the interstate without their knowing she had gone. By the time the police thought to look for her back at the room, she was already asleep in bed from watching television.

"How you like Six Flags?" Dortis Mulkey asked, trying to get a glimpse of her face. "You ride the Scream Machine?"

"I can't remember," Lucille Arp lied. "I rode a bunch."

"Let's go, then."

"It ain't on the way. I got too much unfinished business."

"No you don't. That's the whole thing. Listen here, lady," and he turned halfway around in the seat, trying to get a glimpse of her face. He wanted to tell her something important.

"Drive the car!" Lucille Arp said, beating on his arm, which lay along the back of the seat. "Watch out where you're going."

Dortis Mulkey obeyed immediately, drawing the car back toward the center of the road. He tried to focus his mind the same way he focused his eyes. It was not easy. Nothing was clear except the image of Lucille Arp standing where he had left her beside the road in the midst of the utter desolation and the woman's face he had seen in the window, like something from some other world, some other dimension of time and space, and the sun reflected in the glass such as he had never seen it before—part of this world and some other too—going down across the road beyond the right of way, tangled in the dark of the pines beyond the fence, beyond the overgrown pasture, in the dark earth of the woods. How to tell her that? What was there to say except that he had chosen her just as he had been chosen. He had assumed her by returning to get her, and so was set free, his heart running around in circles like a dog let out of a pen, barking with joy, his old life dead on the highway behind them like a dead possum, everything else in front of them lifting up like the road itself out of nothing, materializing as if by magic.

"Listen, lady," he began, not knowing where to start. But Lucille Arp prevented him.

"I been everywhere there is to go," Lucille Arp said.

"Give me a for instance."

Suddenly her mind went blank. All she could remember were the spring chairs in the side yard under the trees where she used to shell peas and string beans, processing food from innumerable gardens, and where she rocked and rested and talked to Homer and drank iced tea. It seemed for a moment, when Dortis Mulkey asked her, interrupting her train of thoughts with his fool question, that the yard at the side of the house was the only place she had been in her life, twenty feet from the screen door at the side of the house, under the shade of the trees Homer had planted, the ground sparse of grass—clay and sand, tree roots and moss—and overhead the great arches of the water oaks soaring. There were other places she had been. It was more than that; she meant her whole life. It was more than just three spring chairs and a glider.

And then she thought of Shoulderbone Mounds.

"I been to Shoulderbone Mounds. Near Sparta."

"Mounds?" Dortis Mulkey said. "What's a mound?"

"You ignorant boy. I wish I'd had you in my class. You ain't ever heard of Shoulderbone Mounds and Irene, Okmulgee, and Etowah Mounds— all them famous mounds in the state?"

Dortis Mulkey was ashamed. All he could think of were Mound candy bars. "No ma'am," he admitted. He was out of his depth but curious. Being with Lucille Arp was not exactly like being in school. Being in school was like being in an airtight room with the gas turned on and no doors and no windows. With Lucille Arp at least he was driving. The world was there just outside the window. If he chose to—if he knew what one was—he could just drive up to a mound. The image of something hairy with coconut-covered chocolate rose in his mind like a racial memory.

"I did a whole section on mounds," Lucille Arp said. "Every spring. Ain't a person in Unadilla don't know about Shoulderbone Mounds. The ones I didn't teach learned from the others, parent from child and darky from white. They know all about it."

"Yes ma'am. I must have missed that."

"Not all teaches it," Lucille Arp said. "You might have gone to school all your life and never learned a thing about it unless you had the advantage of going to me and hearing me give that two-week section. What grade you get to?" she asked pointedly. It did not seem like a friendly question.

"I finished the tenth grade," Dortis Mulkey lied. He had quit halfway through the eighth to work as a mechanic's helper in Cycle World repairing Japanese motorcycles. By that time he was already beginning on farm tractors, having stolen two or three in the more remote sections of Cherokee County. His method was simply to make sure no one was home and then drive off down the road. He wondered at his temerity now that he had turned professional and used a trailer. Now it was speed; then it was boldness and the ability to blend into the background and drive the dirt roads as though he belonged there all the way back to Cycle World and into the locked shed on the side. It was his introduction to the business.

"You getting your high school equivalency?" Lucille Arp asked. "No need to stay ignorant all your life. No matter how poor you are, you still got that advantage to take if you got the gumption and grit to do it."

"Yes ma'am. What's it look like?"

"What?"

"A mound."

"Like something I ain't never seen. We went to a gristmill. The man that owned it worked at the gristmill at Little Shoulderbone Creek, and he took us, Homer and me. Got in his pickup, me in the front and Homer in a chair in the bed, and drove through the woods and the fields where they used to grow cotton, all in weeds and cockleburs. And then we came to it."

"What?"

"The mounds. Out in the fields, flat growing out of the weeds. Three of them. And we had the map from Colonel Jones and found the spring they used and the burial mound and the platform mound, where they had the temple, and the plaza where they danced and the moat. It was all there under the weeds. You know what it looked like?"

"Woods and dirt," Dortis Mulkey said. He had expected something different but was not entirely surprised. Young as he was, he was beginning to realize that life was like that.

"That's falling short," Lucille Arp said. "Piles of dirt's falling short. It's like them temples in South America. You come on them in the jungle. It's like discovering some far-off time."

"Yes ma'am. Where else you been?"

But Lucille Arp was still remembering. "That man that owned it had a button."

"That right?" Dortis Mulkey murmured, immersed once again in driving.

"Said it was made out of an Indian's ear."

"A what?" It was as though someone had grasped him by the hair and pulled him suddenly out of the water.

"A button made out of an Indian's ear. Said his granddaddy wore it on his vest."

"What for?"

"To hear when they're coming. The Indian Nation began on the other side of the river, and he wore the ear to know when they're coming."

"Where'd he get it?"

"Off a dead Indian, I reckon. He must have found one laying there dead and cut off his ear."

"If he didn't kill him!" Dortis Mulkey said, suddenly aflame again. "Where is it? They still got it? What's it look like?"

"Not much. Like pigskin. White like pigskin after the hair's off. And wrinkled. I wouldn't have known what it was if he hadn't told me."

"You mean it didn't look like an ear?" Dortis Mulkey had imagined an ear fixed on the old man's breast like a question mark asking when they were coming.

"Not to me it didn't. Looked more like a belly button—the inside part, way it folds over."

"You sure it was an ear? Sounds like it might have been something else."

"That's what I thought. I saw that ear, I figured the mice must have eaten up the rest, it was so old, and left the middle, where the hole is, and they puckered it up to sew on the button."

"That right?" The ear was out. Dortis Mulkey would not travel ten feet to see it. "Where else you been?"

"I been to Florida," Lucille Arp said, suddenly remembering. "I been there two times."

"What's it like?"

"Rough," Lucille Arp said. "Florida was rough."

It was before the land boom. They'd driven across the state line to Fernadina. There were cows on the beach and chickens and pigs browsing on sea wrack. They drove the beach at low tide to avoid the dust of the road. They stayed at a fish camp. The cottages were unpainted cypress with kerosene lamps and outdoor privies. It took them four days to get there.

"Florida was rough," Lucille Arp said.

"It ain't now! It's smooth now. Slick as my palm," and he lifted his right hand from the wheel to illustrate how slick his palm was. "Oh Lord, I always wanted to go to Florida, ain't you?"

"I already been, and I found it rough. Florida's all right for men, I reckon. They might like it. But it's too rough for women and children. They got livestock on the beach."

"They ain't now. They cleaned it up. Got more sights than you ever did see."

"I seen it all," Lucille Arp said. "They got roaches big as birds."

"They fly?"

"Some of them do. Some of them crawl in the bed at night."

"That right? I wish I could see it."

"You don't see it. You feel it. Feels like a cat under the covers."

"I don't mean roaches. I mean the whole place. I mean the whole state of Florida from top to bottom and side to side."

"There's more top to bottom than there is side to side," Lucille Arp said, remembering the section she taught on the Geography and Geology of Neighboring States. "It ain't come out of the ocean long. Some parts are still wet."

"That's what I mean," Dortis Mulkey said, his imagination working like a pump. "I told Sandy. I said, 'I ain't staying here. Not when there's Florida I ain't ever seen.' And she said, 'I can't leave my daddy.'"

"Who's Sandy?"

"Girl I'm fixing to marry. I mean I *might* marry when I retire from race-car driving. I told you about that."

"I remember. That's too dangerous. I might have to tell your momma."

"Go on and tell her, you know where she's at. You know where she's at, you know more than I do."

"What happened? She run off?"

"I don't know. I ain't ever seen her. She was gone before my time. I never missed her," he added defensively. Then he fell silent. "I think she's in Tampa. Said she couldn't stay at home, it was too sad."

"What was too sad?"

"Living with me. I made her tired."

"What you mean?"

"Taking care of me when I was a baby. I don't blame her. I'd go too. I wouldn't stay home in Snelville and live in a trailer back of Sandy Mullinax. She said, 'You can get a job, and we'll buy us a trailer and set it up where daddy said, behind his, and hook up like he said—power and water. Won't cost us nothing. So we can have a baby right off.'"

"You looking for your momma in Florida? That why you going?"

"Hell, no! I don't blame her. But I wouldn't go nowhere to see her. If she was walking down the street going one way and I was going down the other, I'd cross over to the other side. I wouldn't even want to see her. She's dead to me. She died when she left."

"That's right. I feel the same way about Hollis, and he ain't even no kin to me. I'd cross the street if I saw him coming."

"Damn right. We ain't going to Tampa, are we? We're going to Miami. That's where we're going. We're going to Panama City, Boca Raton, Fort Myers, Key Largo . . ." It sounded like a long-distance bus driver calling the cities on his route. The words flashed like doubloons.

But not to Lucille Arp. To Lucille Arp, the names smelled of diesel and rough upholstery, of waking all through the night and finding it still dark in the morning—the taste of travel in the mouth, the unwashed face looking through the unwashed window. There was nothing she had done that she would wish to do again and nowhere she had been she wished to revisit except Unadilla and the house she had left there and the business of living to pick up again after putting it down at Hollis's in front of the television set, substituting the lives of strangers for her own life and the gift she was given, which lodged in her useless. She thought of herself as the unprofitable servant who hid his talent under the bushel and rendered it back to his master unused. She thought of the good she might have done, the lives whose direction she might have changed if she had done what her gift instructed instead of denying it like Saint Peter. She often thought of Saint Peter's denial: three times before the cock crowed. She had done it thirty-three times thirty-three. She had done it all her life, not out of fear, but from disbelief and lack of confidence that she would be the one chosen. The knowledge would come, like a voice or great light, and she would deny it, turning to Homer.

She looked at her hands folded in her lap. A great light as from the sun had spilled over them. She looked at her arms. It was all around her, the same sudden light. And she knew that going back to Unadilla was the same as going back to Homer—back to her old life that was dead.

Before her was Florida. She heard a voice speak, loud and distinct as words are distinct, except there were no words, only the true and certain knowledge she knew as her gift, and it was telling her not to go back to Unadilla no matter how much she might want to return.

She looked at the back of Dortis Mulkey's neck and saw the short hairs in the sun like golden wires. She saw his golden hands on the wheel, his golden arms, and she thought of Rooster. It was as though he was still alive, leading her on out of her own life and into his, as one generation leads out of itself into another and then gives way to it. She felt the motion of the car. They were going to Florida, mother and son, to be reunited at last in Tampa. They were already on the way. She knew it the same way she knew her own name.

"You know what I feel like?" Dortis Mulkey said suddenly, turning around in the seat to see her. "I feel like a possum."

"A possum?"

"Yes ma'am. One of them possums dead on the highway. Sandy says that's how they come."

"What comes?"

"Possums. Sandy says that's their natural state. You ever seen one alive? She says that proves it. They're all born dead on the highway."

Lucille Arp snorted. "I don't believe that, you ignorant boy."

"Well that's how I feel. I feel like I'm dead on the highway back yonder and just been born both at the same time."

"What you mean?"

"I got me a future. See that?" He gestured around him. "All that landscape flying past? You don't even know what it is till all of a sudden it's flying past and something else's coming up. It's like you're getting born every minute. Like Disney World. You ever been to Disney World?"

"That some place in California?"

"Orlando, Florida, that's all. You ain't ever heard of that?"

"How far is it from Fernadina?"

"Next to Orlando," Dortis Mulkey said, not certain where Orlando was, or anything else. He had a respectful contempt for geography except as he moved through it himself, and then it was too complex for a map.

"I don't know about Orlando," Lucille Arp said. "I might have been there."

"If you'd have been there you'd have known it. It's the most wonderful place there is. People been there come back and say, 'I wouldn't have missed it. I don't care if I stay here the rest of my life now, right here in this trailer, and never get out as long as I been there.'"

"Who told you that?" Lucille Arp was quick as a chicken.

"Sandy's daddy. They all went last summer."

"He's an ignorant man," Lucille Arp said. "Nobody wants to sit in a trailer the rest of her life. I know. I sat at Charlene's, and it's a whole house."

"That right?" Dortis Mulkey was not listening. He was still thinking about Disney World. "It's a whole other place," he said, unable to contain himself. "You ever hear of Walt Disney?"

"Of course I have, you ignorant boy."

"Well, he's the one made it. You park your car at one of the Dwarfs— Sleepy or Sneezy. One of them in *Snow White*. You ever hear of her?"

Lucille Arp did not deign to answer. She had gone to see *Snow White* so many times she might as well have made it up herself.

"You get inside, they got whole palaces made out of ice. And different lands."

"Different lands?"

"Yes ma'am. They got the Land of the Western Killers."

"Western Killers."

"Yes ma'am. Shoot you down in the streets at noon. And Energy Land, and Space Exploration. Shoot you off in a rocket. And Undersea Land. Put you in a submarine under Lake Buena Vista. Goes on tracks. Plastic fish. Moray eels got teeth in them. Chew on the sides. Chinese Ovaries."

"Chinese Ovaries?"

"Yes ma'am. Four hundred brilliant birds flying from limb to limb."

It was spilling out like household debris floating down a river in flood—crates and chairs, automobiles and plastic spoons, toy ducks, overalls, uprooted trees, mobile homes with corpses still in them.

"You ought to see it," Dortis Mulkey said. "You ain't never seen nothing like it."

Outside the car a billboard advertising Stuckey Pecans and Rest Rooms Ahead gave way to a forest of dark pines. "See that?" Dortis Mulkey said. "It ain't nothing like that. That's ordinary." The red disk of the sun flashed through the trunks of the pines in sudden bursts of illumination. They came to a field, and the sun was there as though rediscovered. It seemed to have nothing to do with this world. It could not even be looked at directly.

"That's just the way it is," Dortis Mulkey said. He gestured contemptuously. "It ain't nothing."

"Well, what are we waiting for?" Lucille Arp shouted so suddenly that for a minute Dortis Mulkey did not know what she was talking about. "Let's go!"

"You mean Disney World?"

"I mean Florida and all the rest." There was still so much he had not seen. He was so young. The whole world still lay spread out before him like music.

"There's lots of things you ain't seen yet, Rooster. I'm going to take you," Lucille Arp said.

"You too. We both go together. You ain't been there either, have you?"

"That's why they put us in Hollis's car." Another piece slid into place, her gift revealing the occult purpose.

Lucille Arp looked out the window. They had come down from the hills of the piedmont to the fields and pine barrens of the coastal plain. The land was flat to the horizon. Furrows stretched until the rows of crops converged in the distance. The soil was gray, made rose by the light that had fallen on it. The sun had sharpened the edges of things—the shadows on the wall of the barn, the boards in their pattern, a particular weed exploded by light. The sand of the fields turned luminous now, almost translucent, the lights seeming to come from within. She never knew the world was so lovely. She never knew she loved it so much.

"You hungry?" Dortis Mulkey asked. "You want you a Coca-Cola?"

"If I was thirsty I might. I never ate a Coca-Cola."

"What?" Dortis Mulkey could not believe it.

"I mean you don't *eat* a Coca-Cola," Lucille Arp said. "Pay attention."

"What do you do with it then?"

"You drink it, you ignorant boy."

"Peanuts, then," Dortis Mulkey said. He was too happy to be put down. "Peanuts and Coca-Cola, how about that? Put them in and shake it up. Ever do that?"

"Of course I have. You think I was born yesterday?"

"No ma'am," Dortis Mulkey said. The idea was inconceivable.

It was years ago when she was a girl, when Coca-Cola was still called dope and served with a dash of spirits of ammonia for kicks. She poured in the salted peanuts, capped the bottle with her thumb, shook it up, and shouted when it exploded all over. She looked out the window. "That's how I feel now," she said suddenly. "I feel like I got peanuts in me. I'm about to pop."

"Me too," Dortis Mulkey said. "That's how I feel ever since we got going to Florida, ain't you? I'm about to pop. That's what made me think about it. That and I'm hungry. You want you some oatmeal?" He looked for her in the rearview mirror.

And that's when he saw it, directly behind them—the State Patrol, moving like any other sedan except it was so close. There was no siren, no lollipop flashing. It had moved up on them when he was not looking, silently, ominously. And then he knew. They were checking the license. Mildred Tuggle! She gave them the number. By this time they probably knew it was stolen.

"Hold on," Dortis Mulkey said and floorboarded it almost by instinct, prepared for the arrival of the State Patrol every day he'd gone to work the last four years. The car surged as though straining to catch up to itself. Lucille Arp was pressed down by her own weight into the grave gray upholstery. It happened before she could even cry out. She felt like a bug on its back until she finally pulled herself upright to beat on Dortis Mulkey's head and shoulders.

"Slow down!" Lucille Arp shouted. "You'll kill us both."

"Look back," Dortis Mulkey said, trying to keep the car in control, threading the lanes of vacationers heading to Florida through central Georgia on Interstate 75.

The police car had begun to wail, lollipop flashing, flat-round-flat-round, like a coin, a disk of light spinning, casting off its geometry like an eccentric circle, the illusion of mass and solidity created by motion. Lucille Arp watched it weaving among the stalled traffic. It was as though every car and truck had stopped: only the noise and the flashing blue light were moving among them.

"Who they after?" Lucille Arp asked.

"Us," Dortis Mulkey said. "They're after us."

Lucille Arp listened as he explained the situation. Hollis. He wanted his car. He would take her back to the house.

"Drive on!" she shouted. "Give him the slip."

She saw a large green sign slide past like the hull of a ship. It said PERRY and then, underneath, UNADILLA NEXT TWO EXITS.

"Unadilla," she said. It was like seeing her own face in a mirror. "Turn off there, you hear me?"

"Yes ma'am."

When they got to Exit 22, Dortis Mulkey leaned right, then left around a pickup truck at the end of the ramp, then left again toward town.

"You're doing fine," Lucille Arp said. "Keep on going."

"I'm going," Dortis Mulkey said.

The State Patrol was still behind them, climbing the ramp. The wail of the siren was like a scream rising and falling.

"I sure wish they'd turn that off, don't you?"

"Yes ma'am," Dortis Mulkey said. They were coming into the center of town.

"Don't stop!" Lucille Arp shouted. They had come to a red light.

Dortis Mulkey drove through a Gulf station to avoid a collision, then kept on straight.

"There's my house," Lucille Arp said as they went past.

"Yes ma'am," Dortis Mulkey said. "Looks nice."

"Don't stop now, keep on to Florida."

The chase lasted almost a quarter of an hour. Most of the traffic in town had stopped, and people were beginning to appear like apparitions in the heat, coming out of stores and houses to stand on the sidewalk or on lawns under trees to watch them pass, scurrying back as, fishtailing, tires screeching, they drew near. It was like a parade that kept reappearing. Occasionally another State Patrol car would join in, or a sheriff's deputy, until there were four or five cars in pursuit. It was hard to tell how many there were since they were all going in different directions as Dortis Mulkey turned in a driveway and drove through backyards or picked his way down a sidewalk and then surged across a field of lawns.

It ended at an intersection where the road jogged right for fifty feet or so and then continued straight. The intersection was blocked by an old woman in a powder-blue Ford Granada. She heard the sirens wailing and caught a glimpse of a clutter of blue lights flashing through the trees. It seemed best to stop right where she was and let it go past. She crept forward until she reached the middle of the intersection, blocking the way in all directions. Then she cut off the engine and waited. Dortis Mulkey would have gone over the sidewalk and across the lawn around the Granada, but the way was blocked by a row of ancient water oaks and a fire hydrant.

In the window of the Granada, Dortis Mulkey saw a face appear as though it had just materialized from another dimension and was still bobbing up and down. Seen in the reflection of the glass it looked like the woman he had seen in the window at Pizza Heaven, except the paper crown was gone. She looked more and more familiar the closer he got until he could almost recognize her. Then he veered left, choosing the fire hydrant. Her face slid past as he hit the brake and started the slide, but it was too late. He knew who it was.

"Look out!" Dortis Mulkey shouted, and he flung his arm out to catch Lucille Arp. But there was no perceptible impact. He felt the car lift up on the fire hydrant and continue across it like something moving under the covers—a hand or a cat. Then it stopped, halfway along.

The patrol car directly behind them picked up speed, siren still wailing, and smashed into the side of the car. Dortis Mulkey was flung forward and backward both at once. His head ricocheted off the steering wheel and hit the dashboard. He fell on the floor beside the heater, which had turned on with the impact and now blew hot air in his face.

Two patrolmen, one black, one white, rushed forward drawing their pistols. The black officer vaulted on top of the hood and crouched there in a firing position. He was aiming at the driver, but Dortis Mulkey was still heaped on the floor under the dashboard. The pistol was pointed directly at Lucille Arp, who was sitting composed on the back seat, arranged for burial among the upholstery. Her eyes were open like a camera with a fish-eye lens, looking out in all directions at once, one hundred and eighty degrees, seeing all the way to Florida, not even recognizing the black officer as the same one who had come for Homer. The surface of her eyes blazed with light.

The other patrolman jerked at the car door. It would not open. He put up his revolver and pulled with both hands, kicking the side of the car for power. The door flew open and Dortis Mulkey tumbled out fresh born, regaining consciousness just as he fell. The patrolmen grabbed him by the collar and dragged him backward toward the patrol car. Dortis Mulkey was half leaning on the patrolman, half running, trying to keep his feet under him, when he saw through the window of Hollis's car the same woman he had seen before. She was hardly visible behind the glare of the glass. She seemed to be receding into another dimension. He could not see if she wore a crown. It was too light to see. Her eyes were like disks, and he knew that he would never see her again—not here and not in Tampa. Not now, not for a while. And he cried out, "Momma! Momma!" And again, as he was pulled away backward, "Momma! Momma! It's Rooster!"

God hath not given us the spirit of fear,
But of virtue and of love, and of a sound mind.

II TIMOTHY I:7

A Joy Forever

"Hello."

Mattie Chadwick stood in the yard and shouted.

"Hello. Anybody there?"

There was somebody there all right. That was well known. There was always somebody there. There was not only always somebody there, there was always somebody up and moving about doing something day and night twenty-four hours a day. They never slept. That's why they had never been robbed. No robber was brave enough. Being just women they carried a gun and passed it about among themselves the same way they did about not ever sleeping. Many a workman came to the door to find one of them creeping around the side of the house with a gun in her hand.

"Hello," Mattie Chadwick shouted. "You in there, Althie?"

She noticed the door was open. Behind the screen was a square of darkness. She felt a bead of sweat creep down her side like a bug. The grass was so short it looked as though it had been grazed by sheep or painted on dirt. She remembered it from when she was a girl. That's all it was then behind the palings—dirt swept in patterns by a twig broom and flowerbeds outlined in rocks like islands. Now there were creatures. She stood among them. Plaster deer and dwarfs of some sort, little men three feet high, and things that caught in the wind and turned as though they had a life of their own—washer women always washing, sunflowers big as Crystal's head when she got back from the beauty parlor, geese flying, windmills turning. The wind stirred them as she watched, and the wings of the goose swept through the air in a swimming motion, lifting and falling. A man in black tailcoat tipped his hat, lifting it and putting it back on his head, greeting the public. I been like that, Mattie Chadwick thought.

"Althie," she shouted. "Althie, Crystal, where are you?"

"Who's that?" It was a voice from inside the house.

Mattie Chadwick looked at the door, but nothing was there. Then she saw, or thought she saw, a figure materialize. The features were obscure except for what looked like a white gaping mouth. Mattie Chadwick recognized it as a piece of cotton attached to the screen to discourage flies. The face was directly behind it.

"Who's that?" Mattie Chadwick asked.

"Althie. Who'd you think it was?"

"I couldn't tell. Looked like some kind of snake to me. I mean in the mouth. The rest was like a regular person. You know what I was thinking about? I was thinking about these things blow in the wind."

"You mean them chimes?"

"I mean these things," Mattie Chadwick said, pointing to the man in top hat. "You ever sit there on the porch and look out at them when the wind was blowing and think, That's me. That's how I do. I ain't got no will. Ever think that? I ain't got no will of my own because I'm afraid?"

"I never have," Althie Grizzle said.

"Well that's what I come to talk to you about. That and how you're a joy forever, following the sun across the sky from sunrise to sunset."

"What you standing out there in the yard for? Why didn't you come up on the porch?" Althie Grizzle asked.

"I was afraid you might shoot me."

"Shoot you? I wouldn't shoot you." She sounded angry, as though if she had a gun she might shoot her.

"I don't mean you," Mattie Chadwick said. "I mean Crystal." The wind rose, and the man beside her lifted his top hat. The goose began swimming. "I was afraid I might startle her if she heard me walking across the porch. She might think it's somebody come to rape her or hold her hostage or perform aggravated sodomy on her."

"Perform what?"

"Aggravated sodomy. That's where they tie your hands behind your back and do something to you in front."

"Do what?"

"You ain't ever read about that in the paper? 'He raped her three times and then performed aggravated sodomy on her'?"

"How many times?"

"It don't come in times," Mattie Chadwick said. "It comes all at once, and then it's over, and they let you go unless they killed you doing it, in which case they burn you with gasoline and bury the bones or strip you naked and put you in the county dump. You ever been afraid of that?"

"No."

"I have. I been afraid of that all my life—somebody attacking me and putting me naked in the county dump after I'm dead. And neighbors come up to dump their garbage—you or your momma or Crystal or Homer— and there I am laying in orange peels, flies crawling all over me. Ain't that awful? Or homeless. I used to think I'd lose all my money, and they'd take my house, and I'd end up under a tree in the dead of winter and night would come on, and I'd get so cold I'd cry out with the pain and look at the stars, and they were all heartless." She stopped and fell silent, overwhelmed with the thought.

"Then what?"

"That's as far as it went," Mattie Chadwick said. "Like dreaming you're falling. You ever hit bottom, that means you're dead."

"I hit bottom and I ain't dead."

"I never said you were. I mean most folks. Most folks hit the bottom, they get so scared their heart stops, and that's what kills them. It ain't the fall. It's the fear of falling. That's what does it. Most folks ain't as brave as you."

"I ain't brave. I just ain't afraid."

"Me neither," Mattie Chadwick said. "Not any more. That's why I'm here. If I was afraid, I wouldn't be here."

"Because I might shoot you?" It was difficult to tell if Althie Grizzle was being ironic. She had the gift of self-assurance.

"Not you. I meant Crystal or one of the others. Forsythia maybe."

"She's at work."

"Mommie then. She might have got startled. I knock on the door, and she whirls around and shoots me right in the soft spot."

"You mean in the top of the head?"

"That's on a baby," Mattie Chadwick said. "I mean here," and she touched herself between the breasts.

"That's a bone there."

"I mean what's behind it."

Althie Grizzle had never stopped to think about what was behind it. She thought of herself as mostly all skin and mucous membranes.

"Your heart," Mattie Chadwick said. "I mean your heart and your tender emotions. They're wrapped up in there like socks in a towel. That's the place where you live or die—that soft spot. That's where you're a joy forever."

Althie Grizzle had a vision of layers of mucous membranes, each one moister and redder than the one before, leading down to where the heart clenched itself like an angry fist. It spurted blood, and she thought of her father. "Mommie don't carry that gun any more." She spoke to keep herself from thinking. "She says it's too heavy. Only time she'll have it is sitting. You set her down, she'll take it and slip it under her skirt."

"That's what I mean," Mattie Chadwick said. "She's sitting twenty-four hours a day."

"That's because she's old," Althie Grizzle said. "If you were as old as she was, you'd sit too." Althie Grizzle loved her momma the same way she loved herself in a mirror.

"Besides, I was thinking about your daddy," Mattie Chadwick said.

Althie Grizzle started. It was as though a great wind had risen and was blowing inside her. It took her breath.

"I was thinking about the time your daddy shot the catcher and went out of the chicken business," Mattie Chadwick said. "Remember that time? They say he even baptized himself. Some say he even did it in blood."

Althie Grizzle felt her heart surge. It spurted blood. Her eyes filled with it. "Don't talk about my daddy," she said. It was a warning.

"I don't mean people's blood," Mattie Chadwick said. "I mean chickens'. Some say he went to the back of the house where the chickens were piling up, killing each other, and picked up the dead ones and baptized himself, he was so sorry for what he did to the catcher. But I don't believe it. Nobody baptized himself in blood."

"Jesus did."

"I mean now. Jesus did a lot of things we don't do now, like raising the dead and healing the lame and the halt and the blind and forgiving the sinners. Besides which, Jesus was baptized with water."

"But he died in blood," Althie Grizzle said. She remembered her father's sermons. Even now they filled her with fear.

"Well, I don't believe it anyway," Mattie Chadwick said. "Way I heard it, he ran to the river, and that's where he did it. Fifteen degrees and the dead of winter, and he stripped naked and walked right in like it was a bathtub. Cracked the ice at the edges, they say, and dove right in and stayed there."

Althie Grizzle listened to her the same way she would to a river. It meant nothing. She was done with that long ago.

"He preached forgiveness the rest of his life," Mattie Chadwick said. "The Lord forgave him, even if he did have to make him crazy to do it."

"He wasn't crazy," Althie Grizzle said. She had said it so often she almost believed it herself. "The Lord took him, and some he takes hard and some he takes easy, and this was hard. He was a hard case."

"I know," Mattie Chadwick said. "I heard him preach on hard cases. Down at the work camp, he said. That's where the hard cases are. Enemies of God and man. I'll never forget it. Made the chills run down my spine and the hair stand up at the back of my neck the way he said it—how they leave children in the dump after they had their way with them. That's where I first heard about it. I was just a child myself."

"What do you want?" Althie Grizzle was suddenly angry. "What did you come here for?"

But Mattie Chadwick kept on going. "He said it took all that sinning and fornicating and beating up on people and such to save him. They carried me off, he said, and put me in the hospital and said I was crazy, but I wasn't crazy. I was saved. If I wasn't a hard case like many another down at the work camp, God wouldn't have to fling me in the river in winter naked as the day I was born and give me new life. Remember that? Said he was proud of every sinful act he ever committed no matter how filthy because they gave God greater glory when he forgave him, and who would want to limit his glory? If he was just like everybody else, God would have called him in church like he's supposed to and not in the dung and filth of a chicken house in the middle of winter with blood on his hands. He'd call him in May when the sun's shining and the air is warm and the wind so calm you can hardly feel it and the trouts in the river leaping and frisking when they put you under and baptize you. That would have been easy. But he was a hard case."

"It was his heart," Althie Grizzle said. "His heart was hard, and that's what killed him."

"I know," Mattie Chadwick said. "But that ain't why I'm here—to talk all day about your daddy. I'm here to tell you, Fear not. You're a joy forever."

Althie Grizzle looked at her and brushed her hair back. It was usually set, but now it had fallen and hung in strands about her face.

"You going to keep me out here all day?" Mattie Chadwick said. "Or are you going to invite me in? I got something big to tell you."

Althie Grizzle suddenly disappeared as though she had swallowed herself and left nothing but the white open mouth still clinging to the screen door. Mattie Chadwick climbed the steps and crossed the porch; it trembled beneath her. The whole house shook, it was so frail. Like most of the other houses in the settlement, it was built by the original owner himself, whether he knew how to do it or not. There was not a professional carpenter or plumber or electrician in twenty-five miles. They were all mill hands and farmers and old-age pensioners and welfare recipients and hard cases of one kind or another.

"Hello," Mattie Chadwick shouted as she stepped inside the screen door. It was like entering another element—hot and dark and smelling of cabbage. "Althie?" she said. "Where are you, Althie?"

Halfway across the room she barked her shins, and someone shouted, "Watch out! Old ladies are brittle."

The first thing Mattie Chadwick thought was, Mommie Grizzle. Oh God. "I'm sorry," she said. "Is that you, Mommie?"

"You almost stomped the breath out of me," Mommie Grizzle said.

"Lucky you knew I was coming, wasn't it?" She still could not make her out, only the vinyl recliner, moved from its usual place beside the heater out to the center of the room.

"Why's that?" Mommie Grizzle asked.

"Because you might shoot me if you didn't know I was coming."

"I didn't know you were coming."

"Didn't know I was coming? I been standing outside talking to Althie the last five minutes."

"I don't pay no attention to outside," Mommie Grizzle said. "I got enough to do with the inside."

"Where's Althie?" Mattie Chadwick asked. "You see where she went? How you doing?"

"Sick as ever," Mommie Grizzle said. "You my age you don't get well, you just get older, and more things happen worse and worse until you die. I think about that every day. But what good's that do me? I'm still getting old. My flesh is melting like fat in a pan. It's running off my body like oil."

"I know what you mean."

"No you don't. I mean my whole body, eyes and all. All the parts I ever loved sliding off like they were greased. It makes me sad."

"That's why I'm here," Mattie Chadwick said. "I'm here to say you're a joy forever. Where's Althie? She got to hear this. And who else? Who else is here?"

"Forsythia's working."

"I know. Where's Crystal?"

"You'll have to ask her," Mommie Grizzle said. It was her regulation not to talk about others. Sins and the Bible and how she was feeling, those were her subjects.

"Crystal, Althie," Mattie Chadwick shouted. "Come here a minute. I got something to tell you." Her eyes had adjusted to the light, and she saw Crystal get up from a chair and walk across the room. Her hair was blonde, short-cropped and curled. The curls looked like they had been put in with a hammer. So did her eyes.

"Why, there you are, honey," Mattie Chadwick said. "You startled me. I didn't know you were in there. You're looking so pretty."

"That's because she ain't dying," Mommie Grizzle said.

"Yes she is," Mattie Chadwick said. "We're all dying sooner or later."

"I mean right now," Mommie Grizzle said.

"Where's Althie?" Mattie Chadwick asked. "You seen her, Crystal?"

"In the bathroom."

"Moving her bowels," Mommie Grizzle explained.

"Here she comes," Mattie Chadwick said, seeing a shadow fall in the room. "Sit down. Sit here." She motioned to the seat beside her. "Crystal, swivel that chair of yours around and listen. They're closing the road."

"What road?"

"The road right here in front of your house."

"They can't do that," Mommie Grizzle said. "That's a county road. They can't close a county road."

"You know who's closing it?" Mattie Chadwick asked. She sounded delighted. Joy shone on her face like sweat. "Benny Easley, that's who."

"Benny Easley," Mommie said. "Benny Easley's in charge of that road."

"That's why he's closing it," Mattie Chadwick said. "He's the county commissioner in charge of roads, opening and closing them both."

"He's crazy," Crystal said. "I don't care if he does have white hair. You know what his wife said when they got divorced. She said he does all sorts of things to men, women, and children both. She says you can't trust him."

"What kind of things?" Althie asked.

"You know," Crystal said.

"You mean aggravated sodomy?"

"I reckon," Crystal said. "Lots of folks would like to kill him."

"We were just talking about that," Mattie Chadwick said. "I was telling about your daddy."

Mommie Grizzle looked up sharply. "What you mean?"

"Shooting that catcher."

Mommie Grizzle looked at her the same way a chicken looks out of the side of its head inspecting something. "You mean that chicken catcher?" she said. "He was just trash. He didn't even come from around here. He just blew in like trash in a corner."

"Well, he shot him, didn't he?" Mattie Chadwick said. "That's what counts. You kill somebody, as long as he's American, it don't matter where he came from. That's what it means."

"What means?"

"Being American. It's against the law. That's why they can't close the road. Road's public property. They don't belong to Benny Easley."

"He didn't shoot him," Mommie Grizzle said. "The filth of his mouth ran like a sewer, and the Lord came down like winds of fire and blew inside him till his brain burned out behind his eyes and all he could hear was the mocking and jeering and devil laughing and cursing and killing his chickens, running like demons and piling up and mashing each other after he raised them and spent all that money on heating them in the dead of winter and carrying fifty gallons of water morning, noon, and night and all that feed where he worked all summer sawmilling to get the money to buy it with and then see it all piling up in the corner mashing itself to death and that catcher in there doing it to them, terrifying them with fear, catching and cursing. And he said, Don't curse. Lay off them chickens. My wife can hear you. Her ears are pure. And that catcher laughed and said he reckoned that's the only hole she had that was. And he said, What? And the catcher said, Pure. You know what he was talking about?" Mommie Grizzle said, breaking off. "He was talking about my openings. You ever hear the likes of that? And your daddy said, You're insulting my woman. And after that he said he didn't even know what happened till he was breaking the ice on the edge of the river and wading out till the current ran through him. The fire was still raging inside him, and the smoke and steam rose up from the river and covered it like in the morning when it's fresh dawn and the smoke rises up from the water and fills the whole valley from side to side. And then it lifted, and he was burned out and his insides melted. He was all hollowed out from the fire and the Lord replaced them with ribs of gold, and the rest of it with chrysolite and crystal packed in like feathers till he was full up like the temple Solomon built to the Lord. And that's when he sang. He didn't even know the words, and he sang every song in the hymnal from page one right on through to page two hundred and thirty-eight."

"How'd he do that?" Mattie Chadwick said. "If he didn't know the words, how did he know what he was singing?"

"Because it was all in praise of the Lord. Like prophesy. Prophets don't ever know what they're saying."

"What happened to the chicken catcher?"

"He said he never did know what happened."

"I mean you. You were there. What happened?"

"I heard him yelling and saw the chickens coming out. They surged around and came out the door in the moonlight like some kind of white water. You couldn't even tell it was chickens, there were so many, and they were coming so fast and fading into one another. It looked solid. One minute it was a door and a road leading to the front, and the next minute it was chickens, solid white like new concrete. And then it was gone. They hit the air and kind of exploded out in the night, some this way and some that. They were on top of the house and in the bed of the pickup truck, in the pine trees, and I don't know where all. Some of them still living down in the woods."

"Descents of them," Crystal explained. "She means later generations."

"What about the catcher?" Mattie Chadwick asked again.

"He was still in there," Mommie replied. "I looked in the door after the chickens were gone, and I saw him there. I thought they stomped him. Turned in their fright and stomped him to death. And I rushed in and said, What happened? That's when I knew my husband was gone. I said, Milton, Milton, where are you? I thought they stomped him too or pecked him to pieces. I was just a girl and didn't know better, and I cried, Milton."

"You loved him, didn't you, Mommie?" Crystal asked.

"I did then."

Althie waved her hand in front of her face as though signaling her mother not to say anything.

"We were just married, and I couldn't get enough of him," Mommie said. "He was my first man."

"And last one too, wasn't it, Mommie?" Crystal had never had a man of her own. She was the youngest and still read Harlequin romances.

Mommie looked at her sharply. "That's right. And after that I was the preacher's wife, and it didn't matter, after that."

Althie was still signaling.

Mommie ignored her. "I looked at that catcher laying there bleeding, and he groaned and opened his eyes. And I said, What you doing there? Where's Milton? And he said how the shit did he know? Excuse the language. I'm saying what he said. Fucker hit him in the head. And I said, What with? He was bleeding over the ear, and he said, A grain shovel, and got up and walked out and said, Tell him I'm quitting. And that's how my whole life changed. After that when they found Milton, I didn't even know who he was, prophesying and talking in strange tongues. And when he came back, he was out of the chicken business. They wouldn't deliver the chicks to him. Gold Kist said there wasn't a man down there drove a truck would come out here and catch for him after what he done to that catcher. Took his ear off. They tried to put it back on, but it wouldn't stay. It mortified on him."

"Well, thank God for that," Mattie Chadwick said.

"What you mean?" Mommie asked. She turned to Althie. "You hear what she said?"

"I mean thank God it was just an ear."

"That's what I said when the sheriff came out. I said, Ears ain't important. Hole's still there to hear out of ain't it, even if the flap is gone? They never did prosecute anyway. Said Milton punished himself enough. But he said it was a blessing. He might have wasted his whole life on chickens instead of attending the Lord's own flock. Meaning people," Mommie explained. "Changed my whole life and the lives of these children." She waved her hand about the room as though surrounded by children of every size and description, like the household of an African king, with wives, children, and all mixed together. "Just one little thing that catcher said about the openings of my body, and the Lord lifted him up and carried him off and sent him back Melchizedeck. He left here Milton Grizzle and came back Melchizedeck, the high priest."

"Except for his heart," Althie said.

"That's right, except for his heart. His heart was weak. He was covered with armor like Saint Paul said, shining in the sun like the angel of light, but inside his heart was weak. And the devil got in there like a worm and ate a hole in it."

"It wasn't weak," Althie said. "It was hard." She had a vision of armor. The heart was plated. It was ringed with eyes and spurted blood. Every opening was filled.

"We ain't going to see his like again in my lifetime," Mommie said. "The time's too short, and I'm fixing to die."

"That's right," Mattie Chadwick said. "But think how happy that's going to make you. After that brief lonely passage, you get to be with him forever and sing in the choir. How about that?"

Mommie looked at her out of the side of her head, as though in a moment the beak would snap and Mattie Chadwick's eye would be gone. "I don't want to have to die to do it," she said levelly.

"It ain't wanting," Mattie Chadwick said. "It's what has to be. The

Lord calls, you going to die no matter what. Now let me tell you about the road."

"They ain't shutting it," Mommie said. "How we going to go in and out on it?"

"They don't mean your part," Mattie Chadwick said.

Mommie looked as though she had just turned off a hearing aid. She was no longer listening to the voices in the room. She was staring into the distance listening to the voices there. They filled the air like radio waves. All it took was a crystal to hear them, and the ability to detach yourself. Old age was the crystal.

"They mean on down where it crosses the river," Mattie Chadwick said. "Somebody bought up the other side. Blackberry Ridge, that's what they call it. Selling new houses on poles all along the river bank. And armed men, they got armed men down there with shotguns in their hands and knives on their hips and I don't know what all. Hats on their heads and some kind of badges. I been to see them. I called out and said, What you doing? And they said, Patrolling. And I said, What? And they said, The river. We're stopping boats and inner tubes. And I said, How come? And they said, This private property now. And I said, The river ain't. The river's water. It ain't property. You can't own a river. And they said, How come? And I said, It's flowing. It moves too fast. Time you sign the paper for it, it's already gone halfway to town. And they said they don't mean the top. They mean the bottom, where it runs. That stays the same. And I said, That ain't where the boats are, is it? Boats on top. They're floating with the rest of it. You arresting leaves and trash? And they said of course not, they weren't lawyers. They were just hired to keep out trespassers and shoot the ones didn't stay out. And I said, Well, at least I ain't floating. I reckon I'm safe, and started to cross the bridge. And they said, Stop there, and scared me to death. Put them guns on me. Felt like cold hands touching my body. And I said, This a public road. My heart was thunking, and my voice was shaking, I was so scared. I said, You can't shoot me for walking on a public road. I'm an American citizen. Besides which, I was raised right here. I used to come down here when I was a baby. I'd lay in that water like a weed caught on a snag and feel it run through me till I forgot where I was or what I was doing I was so cold and the air was so hot. I said, This where I spent my happiest days when I was a child. It's sacred to me. And they said, Yes ma'am. I know how you feel. And I said, No you don't. Not unless you lay in that water till you felt like a tree or a rock on the bottom, you don't understand a thing about it. This where I was baptized, I said. And they said, Yes ma'am. And I said, How you going to keep folks out? And they said they had guns and the sheriff said, Use them. Don't threaten, he said, but make yourself known and be polite, but lean on them. You're there to protect the right to private property. And I said, You wouldn't shoot an old lady. And they said not if they could help it they wouldn't."

"Where they cutting the road off at?" Mommie asked.

"Down at the river. That's where it stops. They bought the land on both sides, and after they take the bridge out, they're going to get a bulldozer and heap the dirt up on the road so you can't get nowhere near. That way they have it all to themselves."

"You can't close a public road," Mommie said. "That road's been here long as I have."

"Longer," Mattie Chadwick said.

"I don't know about that," Mommie said. It was her practice not to talk about things that happened before her time. The world had come into being the moment she was born, and when she died, it would vanish.

"That road goes back to the beginning of time," Mattie Chadwick said. "Before man walked it the Indians did, and before them the animals."

"Indians are men," Crystal said.

"I mean like us. American people. I go back there and think about all that—all them happy times long ago. It's like where they're at. I go down there, and the rocks are the same, and the trees are the same, and the river, it's still the same, and it's like I step back. It's important to me. I can't live just here. Living here without that road open's like plants living without their roots. They shrivel up and die in a day."

"Sometimes you're afraid to go back," Althie said.

Mattie Chadwick ignored her. "I knew I had to get that road open," she said. "But I was afraid if I said something they'd burn my house down."

"He might," Mommie said. "He might have burned more than one, I hear. Benny don't mess around when it's money or something he can hire done in the night where he don't get caught. All it takes is some gasoline and somebody to light the match."

"That's what I know," Mattie Chadwick said. "And not only that, he might kill my dog. That's a well-known fact. He's noted for that."

"If it's him," Mommie said. "Nobody knows. They just seen them dragging their legs where somebody shot them off with a shotgun."

"It's him," Mattie Chadwick said. "They all know who done it."

"He's about like the rest of them, ain't he?" Crystal said. "All them politicians. They got a lot of money in that. They can't afford to be too easy or folks might vote them out of office."

"Just stay away," Mommie said. "That's how I do. Living out here it's too far away to know who I am. I'm safe on my own place and don't make no trouble."

"What if trouble comes to you?" Mattie asked.

"It don't," Mommie said. "Except dying."

"They castrate your dogs anyway, and fling them out in the yard to die."

"That's right," Mommie said. "But not if you don't mess with them. Most of the time they're real gentlemen, except where their own interest's involved."

"Trouble is, it's *too far* out in the country," Crystal said. "Nobody knows what they do out here except the ones they're doing it to, and they ain't fixing to tell for fear they might do it again."

"Or something worse," Althie said. "There's a whole lot worse than dogs. They do it to people."

"I don't doubt it," Mattie said.

"I mean to women," Althie said, and brushed at her face as though brushing away the flies.

"I don't doubt it," Mattie said, "except for the fact that women ain't got nothing down there to cut off."

"Inside," Althie said. "They got it inside." She touched her breast.

"That's right," Mattie Chadwick said. "When I got home, that's just how I felt."

"Bleeding to death," Althie said. "Inside."

"Bleeding to death," Mattie repeated, "where all my tender feelings been cut off and all my memories of all them good times."

"In the dump," Althie said. "In the orange peels and coffee grounds."

Mattie Chadwick stopped short and inspected her. "You all right?" she asked.

"Of course she is," Mommie said. She turned to Althie. "Hush up and listen to Mattie. She got something of interest to tell you. She don't want to hear about how you're dead when you still got so much living to do and so much to be grateful for."

Althie was looking at her hands. Her left hand was curled around the thumb of the right. She stared at them fascinated.

"I know what she means," Mattie Chadwick said. "Except it wasn't just dead I was feeling. I was afraid. I was trembling all over for fear of what might have happened to me. I didn't even know what danger I was in till it was all over—talking like that to men with guns."

"You're braver than I was," Althie said.

Crystal looked at her as though she was crazy. Crystal was not afraid of men. Guns just made them more exciting, like poisonous snakes. "Men ain't so scary," she said. She squeezed her upper thighs together. It was like a secret, the thrill that ran through her. "I ain't never seen a man I was scared of. I ain't got it in me."

"I do," Mattie Chadwick said. "I been scared of men all my life." She paused. "But that's all over. My heart is leaping inside like a fish. Frisking about like a fish in the river. That's why I'm here"—as though suddenly recalled to her purpose. "Now listen to me. Listen what happened. I got home like I said, I started trembling, realizing the danger I was in. I thought, Oh Mattie, you're crazy or something. It don't matter. Times change. People change. Rivers get cut off and dammed up and dried out. You're getting old anyway. Time you let go of them long lost days. And such as that. Talking myself into it, don't you see? Talking myself into forgetting about it. What good does that do you? I said to myself. You can't eat that for dinner, I said. Let it go."

Althie was nodding her head in agreement. "Let it go," she said. "Before it starts to bleeding again." She saw the armed heart surging with blood and knife cuts like scars splitting open and the blood filling them like mouths spilling over. Every opening was filled. She stopped herself and looked about, fixing on the faces around her, nodding earnestly. If she concentrated on them hard enough she would not have to think about it. "Mattie," she said.

"I heard you," Mattie replied. "It's like they say after you've been in a wreck. You ain't scared when it happens. It happens so fast you can't even think to be scared about it, and then when it's over you sit there shaking, and you can't even walk. Like my daddy that time. I thought we were going to have to carry him off to the hospital, and he wasn't even hurt. He couldn't walk, and he couldn't talk, and I thought he must have hurt himself, but it wasn't that. It's like he hadn't caught up with himself—like he was still one place and his body another and the two parts hadn't hitched up yet after he ran off the road that time. That's how it was with me. Fear got in like some kind of animal inside my skin crept in my mouth when I was sleeping. I see it now, sitting there like a cat on my chest breathing when I breathed, lifting and falling, and then creeping in and the hair going down my throat and eating on my stomach in fear."

"What you talking about?" Mommie said.

"The spirit of fear and an unsound mind. I ain't afraid of them that kill the body. I tell you what I'm afraid of. I'm afraid of the spirit of fear that gets inside and gnaws at your guts like a rat at the wires. That's what I'm afraid of."

"Disease and doctors a terrible burden you old as I am and fixing to die," Mommie said. "Sometimes I get feeling sorry for myself having to wake up each morning wondering when I'm going to die."

"I used to be like that," Mattie Chadwick said. "That's what I'm trying to tell you about. Don't fear doctors and diseases. I tell you who it is to fear. Fear them that kill the spirit and get inside and gnaw at your guts like a rat at the wires. That's who to fear."

"And he cast forth demons," Althie recited. "And the spirit of evil and uncleanliness came forth out of their mouth and their name was legion and they ran about amongst the tombstones squealing like hogs, looking for some kind of mouth to get into, some kind of opening, somewhere to hide in. But they were all dead. The tombs were all sealed and the rocks rolled back on them blocking them up. And they rushed about here and there. Remember that?" she said, breaking off. "How Daddy preached the Legion of Demons? He pounded the tombstone and said, This one's dead, and he'd run to another and say, This one too. This a poor woman. Her mouth is sealed. And so on. Rushing from one to the other, rooting and squealing like some kind of hog with its skin inside out looking for shelter, saying, Not this one. This one's dead too. And then he'd come up to somebody. Remember? Somebody standing there just listening, and he'd grab him and shake him and say, This another. You there, sinner! And shake his shoulders and say, You got your mouth open where I can get in there? He said, Open your mouth, and I closed my eyes, and he got inside like some kind of serpent, and it shook in there and tasted like spit, and it was salty, and he said, That's because it's the devil's. If it was mine, it'd tasted like milk. And he said, It's cold too. Mine is hot. That's the difference. Kneel down and pray for forgiveness."

"What are you talking about?" Crystal said. Something stirred deep within, like a body moving in sleep beside her.

"And we knelt down," Althie said, "and I vomited, and it was still salty and hot from being inside me, and it hit the ground and started squealing. And he said, Hush up. Goddamn it, they'll hear you. And it was still squealing and rushing about, and he was still trying to grab me, and I said, The serpent put its tongue in my mouth and started weeping. And he said, Tears don't drown the devil. Unless the blood of repentance goes with it, you might as well stand out in the rain and let it rain on you for all the good it's going to do you. And then he commanded. He quit running around and squealing and said, I command thee. Be gone from her body. And the devils ran forth down to the river and drowned themselves, piling in like they were on fire. It swallowed them up in the waters of Shiloh."

"I remember that," Mattie said, surprised at the incoherent fury. "I heard him preach that. Your daddy's the holiest man I know."

"And one of the best," Mommie said. "The older I get and the longer he's dead, the more I miss him. That's funny, ain't it?"

"Not if you loved him," Crystal said. "You wouldn't miss him if it wasn't for that." The time she spent reading romances had not been entirely wasted.

"You're probably right," Mommie said. "When he was still here preaching and prophesying and casting the gospel seed on the ground, I was too busy to think about that. It's only when you're fixing to die you got time to think about things, and then it's too late."

"I think about things," Mattie said. "I think about things all the time. I might even tell you about them someday, you ain't so busy talking yourselves you ain't got time to hear something so good you're going to say to yourselves it's a marvel. My ears are on fire. Now where was I?"

"Home," Crystal said, "where you been down at the river smart-talking them men with guns."

"That's right," Mattie Chadwick said. "I was thinking how they might have killed me, and I got so scared I called up Benny Easley and said, What's this I hear about what you're doing down at the river? And he said, It ain't me. I'm just the commissioner of roads. I don't own no property down there."

"Wait a minute," Mommie said. "I thought you said you were scared. What you doing calling Benny Easley, you so scared?"

"That's what I mean," Mattie Chadwick said. "I didn't even know what I was doing. And he said, It ain't me. It's the right of private property. How you like it if I used your driveway? And I said, What for? And he said, Driving up and down on it. And I said, What for? And he said, Violating it. And I said, You mean drive up and down my driveway and not come to see me? And he said, That's right. How'd you like that? I said, How long you fixing to do it? And he said, As long as I want to. How'd you like that? And I said, I'd call the sheriff. And he let out a whoop and said, Aha. That's what I mean. And I said, You'd have to be crazy to do that. That's why I'd call him. I'd say, Come get him. He's driving up and down my driveway three or four days now. Looks like he must have gone crazy to me. And he said, Not if I prove my point, I don't. And I said, That's just it. It don't prove your point. And he said, Private property, it does. And I said, We're talking about public roads. My driveway ain't a public road. And he said, It's old. That road ain't used. And I said, I used it. And he said, It's rutted. He said, It's just an old gravel road. The county don't have the money to keep it up. And I said, It's been there all my life and my momma's before me. That road always been kept up. And he said, Not any more it ain't. They run out of money. And I said, That ain't all you run out of. And he said, What's that? And I said, Good sense. But I was the one. I was the one didn't have good sense talking to him like that. But I couldn't help it. I said, That road ain't your road. And he said, I'm the commissioner of roads in this county. And I said, That don't matter. That road belongs to the American people. Anybody wants to can walk on it without fear of guns and getting shot, and unless you open that road again, I'm going to fix you. And then I thought, Oh God, where did that come from? And he got real quiet and said, I hope you will. I sure hope you will, Miss Chadwick. I been looking for a good-looking woman like you to fix me for a long time now. I'm much obliged. And then he hung up. I didn't even know what he was talking about, I was so scared."

"That's because you're a virgin," Mommie said. "All you girls," she said grandly, waving her hand about. "You're all still virgins. That's where you're lacking." She paused a moment. "It ain't so much," she said to herself. "Not when you're fixing to die anyway. It don't help in that."

"He was lying anyway, from what I hear," Crystal said. "From what his wife said about it he'd just soon the chief of police as a woman."

"I don't know what he'd want him for," Mattie Chadwick said, "unless it's to steal the courthouse or something. You steal a public road, ain't no telling what comes next. The prison camp maybe."

"That's right," Crystal said. "That's what I hear, if it got men in it."

"Anyway," Mattie Chadwick said, "I was sitting there with that phone dead in my hand, buzzing like the sound of my own blood in my ear, and the fear crept up into my feet, and they got cold, and on up my legs, and they got cold, and it's like I was buried in water up to my neck."

"Or in the dump," Althie said. "After it's over and you're laying there weeping and not even knowing what it was except it was too big. I like to gagged on it, and it got to bucking and jumping around in there, and then it was dead, and I felt it wet, and I got sick and lay there weeping. And he picked me up and said, You're forgiven. But I couldn't hear him. It's like I was dead. And he stripped me naked and threw me in there, and my face mushed in the mashed potatoes, and my hair got wet from all that juice on it, and it tasted salty, and I didn't know who was going to find me laying there. I was ashamed."

"That some kind of story or what?" Crystal asked. "I might have read something about that." She felt the body shift in her sleep.

"Or seen it in the movies," Mattie said. "There was a movie I saw on TV. They killed this woman and left her naked in the dump."

"That's right," Crystal said. "I saw that movie. And they came and got her and buried her. But she couldn't rest. She was so ashamed at them seeing her naked that she came back and killed the ones did it to her out of revenge."

"Did what to her?" Mommie asked.

"Raped her and performed aggravated sodomy on her," Mattie Chadwick said.

Mommie nodded.

"You know what that is?" Mattie Chadwick asked. She sounded disappointed.

"Of course I do," Mommie said. "I been married, ain't I?"

"It ain't what you're thinking."

"How you know what I'm thinking? You still a virgin?"

Mommie had her penned in a corner. Mattie Chadwick had never married. She nodded her head.

"In that case," Mommie said, "I wouldn't talk about things I wasn't familiar with firsthand, and aggravated sodomy's one of them. I been familiar with that all my life. It's a terrible burden."

"It's something they do to you down there," Althie said. "It ain't your mouth where it gets in, like she said about that thing in her sleep," indicating Mattie Chadwick.

"Seems like everybody's afraid of something," Crystal said. "Except I don't know what it is for me. Flying, I reckon. I ain't ever flown in a plane. When I go to New York, I might have to faint in the aisle."

"When's that?" Mattie asked.

"When I go to audition," Crystal said.

"Crystal's going to be a dancer," Althie explained. "First thing is you got to audition."

Crystal pulled her dress up over her thighs. "My legs are a gift," she said. "They're so pretty I couldn't waste them covering them up."

Mattie nodded. She had always hated her legs. They were too heavy. From the waist up she was a woman. From the waist down the sex was a woman, but the rest belonged to someone else. She had always wanted to be a dancer.

"The lives of most dancers are terrible sad," she said. "They all die of syphilis."

"There's danger in everything you do," Crystal replied, straightening her bare foot, admiring the stretch of the calf. "God give you a gift like that," indicating the twist of her leg, "it's a sin not to dance on it."

Mattie nodded. She was suddenly ashamed of herself. God had taken away her fear and now she wanted to be a dancer.

"Listen," she said. "I sat there with that phone in my hand. I was so scared I could hear my heart beating. I thought, Oh God, what have I done? What did I say? Did I get him mad? And I ran it over in my mind, everything I said on the phone, making it worse, when all of a sudden I got out a mirror and looked at myself. And I didn't even know who I was. I never married because I was too scared. I never left home. I never even had a job. I might as well be that woman on TV they left on the dump. I'm looking for vengeance. That's what I thought. I'm looking for vengeance."

"What do you mean?" Althie asked. She looked excited. Her face was flushed.

"I wasted my life, that's what I mean. I might as well be dead on a dump than sit there afraid of a telephone. And I said, God. God of Abraham, Isaac, and Jacob. Lift this fear off me. And all of a sudden he lifted it off. I felt it back out, just like you said when it ran off squealing, and it's like I was free. My face was on fire and my limbs were twitching, I was so happy. I knew what to do."

"It backed out?" Althie asked.

"Just like you said. You know what I figured? I figured all I had to do was die."

"That's the trouble," Mommie said.

"No it ain't," Mattie said. "Not any more. Once I said that, it was gone."

"What was gone?"

"My fear. Once I figured I'd just soon be dead, that's when I felt it backing up like something I ate, and something else rose in my heart and said, Fear not. You're a joy forever. All you got to do is die."

The words seemed as incongruous as if Mattie Chadwick had reached into her bag and pulled out a bugle and blew on it a call so loud and clear that it reverberated off the walls and met itself coming back from all directions at once like a great light ricocheting about the room.

"Then what?" Mommie asked.

"Then what?" It was as though she had come with a great gift. For a brief moment the air was on fire. The room was full of a kind of light. "I came here to tell you," she began, and then stopped and waved her hand as though the rest was inexpressible. "You're a joy forever," she said finally, driving each word home with a hammer.

"I know that," Mommie said. She sounded disgusted, as though Mattie was a peddler emptying her sack. So far she had seen nothing that interested her. "That's wasting my time," she said. "Come in here to tell me that. Why, if I didn't believe in Jesus already I wouldn't be here. He's my personal savior." It was as disappointing as everything else. Like the taste of salt. The older Mommie got, she noticed, the more everything tasted of salt.

"Why's that, Mommie?" Crystal asked. The words caught her imagination. A Joy Forever. It sounded like the title of a Harlequin romance. She imagined it to be what the man told the woman after he spent the night with her. Meaning what they did in bed—that was the joy part. And how long he would remember it, clenching it in his heart like a fist. That was forever. How could that be a waste of time?

Mommie made an angry gesture in Crystal's direction. "If something's wasting my time," she said levelly, "I ain't fixing to waste my time explaining how it's wasting my time." She turned back to Mattie. "What you said makes me think of Milton. Sometimes I wish he still wasn't dead."

"Why's that?" Althie asked.

"Why's that? To see him again, that's why, and feel his heart beating on mine."

Althie looked at her hands. They were moving in her lap. She made them be still by holding one inside the other.

"I felt his heart beating on mine like a bird in my hand trying to get loose," Mommie said, looking at her. "He pressed it against me."

"You're going to get to see him again," Crystal said, consoling her.

Mommie looked at her as though she had just spit her out. "I don't mean when I'm dead," she said. "I wouldn't want to die to do it."

"We're all going to die," Mattie Chadwick said. "That's what I mean. You're a joy forever."

Mommie pierced her with her eyes. "I know all that. I'm washed in his blood."

"No you ain't," Althie said. "You're washed in water."

"Water means blood."

"No it don't." Althie's hands were turned palm up in her lap as though broken.

Mommie ignored her. "Yes it does. In the Baptist church it does. If I wasn't washed in the blood of my savior, I wouldn't hardly know what to do."

"It don't make no sense," Althie said.

"That's what makes it so true," Mommie said. "Don't you see? Only God'd do something like that. Wade out to your hips in water, and it looks like water, and it feels like water, and it's the same river got water in it every day, but that one day it's blood. That whole river that one day runs full of blood and don't even look like it. If it looked like blood, it wouldn't be nothing. Blood's ordinary. This way it's different."

"Hearts ain't got that much blood in them," Althie said.

"This one does," Mommie said. "This heart's so soft and full of mercy it runs like a river, God feels so sorry. You heard of crying? Well this is worse. God looks out and sees you weeping and full of torment, boiling like water inside your breast from what you been doing, and he's so sorry he starts to sweating and it turns to blood and his heart breaks and flows like a river, and people come and see it flowing and dress up in gay attire and sing hymns of glory and step out in it and wash themselves clean." She paused for effect. "They come out on the other side and dry in the sun, and they shine. The white garments shine in the sun, and they call that place the Distant Shore. You live there forever. That's what it means. A Joy Forever. Means you don't ever come back."

"Dying," Crystal said. "What about living? I ain't even started that yet."

"That's you," Mommie said. "The rest of us are dying already."

"That ain't what I mean," Mattie Chadwick said.

Mommie inspected her from the side without turning in her direction. "That's what it says in the gospel," she said. But in her heart she did not believe it. Nothing she could not see or taste or touch or feel had ever existed. She herself had never existed before she was born, and now that she had miraculously come into being, she was not about to relax and lose it. It was too precious. It meant too much. If she were to lose herself, she knew by some instinctual knowledge deeper than thought that she would lose the whole world. Nothing was worth that.

"Like going to New York, ain't it, Mommie?" Crystal said. "When I go there you'll say, Where's Crystal? And they'll say, She's gone to the Distant Shore dressed in gay apparel dancing her feet off. Making God happy.

Won't that be fine?" She straightened her ankle, and her leg tightened like a bow. Its curve was the absolute curve of beauty.

"That may be," Mommie said. In Mommie's opinion it was better to sit in a chair and stretch like a cat than go to New York. That way you didn't get disappointed.

"That ain't what I was talking about anyway," Mattie said. "The Distant Shore or whatever you call it."

"The New Jerusalem," Althie said. "The City of Lights."

"The City of Lights," Crystal repeated.

"Whatever it is," Mattie said, "that ain't what it meant, not when I heard it. It meant right now. It didn't mean the Distant Shore. It meant right here and now. It won't ever stop. That's what it meant. Sounded like a drum in a tent, and pretty soon here come the dancers. That's how it felt. Like sitting there waiting, and here come the dancers dancing out."

"That's what I mean," Crystal said. She seemed agitated. "It's like I got a life of my own. I mean inside. It's like there's something else going on. That's how I know I'm going to New York."

"You already know how to dance?" Mattie asked.

"She says it don't matter," Althie said.

"It comes with the music," Crystal explained. "That's the first rule of dancing."

"What's the second?" Mattie asked.

"There ain't no second," Crystal said. She paused a moment. "New York City. New York City's the second rule of dancing."

"How you figure that?" Althie asked.

"Because that's where they watch you. I could dance all day on the porch, and who'd know about it?"

"I would," Althie said. "And Mommie."

"I mean who else?" Crystal said. "Where all the ones going to be watching?" She paused again. "And then there's the third rule. Third rule's part of the second."

"What's the third rule?" Mattie asked. She felt like a child playing a game.

"It ain't men," Althie said. "If it was men, they'd have been the first thing she mentioned, but she ain't even thought of them yet, so I know that ain't it."

"Yes it is," Crystal said quickly. "The third rule is men."

Mattie looked at the light outside the window. It framed a tree. The tree was covered with leaves. The wind rose. The leaves rustled. She thought of the creatures in front of the house—the goose swimming, the man tipping his hat, the sunflowers wearily turning their petals like a cheap trick—and she thought of the world and how there is nothing new under the sun. And then she thought, The wise man is wrong. She was not like that.

"Listen to me," she began again. "After the fear fell off me like old clothes and I didn't even know who I was any more, you know what I did? I got on MATS and went to town."

Crystal laughed. "What you mean, mats?"

"She means that bus," Mommie said. "The one goes to town if you know the day and don't mind waiting."

"And don't care about getting back," Althie said.

"The Mountain Area Transportation System," Mattie said. "I called them up, and they said when it was, and I got me a chair and dragged it down to the road and waited, and they picked me up. I was the only one in the bus except Younger, and he was driving."

"He can't drive," Mommie said.

"They think he can. Benny Easley got him the job."

"That don't mean he can drive," Mommie said. "That ain't no recommendation."

"He's a grown man now," Althie said. "He's married now."

"That makes him fit for some things, I reckon," Mommie said. "It don't make him fit for driving."

"Anyway, he got me there," Mattie said, "and I didn't even have to talk to him."

"You couldn't," Mommie said. "You talk, he'd have wrecked you. That's why I never did go on that bus. I said to myself, I know that Younger. Talk to him, it's too dangerous. He'll get confused and run off the road."

"Well, anyway, I got into town," Mattie said, "and went across the square to the courthouse waving my hands so the cars wouldn't hit me and went past them spitters sitting there and said, Stop that. There's somebody coming. I gave them fair warning. And one of them leaned over his back and spit, and another one said, Come on. But I looked at the sidewalk where they been messing it like pigeons and said, You're a disgrace. You're sitting in amber. And one of them said, I got shoes. And I said, The germs go right through the leather. And he said, What germs? And I said, TB and gonorrhea. Pull your feet back. I knew no fear. And they shuffled their feet and tucked them up under the benches, and I went on through like parting the water when Moses left Egypt and the sea gave way and parted in two. I went on up the steps to Mary Phalen in the courthouse and said, Benny locked up? And she said, Locked up? Benny ain't locked up. And I said, Why not? And she said, What for? And I said, For stealing. And she looked at me and said, That ain't funny. And I said, Where is he? And she said, Seeing the chief of police. And I said, That's perfect. He can arrest him. And she said, You can't go in. And I pushed that typewriter table against her and opened the door, and the whole place was full of smoke, and I said, Stop that. I'm coming in. And Mary Phalen stuck her head under my arm where I was holding the door waving it back and forth to get the smoke out, and she said, I'm sorry. She kept saying, I'm sorry. And Benny Easley said, That's all right, Mary. Let her go."

"He's slick as oil," Mommie said.

"And she pulled her head out from under my arm," Mattie Chadwick continued, "and gave me a hard look, but I didn't care. You hurt me, she said. You hurt my foot with that table. And I said, You're lucky you ain't dead. And the chief of police said, Who's that? I said, One of your betters. I don't even know who said it. It's like the words popped out of my mouth, and I kept looking over my shoulder to see who was talking. And he said, Ma'am? and stood up like he thought maybe I was Eleanor Roosevelt and better stand up and act polite till he was certain. And I said, You a public servant? And he said, Yes ma'am. And Benny Easley said, None better."

"Oh," Mommie said, "listen to that oil."

"And I said, You here to arrest that man? And he smiled and said, Who's that? like it was a joke, only he didn't know if he got it or not and it made him uneasy. I could see him looking at me wondering if I was crazy or if I was supposed to act that way—I might have been the governor's momma. So he lay low and laughed a little like it was a joke I was playing on him, and he said, Benny? He said, I'd just soon arrest myself. That's the honestest man I know. I knew what that meant, and I said, In that case, leave us alone. And Benny said, This's Miss Mattie Chadwick. Miss Chadwick lives out in the country, why you don't know her. She don't ever get to town. And the chief of police sat down. He knew I wasn't the governor's momma, and he said to Benny, What the hell is she? And Benny said, I'll get back to you later, Bobby, and walked around behind the desk. And the chief of police got up, and they walked to the door, Benny patting his back and rubbing it like he does when he talks, grabbing at you and rubbing, and said, I'll get back to you later, Bobby. And the chief of police said, She rich, or what? And Benny said, Later, and closed the door on him and said, Now what can I do for you, Mattie? And I said, Miss Chadwick. I don't even know who you are. And he laughed and said, What can I do for you then, Miss Chadwick? and lit a cigarette. And I said, The first thing is put that out. It makes my hair smell of mice. I have to wash it. He laughed and put his feet on the desk, and I said, Put your feet on the floor. They're full of TB and gonorrhea. And he said, What? And I said, That amber outside the court-house. You been walking in that or worse. And he laughed and said, Tell me about the worse. And I said, That's why I'm here. And he said, I figured. That road stays closed. And I said, That remains to be seen. Why you think I came down here after you hung up? And he said, We were cut off, and laughed like he does and clicked his teeth."

"I seen him do that," Mommie said. "Even when he had a set of his own it's like he was snapping. He'd say something and then go to snapping. When he got false ones it was worse. It's like they're rattling—like vibrations in them."

"If it was a fish it'd bite you to death," Mattie said, "you happen to be in the water with him. Like one of them they got in South America. What ɪey call them?"

"Mermaids," Crystal said.

"Miranas," Mattie said. "They go in shoals and you fall in the river and they click at you like that and snap you to pieces. I seen them eat a calf on TV. One minute it was licking the water. The next thing you knew it had a fish on the end of its tongue, and the next thing you knew its legs gave way. The fish ate them. It's like he was melting, and they got a rake and raked in the bones. I seen them do it. One minute it was licking the water, the next minute they were raking in the bones."

"It wasn't real," Mommie said. "A lot of things they do on TV, most of it ain't real. Like the moon. Them men on the moon. They weren't up there. They did that in somebody's barn to fool the Russians."

"This was real," Mattie said. "I saw it happen. And I thought to myself, Lucky Benny ain't got no children. Fall in on a shoal of children like that, you'd be snapped clean before you even said what you're there for."

"God knows what he's doing when he makes them like Benny," Crystal said.

"God don't make them," Althie said. "It's inside the parents."

"Parents ain't got a thing to do with it," Mommie said. "It comes when they get acting nasty with sex."

"They do it in secret," Althie said, flaring up, "where nobody sees them." Her fists were opening and closing like valves. "They don't even know what it is and then it happens, and it's all over. They can't get it back, and they say, What happened? What can I do? They say, Please, please. I won't do it again. And they pray for forgiveness. But it's already done. Christ sweated blood, and he was forgiven. And I said, I'm just a girl."

"Hush up," Mommie said. "I told you about that. Don't talk like that if you can't forgive him."

Althie grasped her hands. It was as though they had been speaking, and she silenced them. The knuckles were white.

Mattie decided to let it go. Whatever it was, it was between them. "Where was I?" she said in the silence that followed.

"Benny was snapping your leg like a fish," Crystal said.

"He was snapping his teeth," Mattie said. "He was still sitting behind he desk and said, We were cut off. He didn't hang up. He never hung up a phone in his life. And I said, Well, I ain't going to argue. What you fixing to do about it? And he said, It's out of my hands. They already bought it. And I said, You can't give a road away. And he said they bought it fair and square, and he's there to protect their right to do it. That's the main right in this country, the right to private property. He said, You take somebody robbing and entering your house. They come in the window, you shoot and kill them, you got a perfect right to do it. You call that murder? And I said, Yes, I do. And he said, You're wrong. That ain't murder. That's self-defense. And I said, How you figure that? And he said, What you are's your property. They come to get it, it's the same as raping and cornholing you."

"Cornholing?" Althie asked.

"Something they do," Mattie said, "like aggravated sodomy. Raping and violating your body. I don't know what it is exactly."

"Nobody does," Mommie said. "Not even me, and I been cornholed all my life."

"You have?" Mattie asked.

"Of course I have," Mommie said. "But I couldn't tell you what it was. It's in the dark. That's one thing. They turn out the light before it begins, and then it's one thing and another. Gets going so thick and fast you can't even tell where one starts and the other leaves off. And they got names for each and everything they do like you got different parts of your arm. This's an elbow," and she pulled at the skin on the back of her elbow. It looked like the wattle of a chicken. "And this's a forearm and this's a backarm," indicating the biceps and the wrist. She flexed her wrist. "And so on to the fingers. They even got names for the parts—tips and the rest."

"What's the middle?" Crystal said. "What you call the middle part of your finger?"

Mommie inspected her from a great distance. "I call it the middle," she said, "same as you. That ain't what I was talking about. I was talking about cornholing. You might want to know what it is."

"Yes ma'am," Crystal said. But she already knew. It happened in every romance she read as soon as the lovers pledged their love.

"Cornholing's a general operation," Mommie said. "Of course, I was married. I was married the whole time, and that made the difference."

"And you loved every minute of it, didn't you, Mommie?" Crystal said. She was thinking of a romance. Two lovers in New York City, one a dancer under the lights. They were cornholing. Crystal did not intend to be like her mother. She would know what it was when it happened, and she would know the name of each function and each individual part. The romances she read were a preparation. New York City would be the great light. The cornholing itself would take place within it.

"Daddy loved you, didn't he, Mommie?" Crystal said.

"He loved God best," Mommie said.

"He loved you and God both," Crystal said. "I bet he couldn't even tell them apart."

"Sometimes he could."

"Sometimes he couldn't," Althie said. "Sometimes he was so full of the love of God his heart got hard, and he came to me and his heart was hard and I said, Don't, and he did anyway."

"He was a terrible man," Mommie agreed. "That's what made him such a good preacher. He knew what he was talking about. Every sin you got on your soul, I got on mine, he used to say. Everything you ever thought of I did at least once. And not only that, I'm still alive. I ain't been struck dead. Ain't that a wonder? That's what made him so good," Mommie said. "He was forgiven."

"No he wasn't," Althie said. "I ain't got it in me."

"It ain't up to you," Mommie said. "God's the one does the forgiving. You just accept it. That's what I been trying to tell you. Pray for acceptance."

"I can't pray," Althie said. "My mouth won't move."

"It ain't your mouth," Mommie said. "Prayer's in the heart. You feel your heart move in your bosom like you're hungry for something you ain't never known. Ain't even tasted. You're sick with desire you want it so much, and God hears you and gives you acceptance. That's what you pray for."

"I can't," Althie said. "I been trying all my life."

"Then try some more," Mommie said. "Just because he beat you—that ain't nothing. The one the Lord loveth, that's the one he chastises the most. And he loved you the most. That's why he did it. Don't harden your heart."

"I ain't like him. My heart ain't hard."

"You're just like him," Mommie said. "I ought to know. I loved you both, and I see you in him." She held up her hand. "Not just the way you look. I see you, it's like looking at him beside me in bed. I mean the way you act. You got a hard heart."

"No I don't," Althie said.

"You're a hard case," Mommie said. "Else you'd already forgive him. He's the only daddy you got. It ain't natural to hate your daddy just because he beat you. That ain't nothing. His daddy beat him, and other people, they all beat him. He was just doing the same thing to you. Look at Crystal. She don't hate him. He beat on her, and she don't even remember it."

"I don't even know when it was," Crystal said. "That's too long ago."

.

"Pray to forgive him," Mommie said, "and Jesus'll wash you clean as a white shirt. You'll shine in the sun." She turned to Mattie. "Now, what were you saying about cornholing?"

"It wasn't me," Mattie said. "It was Benny Easley. He said somebody steals your property it's the same as raping and cornholing you. And I said, Not quite. And he said, What's the difference? And I said, You ever been raped and cornholed? And he laughed and said, No. And I said, If you had been, you wouldn't be laughing. That's the difference. One's a refrigerator or TV—whatever they stole. The other one's you. And he said it was a manner of speaking. I knew what he meant. And I said no, I didn't. Not when it came to raping and cornholing. I never was, and I wasn't fixing to start right then in his office. And he smiled and said, That a proposition or what, Miss Chadwick? And I said, No, I mean the road. And he said, Listen here, and leaned forward and looked hard, snapping at me like his motor was idling. I was so busy watching his teeth I could hardly hear what he said. I'm fixing to tell you one time, and then I ain't going to tell you no more. You're trying my patience. And he shook his finger. And I said, Stop that. And he said, What? And I said, Shaking your finger. I ain't going to listen, you doing like that. And he looked at his hand and put it down and said, That road is closed. Nobody used it. And I said, I did. And he said he meant motor vehicles. It wasn't safe. And he said, Besides which, how much taxes you pay, Miss Chadwick? And I said, Enough. More than what I was getting for it. And he said, Sixty-five dollars and seventy-two cents. That's all you bring in. And I said, What's that got to do with it? And he said, That's you on one side. Sixty-five dollars and seventy-two cents. And on the other side there's Blackberry Ridge. They got houses going up in there, you wouldn't even believe what they cost. There ain't no comparison. Besides which, it's out of my hands. I wish I could do something for you, he said, standing up like he was leaving. And I said, Hold on there. Where you going? And he said, It ain't me, grabbing my arm and lifting me up. But I shook him loose and sat down and said, I ain't leaving here till I'm finished. And he said, Miss Phalen? And Mary Phalen came in. And he said, Miss Chadwick's just leaving. Will you see to it she finds the door? and went back and sat down at the desk. And Mary Phalen looked at me and then looked at him. She took a step in the room and said, Miss Chadwick? And I said, I ain't finished. Go back where you came from. And she started to go. And he said, Miss Phalen? And she said, I can't. And then she said, Miss Chadwick? and pulled at my arm. And I shook her off and said, Get on back. And she got on back and stood in the door and said, Benny? And then she said, Mr. Easley? like she was fixing to ask him a question. And he said, That will be all, Miss Phalen. And she started to leave, and he said, One thing. And she turned around, and he said, Call Bobby. And she said, Bobby? And he said, Yes. He'll know what to do. And I said, You mean that chief of police? If you call him, I'm calling the sheriff. And he said, That won't hardly be necessary. One of them'll be sufficient, and made like he was writing something. I watched a fly crawl on his hand down one finger and over the other. He never even made like he noticed, he was so busy. And then Mary Phalen said something—I never did catch it—and tiptoed out and closed the door and left me in there with him."

"Weren't you scared?" Althie asked.

"Of course I was," Mattie said. "I thought, Oh God what am I doing here? What am I going to do when they come? I kept looking at that fly. I said, You got a fly on your hand, you see it? And he said, Thank you, and brushed it off. And it got on his forehead, and he brushed it off, and it got in his hair, and I could see it walking about. And I said, It sure does like you. And he said, What's that, Miss Chadwick? And I said, That fly. It's in your hair now. And he didn't move a muscle. Just looked at me. And I said, I wonder why it just lights on you? And he looked at me and said, It must be it knows it's my office. If you'll just excuse me, Miss Chadwick, and he brushed at the fly, and it flew up a foot or two and settled back down on his head. I watched that fly crawling and Benny messing around with them figures. He was studying a column of figures, and my heart was racing I was so scared until I couldn't stand it no more. And I said, What's the charge? And he said, Trespassing on private property and unlawful loitering. And I said, Private property? This ain't private property. This belongs to the American people. And he smiled and said, We'll think of something as soon as Bobby comes. And just then there was a knock on the door and Benny smiles and says, If you'll excuse me Miss Chadwick, and yells out, Come in, Bobby. She's sitting here waiting. And Mary Phalen sticks her head in and says, I'm sorry, Mr. Easley. I couldn't find him. He's gone on a call. And he said, Get him. And she said, I don't know how to get him. And he said, The radio. That's why they got them. Get them to call him. Tell him I want him. Tell him it's an emergency. I said, There's a fly on his head. He can't get it off. And she looked at me like I was crazy and said to Benny, You all right? He was clicking his teeth and staring at something on the wall. And she said, Can I get you some coffee? And I said, Yes. And she said, Mr. Easley? And he said, Get her some coffee. I'm all right. The fly was on his collar by then, and I said to Miss Phalen, There it is, and pointed him out. And she said, Mr. Easley. There's a fly on your collar. And he said, Just get the coffee. And she tiptoed out and let me alone in there with him. I felt the fear rising, and I knew if I let it, I'd soon be weeping and begging not to go to jail. So I said the first thing that came in my mind."

"What was that?" Althie said.

"I can't remember. Something about flies and how they're one of the original plagues of Egypt like blood and locusts, and I sure did know why, seeing him troubled like Pharaoh with that one. I don't know what all. This and that, just to be talking. I said, Benny, you're a politician. And he said, Proud of it! like he thought I accused him of something. And I said, I'm sure you are. Ain't nothing to be ashamed of as long as you're honest. And that did it. He started writing on them figures, ignoring me and the fly both. The fly was all over him, and I watched it a while. And he said, Miss Chadwick? He didn't look up. He was watching the fly. It was sitting on a finger nail. He leaned forward and blew on it. The fly flew up on the side of his arm. He said, Miss Chadwick? What can I do for you? My hands are tied. That road's already been deeded over. And I said, They're going to kill somebody. And he said, That ain't my lookout, Miss Chadwick. I'm just the commissioner of roads. And I said, In that case, how we get you out of office? And he laughed and said, I beg your pardon? And I said, You heard me. How we get you out of office? And he said, You vote me out. This is a free country. And I said, When? And he smiled and said, Three years. This is the first of a four-year term. And I said, That's too late. And he said, It is for you, Miss Chadwick. It ain't too late for me. And I said, Don't count on it. You may be dead by then. That stiffened him up."

"I reckon so," Mommie said. "He's still a young man. He ain't like me, fixing to go any minute."

"And he said, Is that a threat? and lifted his eyebrow, and the fly jumped off it. And I said, Yes. And he said, That's another charge. Excuse me, Miss Chadwick. And I said, Wait. How we get you out before then? And he said,

No way. And just then the door opened, and there was Bobby, the chief of police. And he said, This better be important. And Benny said, It is, Bobby, and went over and put his arm on his shoulder and said, I got to get her out of here. This a business office. And Bobby said, There's somebody down at the bridge jumping off. And I said, Oh God, is he dead yet? And Bobby said, Not yet. Son of a bitch fixing to be if I get my hands on him. I'm going to shoot him. And I said, What for? And he said, Trying to kill himself. And Benny said, Bobby, get her out. And Bobby said, How? And Benny said, Pick up the chair and carry her out. And he said, Where to? And Benny said, You figure that out. The charge is trespassing and using foul language, loitering and vagrancy. She's obstructing business. And Bobby said, You coming, lady? And I said, No, and grabbed on the arms of the chair. And Bobby just stood there. And Benny said, Get her. And Bobby said, I got a bad back. I can't lift her up. And Benny said, Shit, excuse the language, and went and sat down where the fly could get at him. The fly was waiting at the desk. And I said, I got to stay here three years. And Bobby said, Three years? like he never figured I was fixing to stay that long. And I said, If that's what it takes. And Bobby said, What? And I said, To get him out of office. I got to stay till the next election. He says it's the only way. And Bobby said, What about a recall? And Benny said, Good God."

"What's a recall?" Althie asked.

"That what I'm fixing to tell you about," Mattie said. "That's the whole reason I'm here. A recall is when you recall them and get them out of office early."

"How you do that?"

"By a petition. Don't rush me. I know all about it. I said to Benny, What's a recall? And he said, Ask Bobby. He's the one knows all about it. And Bobby said, I'm going to get somebody, Benny, as soon as we finish down at the bridge. Shoot him and get it over with, I said. That'll make you both happy. And he said, Ma'am? And I said, Send in Mary Phalen. But he was already out the door. Mary heard and said, You want me? And I said, Explain to me what a recall is. And she told me how if a public official's been caught stealing roads from the county and they still got three years in office, you sign a paper in the courthouse saying what your grievance is and petition for a recall election. Register it at the county clerk and then get the names of half the ones in the county that voted in the last election, and you got you a recall election."

"And wait three years," Althie said. "What good is that?"

"No," Mattie said. "You get to have it right then. As soon as you get the last name on the petition, they got to have a new election."

"What good does that do?" Mommie said. "They just vote him in again."

"Not if you got a petition, they don't. You get half the names in the county, you won right there. All it takes is one more. That's the beauty of a recall. You know where you're at. It ain't like a regular election where you don't know what's going to happen. It's all worked out before you begin. Mary Phalen told me all that. And Benny said, Thank you, Mary. I think that'll be all. And she said, Thank you, Mr. Easley. Thank you, Miss Chadwick, like I was the one done her a favor. And Benny sat down and said, Well, Miss Chadwick? And I said, Well, the fly ain't gone. It was sitting on his shirt. I said, There four people been in this room, and you're the only one it bothered. And he said, That ain't what you came to tell me, like he was real tired like Job from sitting on the dunghill. And I said, No. And he said, You'll need a lawyer. And I said, Not me. They might want the road for a fee. And he said, You mean if you won. And I said, Yes. And he said, You won't. You won't, Miss Chadwick. Recall elections take hundreds of names, and every one on a piece of paper. That's the problem. Keeping them names from burning up. Paper's bad for catching on fire. And I said, Not this. I'll sleep with it."

"He'll burn you too!" Mommie said. "That won't stop him. Oh God!"

"That's what he said," Mattie replied. "He said, You sound like that jumper down at the bridge. And I said, I'd just soon be him as the one that shot him. Besides which, I'd rather be dead than afraid all my life. And I told him about how it came to me when it said I was a joy forever. And he said, You are, and smiled at me and snapped his teeth and said, I can attest to that fact, Miss Chadwick. And I said, As long as we understand each other. Now, where's the clerk's office? And he called Miss Phalen and said, Miss Phalen, would you be so kind as to conduct Miss Chadwick to Gentry's office, since you're the one told her about it. She's going to file for a recall election. And she said, I'm sorry, Benny. And he said, That's all right. She's got a perfect right to do it. All she needs is four thousand six hundred and seventy-two names that won't burn or get lost or blur out in water in six weeks' time beginning from the date when she files. I'll see you, Miss Chadwick. And I said, There's one thing. And he said, What that? And I said, Why don't we work out a compromise? Ain't that how they do in politics? And he said, I'm glad you came to your senses. That'll be all for a minute, Miss Phalen. And she tiptoed out. And he said, What if I get you special permission? You can go down there just like you're rich and bought one of them houses. How about that? Get you a special badge you can wear. And I said, You mean where they won't shoot me? Take more than a badge for that. And then I said what about you?" indicating Mommie. "What about the Grizzle girls?"

"You said that?" Mommie cried. "Oh God! What'd he say?"

"He said he liked you," Mattie replied. "He said you're all right. He said he never heard you complain about nothing."

"And never will," Mommie said fervently.

"That was before the road, I told him. I said, You're going to be surprised how they do when they sign that petition. They owned the mill the whole place was named for, I said. They got an interest in going down there."

"Not me," Mommie said. "I don't go down there. That mill fell in. Besides which, we sold the land."

"That's what he said," Mattie replied. "But I told him the past is sacred. You got to have a way to get back there just like I do. They can't cut you off. You're too old, I told him. Without the past to go back down there, you just shrivel up and die."

"Don't tell him that," Mommie said. "I don't go down there."

"He don't know if you do or not," Mattie said. "And he said, That ain't nothing, Miss Chadwick. We'll get her a badge too. And I said, What about her daughters? And he said, How many? And I said, Three. And he said, That ain't nothing, Miss Chadwick. I'll get as many as thirty-three, one for each person that lives out this way wants to go down there anytime they want to on Sunday. And I said, Sunday? And he said, Sunday afternoon. That's visiting hours for people with badges. And I said, That include hunting season? And he said, They ain't going to shoot them, Miss Chadwick. Not with the badges. Not on Sunday afternoon."

"Oh God, " Mommie said. "How big the badges?"

"That's what I asked him. I said, Them badges big as a sign says, 'Human Being! Don't Shoot'? And he laughed and said, You got a good sense of humor for a woman your age, Miss Chadwick. Them badges about as big as a brooch. Pink and gold for ladies. Black and white for men. We'll get yours encased in plastic where it won't get frayed. Pin it on your coat when you use it. And I said, No thank you. Badges are out. And he looked at me and clicked his teeth like he was thinking. And I watched the fly. That fly was the busiest one in the room."

"That's because he was making his living," Crystal said. She had a special affinity for animals. Next to men she loved them the most.

"I watched the fly to keep from thinking," Mattie said. "The more I thought how quiet it was, the more I realized what I was doing and the more afraid I got."

"I don't blame you," Althie said. "You in there with him."

"It's like he was violating me," Mattie said. "One time they robbed me when I wasn't there. My momma and daddy just died the year before, and I was out down at the river. It was still light, and I got back just before supper, and the door was standing open. It was the fall, and it was cold. When I saw it open, I knew something was wrong, and I crept up and looked in the windows. It's like somebody lifted my skirt."

"Oh God," Althie said. She clutched her hands.

"The whole place was turned over, everything scattered about on the floor. Even flour. I remember looking at that and thinking, They put flour on top of my clothes. And it was like they did something to me—lifted my skirt and did what they do, and I couldn't stop them. That's how I feel about that road—like if I let them, that's what they'd do. So I kept watching that fly and waiting and wondering what I was going to do. It was crawling on the back of his hand. The sun was on it. I could see the hair like golden wires and the wings of the fly where you could see through it. Looked like plastic shower curtains. And all of a sudden it was gone. I couldn't even see what happened, it happened so fast. The hand came down and mushed it in. He didn't hit past it. He hit *on* it and then he mushed it in. When he lifted his hand, I could see a smear of wet on it, part on one hand and part on the other. And he said, Son of a bitch! Excuse me, Miss Chadwick, and reached in the wastebasket and got out a paper and scraped his hands on it. And I said, Ain't you going to wash? And he said,

Later. We got business. Or do we, Miss Chadwick? And I said, What else
you got besides badges? And he said, We could make you a member. We
could all chip in half a million and buy you a new house on the ridge, so you
could go down there whenever you wanted. They wouldn't shoot you
then, Miss Chadwick. And I said, I already got a house. And he got serious
and said he was joking. It was badges or nothing. And I said, Why don't
you just open the road? And he yelled, Miss Phalen! And there was no answer. And he yelled again and went out where she was supposed to be sitting and came back and said, She's gone. I said, Look in the typewriter.
And he came back with a note in his hand. It said, Bobby called. I'm down
at the bridge taking dictation. Love, Mary Phalen. And Benny said, Good
God. What's that mean? And I said, It must be the one they got killing
himself. He's giving her his life story first. And he said, Come with me,
Miss Chadwick. And I said, Where we going? And he said, To fix you up
for a recall. And that's what he did. He took me down there to Gentry's office and said, This's Miss Chadwick. I love her like I do my own momma. I
want you to take care of her. And I said, I'm sorry it's come to this, Benny.
But I can't see no other way. I may be dead if I have to wait to vote you out
of office."

Mommie said, "That's one way. You wait long enough, you die anyway,
and all them happy times die with you. You won't have to go down there,
you wait long enough."

"I thought of that," Mattie said. "But it's too uncertain. And Benny
said, It sure was good to see you again, Miss Chadwick. I appreciate the
confidence. Whatever that means. And I said, You won't reconsider? And
he said if it was just him he would. If it was just him, that road'd be scraped
and graveled tomorrow. Might even pave it. But it was private property.
That's the thing holding him back. And I said, Then I'll see you in court.
And he laughed and said, It amuses you, don't it? and clicked his teeth like
he was getting a message and they were the answer in Morse code. And
that surprised me. That's the first thing he said that surprised me. And I
said, Benny, it don't amuse me. It scares me to death. And he said, You're
too old, Miss Chadwick. And I said, That's why I'm doing it, Benny. I
don't care if I die, anyway. I figure I'm a joy forever. And he said, Gentry,
fix her up for a recall, Gentry. Do up the papers, and give her a few extra
forms for petitions in case something happens to the ones she got. And I

said, Is that a threat, or what? I figured I had me a witness. And he said, No, no. I meant get lost or burned in the fire, thrown out in the trash. You got six weeks. Four thousand six hundred and seventy-two names. And I said, Seventy-three. That extra one's the tie breaker. And he smiled and said, You think ahead. And I said, That's how I got as old as I am. Otherwise I might be dead crossing the street. And he said, Miss Chadwick, my best to you, ma'am. And he said to Gentry, Anybody looking for me tell them I gone down to the bridge to look at the jumper killing himself. And I said, Don't shoot him. And he smiled and said, Dear Miss Chadwick, you exaggerate my importance, and opened the door and said, I ain't the chief of police. And then he was gone, and Gentry said, He's just the county commissioner. And I said, Not for long. Where are them forms? And he gave me a pile of petitions big as a phone book."

"How many names you got?" Mommie asked.

"I just started," Mattie said. "You're the first ones I asked except Homer. I met him coming back on the bus. I signed it, and then he signed it, and Younger signed it. That's three already."

"Younger signed it!" Mommie said. "He can't write his own name."

"He voted in the last election," Mattie replied. "That makes him eligible."

"Let me see it," Mommie said. Crystal ran over to look at the petition with her. Althie got up and left the room.

"Where's she going?" Mattie asked.

"Bathroom," Crystal said. "I need the mirror sometimes, but she's always in there. She spends half her life in the bathroom moving her bowels."

"That ain't a signature," Mommie said.

"Looks like something cast by a worm," Crystal said. "It's all on top of one another."

"That settles it," Mommie said. "I ain't signing nothing Younger signed looking like that. He can't even sign his name."

"Then sign this one," Mattie said and gave her a clean sheet. "Start a new page. That's the best way anyway. That road goes in front of your house, and they still call it Grizzle Mill even if the mill ain't there now. They see the name of Pearly Grizzle standing there first, that'll show what they're up against. 'Local Citizens Up in Arms.' That's what the newspaper head-lines'll say. 'Pearly Grizzle First on the List.'"

"I ain't signing," Mommie said.

"You ain't signing?"

"I ain't signing my name to things. I wouldn't want them to know who I was."

"They already know. You're famous already."

"I ain't signing."

Mattie looked at her. "It's right in front of your own house. It's your road."

"I don't care. I don't want them to get my name down."

"What do you mean?"

Mommie waved her hand about grandly. The skin sagged and slid to-ward her elbow. "All this," she said, taking in the entire room. It might have been Queen Victoria speaking of India. "They might want to get it."

"Who?" Mattie asked.

"The ones at the courthouse," Mommie said. "Like that time the sheriff came out here and said, How you doing? And I said, Not as good as I used to. And he said, That's too bad. That's why I'm here. Old folks got special rights and privileges they might not even know about. And I said, You sell-ing tombstones, or what? And he shook in the chair. He's a big-bellied man, and he said, Your mind's still good. And I said, That's the top of the candle. That's going to be the last thing to go. And he looked like he didn't know what that meant and leaned forward like he was going to tell me something I wished I knew and said, Mrs. Grizzle. We're missing your vote. That's why I'm here. We got you an absentee ballot. And I said, What's that? And he said, A way to vote for the man of your choice without getting up from that chair. And I said, The man of my choice died two years ago. And he looked like he didn't know what I meant and said, This ain't the presidential election. This ballot's just for the race in the county. And I said, I'm speaking of Reverend Grizzle. And he said, Yes ma'am. You lost me there, and pulled out this paper and said, I already filled it out. All you got to do is sign it. And I said, I don't sign my name. And he said, Then mark it. I'm a notary public. And I said, I know how to write. I don't want them to have my name. That way they can't come and get it. And he said,

What? And I said, Whatever they want. Come and take it. And he said, Who? And I said, Lawyers and politicians. They been known to steal county roads."

"You told him that!" Mattie said.

"I can't remember. And he said, What about the deeds to your land? You got them recorded? And I said, No. I keep them here with me. And he said, I'll be damned. What about taxes? And I said, I pay them. You don't have to sign to do that. And he said, I'll be damned. Mrs. Grizzle, you sure you're married? and shook in the chair like he was laughing. And I looked at him like it was the first time I saw he was there and said, Reverend Grizzle signed for that. He's the one with his name on the license. Then I let him have it. I said, I'm married, but I don't vote. And he said, Don't vote? and pushed his chair back and stood up. He was so close all I could see was his belly and on top a star. I couldn't even see his head. And I said, No. You vote, they put you on jury duty, and what if it's rape? What if it's murder? And you say he's guilty, and all his kin folks come and get you and burn down your house or shoot out your car or castrate your husband or child. Voting ain't worth it. And then he leaned down, and I could see the brim of his hat. And he said, You ain't on the rolls? And I said, That's right. And he said, In that case I'm wasting my time. And I said, I'm sorry, but that's a regulation of mine. If it takes my name, I ain't signing. And he bent over, and I could see his face. It reminded me of my granddaddy when I was sitting in his lap. I thought for a minute he was trying to kiss me, but all he said was he understood. Old as I am, he knew how I felt. He was just going to leave the ballot in case I thought of somebody who might want to sign it. And I said, What for? And he said, To save the trouble of standing in line. Just mail it in. And I said, Thank you. And he said he's happy to oblige. We got any trouble? And I said not since my husband died. That's trouble enough. And he said, Yes ma'am. Reverend Grizzle."

"You want me to fill this petition out so you can mail it in?" Mattie asked. "That what you're saying?"

"That's what the sheriff did."

"What happened to it?"

"I signed the sheriff's name on it and mailed it on in," Mommie said. Mattie laughed. "Then I ain't leaving this one," she said.

"I might change my mind," Mommie said. "Besides that, Forsythia ain't here. She might want to sign."

"What about you?" Mattie asked Crystal.

"I'm going to New York," Crystal said. "I won't be keeping up with that road."

"What about Althie?"

"She's in the bathroom," Crystal said, and then looked up as something passed over her. Althie's shadow entered the room. A moment later Althie appeared framed in the light of the open door.

"Oh my God!" Mommie cried. "Oh my baby. God, what happened?" Althie's face was covered with blood. It was smeared on her cheeks and over her forehead. It matted her hair and eyebrows and dripped on the collar of her dress. One ear looked as though it had been ripped off, and her nose was missing. That was the first shocked impression. The blood that darkened it made it look like a hole in her face.

"Oh my God!" Mommie cried. She tried to struggle out of her recliner but succeeded only in making it flip back and extend its footrest. Mommie was flung flat on her back, looking at the ceiling crying, "Get her up. I can't get loose of here. Help her up"—unable to distinguish between herself and Althie.

Crystal stood immobilized, not knowing which one to help first, Mommie or Althie. She finally decided against them both and ran out the screen door into the yard among the wind turners. "What happened?" she shouted, and then her mouth filled with saliva. She swallowed hard, trying to keep ahead of it. Then she got sick, bent at the waist like the washerwoman. Around her a garden of sunflowers spun insanely in the wind.

Mattie put her weight against the back of Mommie's chair and tipped her upright. Mommie was already climbing out before it had even come to rest. A gun clattered to the floor, and Mommie kicked it under a table. She was at Althie's side, holding her face in her hands. It looked as though the head had been severed and Mommie was trying to put it back on.

"Oh my baby. God, what happened?" she said, swaying with the head in her hands.

"You cut yourself, or what?" Mattie asked, coming forward to get a better look.

Just then the porch heaved and shuddered as Crystal ran across it. Then she was in the room. "I was sick," she announced.

"That ain't nothing," Mattie said. "Look at your sister."

"That's what made me sick," Crystal said. "What happened to her? Looks like an automobile accident, except it happened in the bathroom."

"I baptized myself," Althie said.

"Where the blood come from?" Mommie said. "It's all over you."

"It's my blood," Althie said.

"Your blood," Mommie said, dropping her hands, setting the head free. "I know it's your blood."

"I mean it's my own blood," Althie said. "I ain't hurt."

"You mean it's your blood?" Mattie asked.

Althie nodded.

"That's disgusting," Mommie said. "Oh God, that's disgusting."

"I'm going to be sick," Crystal shouted. But she stood there, fascinated. "You got that blood all over your face." Nothing she had read in the romances prepared her for this. She had read of perfect lovers so obsessed with each other that they gave up not only home, wife, children, job, and nationality, but food, drink, sleep, and sex—even sex—to maintain their passion. But this had the true ring of excess. This was really crazy. That's what made it so fascinating. "You mean you got it and rubbed it on you?" Crystal said. She wanted the details.

"Hush up, Crystal," Mattie said. She turned to Althie. "Why you want to do yourself like that? You want me to wash it? You all right? You want to sit down?"

Mommie crept across the room, rushing for support from stool to table to chair to recliner, holding out her hand the last few tentative steps to Crystal, who ran forward just in time to catch her. They swayed together. Crystal finally gained control and turned Mommie slowly like a television aerial too heavy to handle alone, catching the balance and then catching it again. When Mommie was finally turned with her back to the chair, Crystal shoved her and caught her, both at once. Mommie eased into the recliner. The footrest leaped out like an animal, but Mommie immediately pushed against the arms and swept herself upright. She sighed and whistled from the effort, then pointed across the room. "The gun's over there," she said. It looked like a snake coiled in the corner, scales oiled in the light.

Althie started to go and get it when Mommie said, "Not you. I don't want you to touch it." She turned to Crystal. "Go get it, honey. Your hands are clean." Crystal got it and gave it to her and Mommie tucked it under her skirt.

"I almost had a heart attack," Mommie said. She turned to Althie. "Go wash it," she said. "That ain't clean."

"Neither was Jesus," Althie said. "He had dirt and blood all over."

"He died on the cross for your sins," Mommie said. "His blood was holy. It wasn't like that. It was like gold. It didn't even smell like blood. His blood was like water. It washed you clean."

"Made *me* sick," Crystal said, as though that was accusation enough.

Mommie ignored her. "You know how blood smells? Like smelling an animal. You put your nose inside their fur and smell their skin. Well, his wasn't like that. His smelled like perfume. Remember that woman sleeping with men all her life and came to him with the sweat and sperm of the bed still on her and washed his feet in her own tears and dried them with her golden hair and oiled them with precious oil? That's what it smelled like. His blood was sweet like you feel in your heart when you know you're forgiven. Jesus's my savior, my own sweet lord. He ain't like you."

"I don't care. I couldn't forgive him," Althie said. "I couldn't pray. My mouth wouldn't open, and my heart wouldn't move. All my life it kept squeezing on something like I had something inside my fist I kept squeezing on, and I didn't know why I couldn't let go."

"So you baptized yourself," Mattie said.

Althie nodded. "He was laying in bed and called me and kept calling, and I wouldn't come, and he still kept calling, and Mommie said, Why don't you go? And I said, I can't. And she went to the door and said, Milton. She won't come. And he kept calling, and I went to the door, and he said, Come in. And I said, No. And he said, Come in here where I can talk to you. And I said, Talk from there. I can hear you. And he said, Come sit by his bed. He got to whisper. And I said, No. And he said he was dying. Did I know that? And I said, Maybe. The doctor was there, and he said he might die. But I wasn't taking no chances. I said, I can hear you from here. And he said, Althie, I'm sorry. I came to ask your forgiveness. And I said, You didn't come. I did. I started to go, and he said, I had a heart attack. I'm covered with blood except you can't see it. It's leaking inside. And I said,

What about the chrysolite and marble packed in like feathers? I thought your body was replaced. And he said it was, his immortal body. He meant his mortal. And it's like I could see it tucked inside him like stacks of laundry, and the heart was inside them folded up in there, and I pulled the towels back and the sheets and the dishrags one by one, and I pull off the last one, and there it is, plated with armor and ringed with eyes, beating. He said it's bleeding inside his body. All the cavities were full. He couldn't breathe. He said, Forgive me. He said God did. And I said, How you know that? And he said, He got to as long as you're baptized and tell him you're sorry. That's his nature. Why else you think he died on the cross? And I said, You got what you wanted. What you need me for? And he said, You're the one I did it to. And I said, You did it to God. He said, I know that. All them sins go in like nails. Every one's a thorn in the crown pressing his flesh making him blind where he can't see from all the blood dripping in his eyes till finally he don't even know what you're doing, he still forgives you. Blind as he is, his heart's full of love. But you're the one, he said. You know what happened. And I said, No I don't, and left. And he called me back. And Mommie said, My nerves can't stand it. I got to fix dinner. Forsythia's coming home in a minute. And I went back there, and he said, I'm sorry. And I didn't say nothing. I leaned in the doorway. And he said, Forgive me. And then he started yelling and thrashing about, holding himself where he was bent double and rolling around. I looked at him. I thought it was some trick. And Mommie came up, and she said, What happened? And then she said, Oh my God."

"I knew he was dying as soon as I saw him," Mommie said. "He died in my arms."

"He was already dead," Althie said. "The pyjamas rode up on his legs, and they were sticking out. There wasn't any hair on them. They looked like lard or bacon grease. The top was all twisted around his neck like he'd stood still and his clothes kept on twisting after he died. And his head was turned backwards—his face was down, and the rest of him was on its back. I could see buttons in the front and no face, and I figured at first it wasn't him. It was something else laying there twisted up in his pyjamas. I couldn't even ask for forgiveness."

"That's where you made your first mistake," Mommie said. "If I didn't ask for forgiveness and pray, I couldn't keep going."

"I couldn't keep going," Althie said. "It looked like something else he'd killed and put there in his pyjamas and left it. And we got to take it and straighten it out and wash it and set a smile on its face and put on new clothes."

"I did the makeup," Crystal said. "I didn't even wear it myself. I was too young. But they let me do it. Said it was good practice. Besides which, she got the interest, they said. She'll do a fine job. I was going to be a cosmetician before my legs started to shape up. Then I switched over to being a dancer."

"You hated him," Mommie said.

"I didn't hate him," Althie replied. "I thought it was me laying there, and they'd come and strip me and see who it was, and I didn't even care. I didn't hate him. That was the trouble. I didn't feel nothing, and he couldn't hear me. He was dead." She rubbed at her cheek. Grains of dried blood came off on her hand. She examined it. "Feels like dirt."

"Let me wash you and get you new clothes," Mattie Chadwick said. "You got blood all over your neck and down the collar." She went over and took Althie by the arm.

Althie flung her off. "I got something I got to tell Mommie," she said. "I didn't mind him beating me, Mommie. That was his way."

Mommie looked at her and nodded.

"It's what he done to me," Althie said. The words had come. They stood at the edge of her mind and looked out as out of the entrance of a cave. She saw her father. It was no demon. It throbbed at her temples like the sound of her blood and beat on the sides of her head for release. She was polluted, the words were saying. The corpse had been buried so deep in her heart that she did not even know where to find it until now when it had come and looked out and the words had formed around it like flesh. It was no pig: it was herself she had heard squealing. The words were there waiting to be spoken. She looked at her mother. Her mother's eyes were clear blue. Her face was all lines going in all directions at once, meaning nothing except how long she had lived and how much she had been through and how fearful she had been and how she had lived with him and now she was dying. Mommie looked at Althie trusting that nothing Althie said could ever harm her. And Althie felt it give way. Whatever had gathered inside her heart and was about to name itself gave way and ran among the tombstones squealing. He had come, and she had vomited him out, and she knew that she could never tell her mother. It was as though a road had opened up inside her.

"Don't tell me nothing," Mommie said. "I already know. I don't want to hear about it."

"Come on," Mattie said to Althie, and drew her away.

"Go wash it off," Crystal said. "It's nasty to look at. That'll make us all feel better." They left the room, and Crystal said to Mommie, "Good thing it was Mattie, wasn't it, Mommie? At least she's a woman. Supposing it was somebody else."

"Like who?" Mommie asked. She had not known what Althie was going to tell her, but she feared in her heart that she already knew.

"Like the preacher," Crystal said.

"She might not have had the provocation if it was the preacher."

"Provocation?" Crystal said. "What provocation?"

"All that talk about opening the road and going back there where you were a child and all that talk about old lives. That got her stirred up and thinking about things she wished she hadn't. Let sleeping dogs lie. Better just to forget about some things. We do what we can. That's all we know how to. And sometimes our children forgive us, and sometimes they don't."

"I forgive you," Crystal said.

"What for?" Mommie asked.

"Whatever you're talking about."

"I wasn't talking about you," Mommie said. "I was talking about . . ." She paused. "I meant Althie."

"Why she put that blood on her?" Crystal asked. "She crazy, or what?"

"It's hard to explain," Mommie said.

"Why's that?"

"If I knew how, I'd tell you," Mommie said. "You get as old as I am there're too many things happened to explain them all. It's like there're too many things in the way come crowding in all together, and you get hold of one of them, all the other ones get loose."

"All the other what, Mommie?"

"Things you were saying," Mommie said patiently. "Things that it meant. Sometimes they're all scattered and littered over years of your life, and you got to go back and pick them up, and by the time you get some, all the others blow away. I wish I could talk about half that I know."

"I talk about everything I know," Crystal said. "I ain't so old I get cluttered up."

"It ain't that," Mommie said. "It's knowing too much."

"And living too long," Crystal said, trying to appear sympathetic.

"That ain't it," Mommie said. "There ain't no such thing as living too long."

"What if you're cluttered?" Crystal said. "That's a terrible burden, ain't it?"

"It's a terrible burden," Mommie said. "That's how it comes. I just take it as it is."

"You reckon they're finished?" Crystal said. "I got to set my hair, not to mention what else I got to do I ain't telling." She leaned forward and spoke in confidence. "When you reckon she's going to go? I get tired of her being here, don't you?"

"She's a pitiful case," Mommie said. "Ever since her momma and daddy were killed in that car wreck she ain't ever been the same. You hear how she talked about Benny Easley, and most of it lies? She's too scared to sit in her own shadow."

"Why's that?" Crystal asked, already knowing. It was a small kindness to accept Mommie's jokes.

"For fear she'll catch cold," Mommie said. Her mouth grew round like a hole in the wall, and she wheezed through it. "You ain't ever heard that old joke?"

"I might have," Crystal lied. "I can't remember." She was good-hearted and loved Mommie almost as much as she loved herself. They were old friends, easy and comfortable together. The only real difference between them were Crystal's romances and Mommie's memories. Both were rich sources of fantasy.

Althie and Mattie came back in the room. Althie's face was clean, and her hair was damp and drawn back from her forehead as though she had drowned in the river and had just been restored to life. She wore no makeup, and her lips were blue. Her eyes were brown and heavy-lidded. They looked hooded. Her nose and forehead and ears were pink from scrubbing and glowed in the wash of light from the screen door. The high spots were shiny. She wore a dress of worn blue cotton so faded it was almost white.

"Here she is," Mattie said. "Good as new."

"You got it all off?" Crystal asked unnecessarily.

Althie nodded. "Inside and out." She paused. "I ain't crazy."

"I know you ain't," Mommie said.

"I think she is," Crystal said. "I wouldn't do that. That's nasty as something else I can think of. Two or three things."

"Gives you something to do," Mommie said and made the hole in the wall again and blew through it.

"That's one thing," Mattie said laughing. "It ain't boring, is it? That's one thing you can say for it. You all right?" she asked Althie. Althie nodded. "Well, I got to be going. It sure was good to see you all. Crystal, you're looking mighty pretty, and Mommie, your face is shining with health. You're the picture of health and happiness."

Mommie waved her arms about so violently, denying both health and happiness, that the pistol clattered out from between her legs and fell to the floor. Mommie kicked at it spontaneously, almost involuntarily, she was so used to forgetting about it and having it fall to her feet whenever she got up out of the chair. It went rushing and clattering across the room toward Mattie, who lurched out of her chair just as the pistol went under. It might have been a rat or a snake it went so fast. Mattie cried, and the gun went off. The room filled with smoke and the smell of fear. It was metallic like tomatoes.

"I might have killed myself," Mommie said, her voice rising from the smoke like the peak of Mount Ararat after the flood.

Althie rushed to her. "You okay?" Mommie was lying back in the chair looking up at the ceiling.

"If I ain't dead," Mommie shouted. "I might be shot. I don't know."

"Check her chest," Mattie said.

"Oh God!" Crystal cried. "What if she's dead?"

"I wouldn't be talking if I was dead," Mommie said. "Hush up and do like she said."

"Here it is," Mattie said. There was a hole in a shade at the window and behind it the glass had a hole in it as round and wrinkled as Mommie's mouth when she laughed. "It ain't nowhere near her."

"Thank God for that," Mommie said. "Help me up," and she pushed at the arms of the recliner.

"You want that gun?" Mattie said. She bent over and picked it up.

"I thought you were afraid of guns," Mommie said.

"I was," Mattie said. "I told you it left me."

"That goes for guns too?"

"That goes for everything," Mattie said. "I don't care if I live or die."

"Me neither," Althie said. "That what I thought when I put that blood on me."

"I reckon you did. You been in the bathroom too much," Crystal said.

"Whatever that means," Mattie said.

"I don't have to mean something every time I talk," Crystal said. "I ain't like you, always thinking about something or other."

"Well, I got to be going," Mattie said.

"Come by next week. We'll do it again," Mommie said. She made the hole again and blew through it. "Always good to see you, Mattie. You stay awhile. We got something to eat for supper and someplace to sleep."

"I got to go," Mattie said. "I only got six weeks."

"You mean the petition?" Althie said. "Give it to me. I haven't signed it."

Crystal was staring at her, shaking her head back and forth. The ringlets leaped about like worms. Mommie's eyes were downcast. She reached under her skirt and rearranged the pistol.

Mattie handed Althie a copy of the petition. Then she rooted about in her bag and came up with a ballpoint pen. "Wait a minute," Mattie said. "Give me that back. That one already got names on it. You sign a new sheet."

Althie leaned over and signed on the floor. The blood rushed to her face as though she was holding her breath underwater. Then she rose to the surface again. "There you are. That makes six."

"Four," Mattie said.

Althie turned to Mommie. "You didn't sign it?"

"I told her it wasn't my business. I'm too old to go down that road. I don't even get off the porch. I live too far out. I didn't want them to have my name. I might die tomorrow."

"What she means is she didn't want to," Crystal said. "And I don't either. I'm going to New York. They might burn the house down. I might not get to go."

"What about standing up for your rights and flying your colors?" Althie asked.

"What about it?" Mommie said.

"Sometimes you got to," Althie said and bent over from the waist. It looked as though she was tying her shoe.

"What that?" Mommie said looking at her. "What you doing?"

Althie's face was red as a slab of fresh meat. She was writing something on the petition. "Signing your name," Althie grunted.

Mommie was out of the chair before Crystal. "Whose name?" Mommie said.

"She signing my name?" Crystal asked her.

"Give me that," Mommie said, just as the pistol caught up with her. She kicked at it viciously as one might kick a terrier dog snapping at one's heels. The pistol went clattering across the room, and Mattie held out a foot as though to stop it, then pulled it back remembering her grandfather who'd fought at Chickamauga before he had enough and came home minus a foot where he held it out to stop a cannon ball that was rolling along in the dirt. The cannon ball kept on going and took his foot with it before it came to rest among the roots of a pine tree. Mattie still used it as a doorstop. Son of a bitch good for something, her grandfather'd said. There's a destiny even in that. The pistol pulled up against the wall and ricocheted about in the corner as though it had gone mad and was looking for a way out.

"Give it to me," Mommie said, snatching at the petition.

Althie held it away from her. She did not notice Crystal ease herself alongside the chair. As soon as she got close enough, Crystal lunged suddenly and snatched the petition. She lost her balance and lurched halfway across the room before she pulled up short at a table.

"She got my name down there?" Mommie asked.

Crystal said, "No."

"Whose name is it?"

"Althie Grizzle."

"What else?"

"Immanuel."

"Immanuel what?"

"Immanuel. That's on the first line. And then on the second, Forsythia."

"Forsythia who?"

"Your daughter," Crystal said. "Forsythia Grizzle."

"Where's my name?" Mommie asked. She sounded disappointed.

"It ain't down here," Crystal said. "Mine ain't either."

"Give it to me," Mommie said. She took the petition. "Now give me the pen."

Mattie took the pen to her. Mommie leaned over the table and wrote in a jagged but curiously rounded, childish hand "Crystal Grizzle" on one line and under that, "Pearl Grizzle." She paused as though thinking or remembering. Then she bent over the table again and wrote on the next line "Rev. Milton Grizzle." She waved the paper about in the air to dry the ink. Then she stopped and leaned over the table again. Mattie saw what she'd written and laughed.

"What she write?" Althie asked.

"Immanuel Grizzle. We're going to get in trouble, they ever come out here looking for Immanuel Grizzle."

"You scared?" Mommie asked. "They won't even know who it is. We're too far out here, and there're too many Grizzles for them to keep up with. Besides which, I'll be dead by then. I won't live to see a recall."

"That what I figure," Althie said, and then, seeing the stricken look on Mommie's face, said, "I mean for me. I don't care if I am or not."

"And I'll be in New York," Crystal said. "I ain't waiting around for them to open that road. Dancing won't wait."

"Thank you," Mattie said. "He's good as out of office. People won't stand for him closing the road. That's an injustice."

"Give me some of them papers," Mommie said. "We'll get them signed. Crystal," she said. "Go down to the mailbox and wait till Cooper comes and get him to sign it. He drives the roads delivering mail every day and might not like it if they're fixing to close them." Crystal protested but left the room, the porch trembling after her passage.

"Forsythia needs some," Mommie said. "She got lots of folks at work she talks about. I don't even know their names. But there's a bunch. They say they might shoot him themselves—I mean Benny—if they wouldn't put them in jail."

"You know what they say?" Althie said. "They say, Don't worry about going to jail. They won't put you in jail just for shooting Benny Easley. That's a mercy killing, they say."

"We're going to win," Mattie said, and got up as though to go.

"Give me some too," Althie said. "I'm starting work."

"Oh?" Mattie said. Althie had always stayed at home and helped her mother. She never worked.

"Work?" Mommie said. "Who's going to hire you to work?"

"I'm going to work on this petition," Althie said.

"That ain't work," Mommie said. "They ain't going to pay you for that. Work means they pay you."

"This don't," Althie said. She turned to Mattie. "Give me some papers. I'm going to town in the morning on MATS and take a chair and table with me." She paused. "Two chairs and a table. One for me and one for Mommie."

"I ain't going," Mommie said. "You take Crystal, you got to have somebody go with you. Take her on the way to New York."

"And we'll set up in front of the Red Dot," Althie said, "and get them to sign when they come out with the groceries."

"Not me you ain't," Mommie said. "They might put me in jail already. You're putting your head in the jaws of trouble."

"We'll do that for six weeks," Althie said. "Every day for six weeks but Sunday."

"How many you reckon you need?" Mattie asked.

"How many you got?"

"Nine hundred and ninety-eight blank ones and two with names on them."

"Give me half," Althie said. "You keep the ones already got names."

"She don't need that many," Mommie said. "Just give her a few. I ain't going."

"You're going, all right," Althie said. "Your period of mourning is over."

Mommie smiled. She was delighted.

"I won't even get to cook the dinner," Mommie said. "We might have to buy it in town and eat it in front of the TV set. I'll be too busy to do the dishes."

Mattie handed Althie half the petitions she had with her. "I'll get the others next time I see you."

"Don't wait too long," Althie said. "They're going to go fast."

"Let me keep them," Mommie said. "I'll guard them for you. Go get the pistol." She took it from Althie and went to the door. "I'm going to help Crystal," Mommie said. "She might forget what she's down there for."

"You all right?" Mattie asked Althie after she left.

Althie nodded. "I'm all right. I'm sorry I did that."

"I ain't," Mattie said.

Althie paused. "I ain't either. I'm sorry I'm crazy."

"You ain't crazy."

Althie laughed. "I ain't as crazy as Crystal," she said, as though that was consolation enough.

"Crystal ain't crazy. Crystal's young."

"Well, then Mommie."

Mattie laughed and hugged her. "She ain't crazy," she said. "She's just old. We're all crazy."

"Some more than others."

"And some get cured by the grace of God in ways they don't even know how it happened," Mattie said, "except they give thanks and laugh they're so happy. Their heart overflows and makes a glad sound. That's what the Lord's yearning to hear. He likes that more than music." She went to the door. "Goodbye, honey. Looks like we're both feeling better. I'm glad."

"I'm glad too," Althie said. "You're some kind of angel."

"Come go with me down to the mailbox," Mattie said. "I see them still down waiting there."

They went out the door and moved over the tremulous porch. At the edge the sun struck them viciously, blinding their eyes. The wind was still, and the wind turners stood slack in the yard. Further beyond at the mailbox Mommie was pacing. Crystal was seated on a rock.

"Put up your gun," Althie shouted. "Cooper won't stop if he thinks you might shoot him."

Mommie opened the mailbox and put it inside.

Mattie laughed. "He won't think of looking in there if he's delivering the mail."

"Not when I'm here collecting it. I'll take it with me after I'm through," Mommie said.

Just then Mr. Cooper's light green Toyota came over the crest of the hill heading for Mommie. She stood in the middle of the road flagging him down. Crystal got up and brushed her seat. The wind rose and drove the dust toward them. The wind turners creaked in protest, then set up a high wail as they were driven like Sisyphus to perform the same mindless act over and over. They sounded as though they were driven by furies. Mommie was standing with her head stuck in the window beside Mr. Cooper. It looked as though she was bitten in two—only the bottom half protruded. Then she emerged and motioned to Crystal. Crystal started to open the mailbox, but Mommie was on her before she got to it and took the paper from her hand. Crystal went back to the rock and sat down. She held her legs out as though offering them up as a sacrifice. Then she moved them about in a dance. They leaped here and there, pivoting from out of the rock. Mommie was back inside the car. It looked as though she was trying to climb in. The door opened. Mommie leaped back out of the way, and Mr. Cooper emerged. First his black shoes, then his black heart.

"He says he won't sign it," Mommie shouted. "He says he's too scared. He says they might shoot him."

"Tell him they can't shoot us all," Mattie shouted.

"He says he ain't worried about you," Mommie said. "He got to carry the mail all over. There's a hundred thousand trees in this county and every one a man behind them if they want to shoot him. He says it ain't worth it."

"Tell him it's worth it," Althie shouted. "Look at me."

"He says he's looking," Mommie shouted.

"Tell him to look inside the mailbox," Mattie said.

Mr. Cooper opened the mailbox and recoiled as though he had seen a snake.

"He says he'll sign it," Mommie shouted. "What does he care?"

Then he was gone, the green Toyota turning to dust.

Mattie Chadwick hugged Althie Grizzle again and waved to Mommie, who had the gun in one hand and the mail in the other. Crystal was still dancing alone, holding the petition. Mattie looked down the road to the river. The dust from Mr. Cooper was clearing. It drifted toward the tops of the trees like smoke. The weeds on both sides of the road were covered with dust, and the road looked disused, as though it had been locked up for fifty years. It made her think of her momma and daddy. Their eyes were dust. But her heart was too full to be sad. The whole road lay before her either way she wished to go, down to the river or back to home, and she realized they were both the same, just as north and south are both the same. Any road leads into all others if you follow it out far enough, and all roads take you back to the same place you started from if you just keep on going long enough and don't let them close it. She turned and began walking. Her shoes were dusty, the air was hot, the sun struck at her again and again. But inside she was like an army. Her heart called the cadence. It beat inside her like a great drum.

Design by David Bullen
Typeset in Mergenthaler Galliard
by Wilsted & Taylor
with Metropolis Bold display
Printed by Maple-Vail
on acid-free paper